THE
MULHOLLAND
FILES

Sandy Jones

x

THE MULHOLLAND FILES

SANDY JONES

Matador
9 Priory Business Park,
Wistow Road, Kibworth Beauchamp,
Leicestershire, LE8 0RX
Tel: 0116 279 2299
Email: books@troubador.co.uk
Web: www.troubador.co.uk/matador
Twitter: @matadorbooks

ISBN 978 1838591 472

British Library Cataloguing in Publication Data.
A catalogue record for this book is available from the British Library.

Printed and bound in Great Britain by 4edge Limited
Typeset in 11pt Sabon by Troubador Publishing Ltd, Leicester, UK

Matador is an imprint of Troubador Publishing Ltd

A love letter to my husband

Three years before

A slight mist curled up the valley, hanging over the river and hugging the meadow. It brought with it a chill despite the time of year. Spring was Edward's favourite season, and no early morning mist would put him off his jog through the nature reserve. This was the best time of day, before the dog walkers came out in force. Gossiping in groups they slowed him down or, worse still, tripped him up. It would be another hour or so before they appeared.

He crossed the bridge and began the gentle descent to the railway line where an unmanned foot crossing gave access to the hill leading back into town. His breath formed clouds in front of his face as he ran; his fitness level was not where he would have liked it to be, and he coughed slightly as the path twisted towards the gate. Slowing down he looked up and saw the woman coming down the hill on the other side of the track. He'd seen her before and knew who she was. Her husband had died recently in a nasty accident involving a train hitting his car.

Why was she out so early? She had her head down and was dashing now towards the gate. Edward had a sudden thought and his instincts told him to act on it. He picked up speed, running down the slope as fast as the terrain allowed. His heart pounded with the exertion.

She had reached the railway tracks and stood as still as a statue looking straight ahead. The London train was due any minute and Edward heard the driver sound the horn as it passed the road crossing further up the line. By the time it reached the gate it would be travelling at over sixty miles an hour. Swirls of mist obscured the view, and the woman, dressed in grey, would be invisible to the train driver, even if he could stop in time.

Edward was within fifty feet of the crossing now. He saw her pale face, dark eyes staring at the track as she took one step from the gate. His heart pounded as he lunged forward and shouted:

'Abigail Rayner! Don't do it!'

The train was on them, heat and noise and the startled faces of commuters staring back at him. Then it was gone. He realised he'd been holding his breath, preparing for the worst, but as the train continued its journey he saw a small figure crumpled on the bank on the other side of the line. He ran to her and put his arm around her as she sobbed.

'You saved me. I don't even know you. Why...?'

'Because it's not the right thing to do. You must carry on. You're so young; your whole life is in front of you. He wouldn't have wanted this, would he? Rob would have wanted you to be happy.'

She looked up at him, pale as a china doll with tear tracks running down each cheek. Her eyes were like saucers and he recognised that look; he'd seen it before. Her voice was muted. *The drug must be strong stuff*, he thought.

'Did you know him?'

He hesitated and said, 'No, I never met him.' Which was the truth, just not the whole truth. Edward helped her to her feet.

'I'll take you home. Is there anyone you can call to be with you?'

She shook her head. Rubbing the back of her hand across her face she took a deep shuddering breath.

'I don't want to go home yet.'

Then Edward did something completely out of character: he offered to make her tea at his cottage. And that was the start of it all.

Chapter 1

Edward closed his heavy front door and stamped his feet, shaking the snow from his boots. As he bent to untie his shoelaces, he spotted the small white envelope lying three feet back from the doormat. He kicked off his boots, leaving them dripping on the mat, and picked it up. There was no address, just his name neatly typed in bold letters – Edward Covington.

Padding into the kitchen he draped his coat over the back of one of his old oak chairs and dropped the letter on the table. The Aga was doing its job well, warming the room to a cosy temperature. The old house was difficult to keep warm and Edward spent most days in the kitchen unless he lit the fire in his low-ceilinged living room. Today was no exception. Kettle bubbling on the stove he turned his attention back to the letter. Junk mail wasn't usually personally addressed.

When Abby came for her morning coffee, she found him sitting at the table frowning over a photograph. He looked up as she bounded in, pink cheeked from the cold air, wrapped up like a Peruvian mummy.

'Hello, Abby. The kettle's boiled. Help yourself.'

'Morning, Edward. Thanks, I'm dying for a decent coffee. It's foul out there.'

Abby found a mug and helped herself to coffee before joining Edward at the table.

'What have you got there? Family picture?'

He handed her the photo. It was a small black-and-white portrait shot of a woman in dark clothing. Abby stared at it.

'Who is she? A relative of yours? She's quite attractive.' She looked up at him. 'It's not an old flame, is it?'

Edward laughed. 'I'm afraid not. I have no idea who she is or where she came from.' Then he told her how he'd found it on his doormat when he came back from his morning walk.

'How fascinating! Who is she, and why send it to you?' Abby tossed her dark hair back from her face and peered closer at the picture. 'Do you have any ideas at all? Are you sure she's not someone from your past?' She unwound her long woollen scarf as she spoke.

Abby always unwrapped herself bit by bit: hat, gloves, coat then scarf. Edward found it amusing, but today he was preoccupied and didn't notice.

'No, I don't recognise her. I never forget a face. Also, look at her hair and the style of her dress. I think it dates from the mid-sixties, maybe earlier, before my time.'

Abby looked closer at the woman in the photo. Her hair fell forward again as she leant over it. Edward reminded himself that he was nearly old enough to be her father. He stood up and offered another mug of coffee. She took off another layer, looking less Peruvian and more Home Counties. He smiled at her and found a tin of shortbread biscuits saved from Christmas.

Putting two steaming mugs on the table he reached for the photo and said, 'There are several things about this that puzzle me. Who sent it, and who is the woman? And why me? I'm fairly sure I don't know her. How old do you think she is?'

'Probably about thirty, possibly younger, around my age I'd say. I find it hard to guess with these old photos; everyone looked older then. I've got photos of my grandparents looking really old and they were only about fifty when the pictures were taken.'

Edward smiled at Abby. He wondered what she thought about him. Did he look old to her? She looked up and caught him staring at her.

'What? What did I say? Oh, Edward, don't go on about age or I'll start calling you an old fart...' she pulled a face at him, '... and mean it!'

He held his hands up in submission. She had a way of drawing him out of his shell. He never felt old when she was around.

Tapping the photo with her red nails Abby said, 'Back to the photo; what I was going to say was that looking at her dress I'd say she was middle class, not wealthy but definitely not poor either. Look closely; see her necklace? And it looks like a diamond ring on her finger but no wedding band. So she was engaged but not married.'

'How do you know it's a diamond?'

'By the way it's caught the light. See the flash? I don't think paste would produce that sparkle.'

Edward stood up, pushing his chair back. 'I've got a magnifying glass in my study. Let's take a closer look.'

They went through to his study. It was a small room accessed from a door in the panelling of the living room and had views of the garden. He called it his inner sanctum and no one other than Abby had ever been allowed in. The smell from last evening's fire lingered in the air. Edward switched on his desk lamp, casting a dusty shaft of light over the unpolished surface. He was suddenly conscious of the mess and pushed aside the pile of papers and journals cluttering the top.

Abby perched on the deep windowsill and watched him search through the drawers looking for the glass. His thick silver blond hair shone in the artificial light as he leant over the desk.

'Here it is. Can you pass me the photo?'

They leaned over the picture together as Edward held the glass over it. The ring and necklace were brought into sharp focus. Abby had been right about the quality of the pieces. There was very little else to go on. Her face was pleasant rather than attractive and there was nothing in the picture to date or place her. The photo was of a professional standard so suggested a studio portrait. Edward was puzzled. In his experience there was a reason why he had this photo; some mystery to be unravelled where his skills would be put to good use. He frowned.

Abby took the picture from his hand and held the glass over it. She stared intently at every inch and then sighed. 'I thought there may be a mark or something to identify the photographer but there isn't.'

'Let me look again.' Edward almost snatched the picture from her, holding it up against the light, first front then back. 'You are a clever girl, Abby. There is a mark. It's in the paper, like a watermark.'

'Really? That's good.'

'Ah, I'm afraid not. It says Agfa.'

'Agfa? What's that?'

'The film the photographer used. I think we've drawn a blank. All we have to go on is the woman.'

'There must be a connection to you. Why else would someone send it to you? Perhaps they forgot to put a letter in with it, and when they realise they'll send that too.'

Edward thought this was some kind of test. He was missing the point. He stared at the woman's face again. What was it? He was beginning to think that maybe she did look familiar but he still had no idea who she was.

By Tuesday the snow had stopped. When Edward went for his usual early walk, the trees were already dripping. The thaw had begun. It was two days since the mysterious envelope had dropped through his door and he was no nearer to knowing why. It was also two days since he'd seen Abby.

Back home he unfolded his magazine and made some coffee. As he reached for his mug, the doorbell rang. He glanced at his watch. It was late for the postman and he wasn't expecting a delivery. Even after all this time he still felt tense when something unexpected happened. He no longer carried a gun but kept a sturdy baseball bat by the front door, hidden by the coat rack.

He used his peephole but could see no one. With one hand outstretched towards the bat he slowly opened the door. Both his porch and the short path to the lane were empty. There was nobody in sight. Quickly he did a mental check of the house; all doors and windows were locked so this was the only way in. Edward realised he'd been holding his breath. He released it, shook himself and closed the door. As he stepped back, he saw a buff-coloured envelope on the mat. He'd stepped on it as he looked out of the porch.

He was slipping. How could he miss that? He took it through to the kitchen and opened it. A single slip of paper fell onto the table. *No more photos, then*, he thought. He left it where it fell and read the few typed words. It read simply: "Try looking in Bath. Goodrich & Wellbody", followed by "More to follow when you've solved this one".

Edward knew for sure now that this was a test. What bothered him was who and why. He'd left those days behind and had enjoyed the peace of this small Wiltshire town for several years now. It was possible, even likely, that they wanted him back for some operation or special job, but he'd survived enough code one operations to last a lifetime. Most of his colleagues had not been so lucky. That murky world had no appeal for him. The thought of returning to it left him feeling queasy.

He sat at the table, fingers spread either side of the sheet of paper, not wanting to touch it. His coffee had gone cold. He knew he'd no choice but to follow the clue. It may provide him with the answer as to who was contacting him. Sighing, he went to get his laptop.

A few hours later Abby tapped on his window, mouthing she couldn't get in. He jumped up from the table and opened the door.

'I must have forgotten to unlock it this morning, sorry. Would you like a coffee? I was just going to make another.'

'That sounds like a good idea. I'll make it. You look busy.' She filled the kettle and put it on the hotplate of the

Aga. He watched her and thought how lovely she looked in her dark red top. She turned and smiled at him.

'Have you heard any more about that photo?'

Edward smiled back. He was too slow in answering and she jumped in, 'You have! I can tell. Don't try to lie to me, Edward, you know I can tell when you're hiding things.'

He thought he'd like to test that theory but decided not right now. Stretching his arms out he yawned.

'Yes. You were right about them forgetting to put a note in.'

'I knew it! What did it say? Who is she?'

Edward handed over the slip of paper, watching her face as she read it. She looked puzzled.

'Is that it? Nothing else?'

'That's it. I looked them up. They were a photography studio in Bath from 1919 to 1968. When Mr Wellbody died, they were bought out by Pinkerton's and moved to a bigger store. Pinkerton's still exists.'

Abby grinned. 'Then they might have the old records. She might be in their archive somewhere. We could go and see them.'

Edward noticed the "we" and was just about to say he didn't think it was worth chasing, but she'd left the room. She came back with the telephone directory.

'Abby, we can't go bothering them with some old photo. We have no way of identifying it. If their records go back that far there will be hundreds, even thousands...'

Abby held up her hand to stop him. She already had her mobile in her other hand and was tapping in a number. Edward weighed up his options. He could just let her have her way and hope it would come to nothing, or somehow deflect her, stop her getting involved. He made an instant decision to let her join him in this one pursuit and then keep any subsequent contact secret. Damage limitation, he thought.

Pinkerton's agreed to meet them as they did indeed have an extensive archive of original proofs going back over eighty years. Abby told them it was for family research – she was 'doing the family tree'. Edward listened to her charm the studio assistant and thought she'd missed her vocation. She could have been one of his team gathering information and feeding it back to the field operatives. He shook the thought away swiftly.

Abby put her phone down. Her eyes were sparkling. She laughed at him.

'That was easy. I should do this for a living. Perhaps we could start up a detective agency?'

He knew she was joking, but he didn't laugh. She frowned at him.

'Don't be stuffy, Edward. It was only a little lie. I've arranged for us to go on Thursday at ten o'clock to meet a Mr Winterbourne. If that's okay with you?'

'Of course it is. Then we can go for lunch somewhere. My way of saying thank you.'

'Thank you for what?'

'For putting up with me. I know I can be a boring old fart sometimes...'

Abby rolled her eyes and turned back to the stove to take the kettle off the hotplate. She had her back to him when she said, 'Edward, you are the nicest man I know so don't call yourself old.'

He was glad she couldn't see his face. He found it difficult to hide his feelings from her. It would be tough keeping her out of whatever was developing.

Chapter 2

The Georgian townhouse stood in a row of Bath stone buildings above Walcot Street. Edward took ages to find somewhere to park his old Mercedes, so they arrived breathless and slightly damp from the drizzle.

Pinkerton's took up the ground floor of the old building. From the outside it looked like any of its neighbours, but as they pushed through the entrance a huge pale room, the colour of an ancient whale bone, greeted them. High windows provided natural daylight, enhanced by strings of overhead spotlights suspended above them like rows of fairy lights.

Edward followed Abby to the reception area. A young woman sat, smiling, behind a glass and chrome desk.

'Hello. My name is Tamara. Can I help you?' Her voice had a singsong tone that Edward thought was affected.

Abby said, 'Hi, Tamara. I'm Abby Rayner. We have an appointment with Mr Winterbourne.'

As Tamara went in search of the archivist, they strolled amongst the displays. All the photographs were in black-and-white or sepia, adding to the washed-out appearance of the room.

Abby whispered to Edward, 'Did you notice how the receptionist matches the room? Everything's so wishy-washy.'

Except for you, he thought. He leaned towards her, catching a trace of her scent.

'Why are we whispering?'

Abby giggled. 'I don't know. It feels like a library. I suppose it's a collection of pictures instead of books, but it seems a bit sterile somehow.'

'Watch out, here comes the head librarian,' Edward teased as he spotted a man striding towards them across the empty space.

Winterbourne stretched his hand out in greeting. 'Mrs Rayner, I presume, and…'

Edward gave his hand to shake and said, 'Edward Covington, a family friend.'

'Ah, nice to meet you both. Come this way.'

He spun on his heels and strode towards a door at the far end of the room. Edward struggled to keep up and could see Abby had broken into a trot beside him.

She hissed in his ear, 'God, he's so tall. Like a daddy-long-legs.'

Away from the exhibition space, the building retained its old-fashioned charm. Winterbourne led them down several dimly lit corridors to his archive. This room was more like a library, with rows of shelving rolled together. Each row had a large metal wheel, like a ship's helm, to steer it across the floor. There were neat reference labels everywhere.

'Welcome to my den.' Winterbourne threw his tweed jacket over a chair by the table in the corner. 'This is where we keep all of our photographic records, going back to the middle of the last century. No, I mean the one before that. I forget we are in the twenty-first century now.'

Edward thought, *I bet you do*. He couldn't judge the man's age by dress style or features. His pale complexion, limpid eyes half hidden behind large glasses, and old-fashioned clothing made him appear like a relic from the last century. He watched Winterbourne talking to Abby, noticing he wasn't immune to her charm.

'So, Mrs Rayner, you want to find out who is in your picture? May I?' Winterbourne stretched out his bony hand to take the photograph from Abby.

'Please call me Abby.' She gave it to him with a smile.

'What a nice portrait. Yes, I've seen this young lady before. I have a photographic memory; very useful in this line of work. Now then, she lives in nineteen sixty-six, if I'm not mistaken.' He rolled back one row of shelving, allowing himself enough room to squeeze between them. They could hear him talking to himself as he searched for the file he wanted. 'Ah, here it is.'

Winterbourne slipped out from between the rows with an old brown box, placing it on the table. Inside were photographic proof sheets, each one numbered and clearly referenced. He took one out for Abby and Edward to see.

'Here she is. Your relative, Mrs... Abby, is a lady by the name of...' he peered at the small label through his thick glasses, '... Judith Mulholland.'

The rest of what Winterbourne had to say was lost to Edward. He couldn't believe the name he'd just heard. Why hadn't he recognised her? Hiding his surprise, he leaned forward and looked at the sheet. Abby picked it up. She turned to Edward, 'Great-aunt Judith. Who'd have thought it?'

'Can you tell us any more about the sitting?' Edward asked.

'Let me see.' Winterbourne took the sheet back from Abby. 'It was privately funded. It was taken for a newspaper announcement of the young lady's twenty-first birthday and engagement to be married.'

Edward said, 'Can you tell which newspaper?'

'Unfortunately not, but my guess would be *The Times* and possibly the local one as well.'

Abby smiled at Winterbourne. 'That's very helpful. You say it was privately funded. Would that have been her parents?'

'I believe so. All I have here is a Mr G Mulholland of Sion Hill, Bath.'

Edward remembered her telling him once that her father had been 'in banking', which would explain the prestigious address. It must be nearly twenty years since he'd seen Judith, he thought.

Abby was winding up the conversation with Winterbourne, thanking him for his help and promising to come back again to see their next exhibition. He pulled a plain white business card from his jacket pocket and gave it to her. They shook his limp hand and made their way back through the corridors to the exhibition space. There were several Japanese tourists looking at the pictures, bringing a splash of colour to the room. Outside the drizzle had stopped.

Edward guided Abby across the road to where he'd parked his car.

'Where would you like to go for lunch?' He opened the door for her.

'I'm easy. Wherever you like, Edward.' She slid onto the smooth leather seat, revealing just a glimpse of leg as her dress rode up slightly. It was a pretty vintage style, and Edward thought he ought to compliment her. As he climbed in beside her, she looked at him. 'You know her, don't you?'

'What makes you think that?'

She sighed, 'Edward, I know you. I saw your face when Winterbourne mentioned her name. Nobody else would have spotted it but I saw your mouth twitch. Did you know you do that when you're trying to hide something?'

'No, I wasn't aware of it.' He heard his voice, thought how formal he sounded. 'Sorry, that sounded rude. You just surprise me every time, with your ability to see through people.'

'Not people, Edward. Just you. Now, take me to lunch and tell me all about Judith Mulholland.'

They went to a favourite of his a few miles out of Bath, an old-fashioned pub on the banks of the canal. Inside, a log fire gave welcoming warmth to the few customers. Edward found a table in the corner away from the bar.

Over lunch he told her about Judith. She had been his section head when he joined the service as a young man. He was careful to avoid any detail and told Abby that he had worked in London for the civil service.

'Why didn't you recognise her?' Abby sipped her drink, rolling the ice around in her glass with a straw. Her dark eyes turned up to him. 'Had she changed so much?'

'Yes, she had. When I knew her, she would have been about forty-five or so, worn down by the job. It was a big deal then, to be female and in a senior position. Her hairstyle had changed, and she always looked rather sad.' He hadn't thought about it before but realised now that that was how she'd looked, as if she carried the cares of the world on her shoulders.

Abby frowned then said, 'If you knew her as Mulholland then she must never have married.'

Edward smiled at her. 'Abby, you're so quick. You miss nothing.' He thought back to the days he'd worked with Judith. She had been approachable, friendly even, which was unusual then. But she never spoke about her own past. He didn't know she'd been engaged. She'd never mentioned it. 'I wonder why her picture was dropped through my door. I've had nothing to do with her for years.'

'Perhaps it's a calling card, and she'll get in touch.' Abby crunched the ice, stirring the remains of her drink. 'Or maybe she's retired, and she's going to send you an invite to some do?'

Edward frowned, working out how old Judith would be now.

'She must have retired years ago, but you may be right about it being a calling card.' That bothered him. It spelled trouble if Judith Mulholland had sent the photo.

'But why send you a photo of herself as a young woman?' Abby was frowning too. 'It doesn't make any sense.'

Edward thought, *In my world nothing makes sense until you break the code*, but he couldn't say that to Abby. He just agreed it made no sense whatsoever.

Chapter 3

Rain was beating on the window. Judith crossed the room and pulled the blind down. She slid open a door in the oak panelling, then turned back to Edward.

'Can I get you a drink? Scotch? Or are you a beer man?' She reached into the cabinet and pulled out two tumblers.

Edward said, 'No thanks. I'd rather keep sharp.'

'Please yourself. You don't mind if I carry on without you?'

'Not at all.' He wondered if that sounded abrupt, but she didn't seem to mind, pouring herself a slug of Scotland's finest malt. He watched her as she swigged it back before taking a cigarette from a silver box on her desk, lighting it deftly. She smoked some French brand that smelled of sweet wine and drew the smoke deep into her lungs before exhaling slowly with eyes closed.

'Now, Edward, down to business. Do you know why I've asked you here tonight?' She continued, obviously not expecting an answer from him, 'I need you to do a little job for me. I want you to find out who's planning to kill me.'

He must have looked surprised because she laughed, a rarity for Judith. Her powdered face creased, and her red lips parted, revealing yellowing teeth. She coughed.

'Yes, you heard right. Someone is plotting to have me permanently removed and I would like to know who, and why. Do you think you're up to the challenge, Edward? I can't trust anyone else in this damn organisation.' She turned her back on him, going back to the drinks cabinet to pour another scotch.

Edward looked at his brogues, considered his response, and said, 'I suppose that's a compliment. How do you know someone's planning to remove you?'

She fiddled with her pearl earring, twisting it round and round in her ear. He thought, even though she was at least twenty-five years his senior, that she was still an attractive woman.

'Edward, I know everything that goes on in this building, and beyond; who's sleeping with the enemy, who's trading and who's playing for the other side.' She laughed, although it sounded more like a cough. 'I need you to infiltrate. Persuade them you're on their team and report back to me. Can you do that for me?' She leaned forward over the desk. He caught a whiff of whisky intermingled with a musky scent and French tobacco.

'Where do you want me to start?'

'I'll send you the file. Read it carefully and we'll meet again on Wednesday.'

Edward could hear the rain hammering against the window. It was getting dark in that room and very hot. Why was he so hot? He looked at his feet. His brogues had changed to slippers, and he seemed to be wearing pyjamas. Confused, he stood up. Judith had disappeared.

Her desk was covered in piles of jewellery, bright sparkly rings and strings of pearls. He slowly moved towards it, his legs like jelly. Where had Judith gone? Amongst all the jewels was a small black-and-white photograph of a young woman. She looked strangely familiar. He picked it up. His fingers felt wet. He held up his hand in front of his face. His fingers were dripping with blood. The rain was getting louder…

Edward woke up with a start. His heart was pounding. He recognised the adrenaline rush. He hadn't felt like that for a long time. The duvet had wrapped itself around his body; no wonder he was so hot. He rubbed his eyes, looked at the clock beside his bed, it was five thirty, and heard the storm outside. What the hell had that dream been all about? Judith Mulholland had never entrusted him with such a job, so why had it seemed so vivid? He closed his eyes, searching his memory for a clue to explain the dream. The room had been her office. The drinks cabinet hidden in the panelling, the big mahogany desk and the smell of those damn French cigarettes had all been authentic. Everything else was a sham, except the photo.

The fields next to the river were sodden after so much rain. Edward jogged up the slope, panting from his exertion and damp from the persistent drizzle. He knew he was getting fitter. Last week he had walked up, now he was determined to reach the top before he slowed down.

The weather had deterred the local dog walkers, so there were no leads to trip over or chatty groups to dodge. He ran easily to the top and slowed to catch his breath before jogging back towards home. Abby had told him she thought he was mad running in this weather. She hated getting wet.

Edward felt good. Since giving up smoking seven years ago he had slowly improved his stamina and regained muscle. Back at home he showered, made coffee and caught up with some bill paying. Abby would be late today, so he'd offered to cook her some lunch.

He heard the clatter of the letter box from his study. It was twelve o'clock, the post had already been delivered, and the local paper wouldn't appear till late afternoon. He guessed it was another message; he'd been expecting one since the last had dropped on his mat. Edward ran through the house and flung open the door, but there was no one in sight. Whoever was leaving these was quick on their feet.

He bent to pick up the envelope, white and handwritten – "For Edward Covington". Opening it carefully he found a handwritten note addressed to him. As he began reading it, he heard Abby's voice outside. She'd arrived by taxi and was paying her fare, the rain bouncing off the roof of the cab. He waved at her from the porch.

'Abby, come in this way. Did you see anyone as you came up the lane? I've just had another message.' He ushered her in and shut the door against the rain. She threw her hood back, shaking water onto the floor, and unbuttoned her coat.

'God, the rain's awful again. Was it a woman?'

'I don't know. I didn't see anybody.'

'We saw a woman rushing down the lane. The taxi driver commented because he recognised her and said she didn't live around here.'

Edward took Abby's coat and hung it on the rack to drip on the stone-floored porch. 'What else did he say?' He knew that taxi drivers could be useful sources of local information.

'He said she worked at a nursing home just the other side of Bath, the big mansion that was converted a few years ago. Oh yes, and she lived at number twenty-nine Orchard Way, and has a cat that needs to go to the vet once a fortnight.'

Edward laughed. 'All that in less than five minutes.'

'He was a mine of local gossip, knew everyone, and you wouldn't believe who he's had in his taxi.'

Edward rolled his eyes, laughed again and said, 'Let me get you a warm drink and we can read this together.'

The letter was short and to the point. Edward read it out to Abby as they waited for the kettle to come to a boil.

'By now you will know who is in the photo. Judith told me you're clever. I said I'd help but I'm scared. She wanted me to meet you, but I don't know if that's a good idea. I think they may be watching me, and I took a risk today delivering this. She said I should write to you and post it as they would monitor my emails and my texts. This is serious stuff. I don't know what to do. Please help me. I've bought an old mobile with a pay-as-you-go SIM. Please use this number to contact me. I'm scared.'

'Bloody hell. What do you think she's talking about? Why you, Edward?' Abby frowned at him.

Edward shrugged, hoping he was convincing. 'I have no idea what's going on or what Judith Mulholland's been telling her.' He paused. 'Perhaps the old lady has gone senile and developed some kind of paranoia. You know the sort of thing; everyone is out to kill her or steal her money.'

Abby looked unconvinced. 'It seems a bit extreme to me though, and a care worker would meet lots of old people with dementia. Why would she go to all this trouble?'

Edward turned away from her to make the tea. He remembered his dream. This felt like an extension of it. It was all very strange. He turned back to find Abby tapping the number into her phone.

'Abby, what are you doing?' He spilt tea as he put the mugs down, reaching across to take her phone. She glared at him, stepping back out of reach. He stopped. 'Don't ring that number. We know nothing about this woman or what she wants. Just promise me you won't ring her, at least until I've tried to contact Judith.'

She stared at him but cancelled the call as he'd asked.

'There's a lot you're not telling me. I'm not stupid, you know. I didn't buy into that civil-service-mundane-work-in-London scenario. There's no way you were ever just a dusty pen-pusher.' She held up her hand as he opened his mouth. 'It's okay, I understand you can't tell me things. I guess you're bound by the Official Secrets Act or something. But please trust me now, Edward. I want to help.'

She stood, phone in hand, slightly flushed, and looked so appealing that Edward forgot who he'd been, even forgot the age difference. He moved quickly, took hold of her face and kissed her. She surprised him by responding passionately, wrapping her arms round his neck so he couldn't back away. When she let him go, he could see tears in her eyes.

He took a deep breath. 'I'm sorry, Abby. I shouldn't—'

She stopped him, putting her fingers across his lips. 'Don't you dare say sorry for kissing me. I've been waiting a long time for you to wake up, Edward Covington. I was beginning to think I'd got it wrong.'

'Sorry,' he paused, 'and I'm not sorry for kissing you. You're a lovely girl, Abby.'

She frowned and threw her phone down. 'For God's sake, Edward! I'm not a girl and you're not an old man! I think you're incredibly sexy. Don't look so surprised. I've been dying for you to show you felt the same about me.'

He took a deep breath, thinking what a fool he'd been. An invisible boundary had been crossed, but he still wanted to protect her. He couldn't think what to say so he kissed her again. It felt so good to have her body pressed against his, to smell the lavender scent from her hair and feel the soft warmth of her lips. She held him tight.

'What do we do now?' She spoke quietly without looking up at him.

'I think we should drink our tea before it gets any colder.'

Abby laughed. 'Tea, of course, how British!'

'Abby, just shut up. Tea always comes first.' He laughed too, feeling slightly lightheaded. He realised he was happy, a strange sensation of well-being that he'd almost forgotten. 'Then I'll make you lunch if you're good.'

'I'm always good.'

Later that evening after Abby had gone home, Edward relaxed in his old leather armchair in front of a crackling fire. He watched the flames licking round the logs and thought about her. They had crossed a line today, and he wondered where it would take them. The letter worried him. If there was any truth in what the woman had written, there was trouble ahead.

Chapter 4

It was nearly a week since the last note had been dropped through Edward's door. He persuaded Abby not to contact the care worker while he did some background research. His head told him to ignore the communications, but he worried what might happen to an innocent bystander like the care worker. Judith had been ruthless at times, and Edward knew she'd made sacrifices to achieve results as long as she wasn't the one who got hurt. He felt he was being manoeuvred into something he didn't want to do.

There wasn't much on the internet about the care home. Their website was basic, the costs of living there very expensive, suggesting exclusivity. Having found little to go on, Edward decided he would need to speak to the woman to find out more. He thought if Judith Mulholland was in trouble he needed to tread carefully.

Abby was coming to dinner, so Edward cleaned the house, dusted and polished, until his table gleamed and the glass sparkled. He was stirring the casserole when his phone rang. It was Abby's number.

He picked it up, still stirring, 'Hi, Abby…'

'Edward, are you watching the early evening news? The BBC?' Her voice sounded urgent, even slightly panicky.

Edward turned to reach for his television remote. 'What is it?'

He switched on the small TV on his kitchen worktop. The news item was already halfway through; a news reporter was standing in a suburban street talking about the mysterious death of one of its residents. Abby said, 'Just watch,' in his ear. The reporter said '... the police are appealing for witnesses, although their spokesperson said there are no visible signs of entry or evidence that anyone else was involved. The investigation is ongoing...'

'Abby, what's it all about?' Edward thought he knew what the answer would be, and she confirmed his fears.

'Edward,' her voice sounded agitated, 'it's her, the woman who worked at the care home. She's been found dead in her house. There's no explanation, no evidence, nothing stolen or broken...'

Edward spoke quietly and calmly, 'Abby, listen to me. We'll talk later. This is not a conversation I want to have by phone. I'll check the other news programmes and see if I can work out what's happened. Don't worry. Come round as planned. Seven thirty, okay?'

She said, 'Yes, okay. I'm fine really. It just shook me up a bit. Poor woman.'

After the call, Edward flicked through all the channels looking for the report, but there was very little about it. He knew the tabloids would probably run with it. The slightest whiff of scandal, an unexplained death, would draw them in like vultures. Abby was right; the poor woman hadn't deserved that.

They talked about the mysterious death over dinner. Edward tried to play it down, not wanting to worry Abby.

Afterwards, they sat together on his leather sofa and watched the news. The story was growing. A young female reporter stood outside a semi-detached red-brick house, typically suburban, and spoke solemnly to camera, '… It seems Miss Trent lived alone with her cat. Neighbours say she kept to herself but appeared friendly. Police are saying very little about the death, other than it is, at present, unexplained. Reports are suggesting there was no break in, and the doors were locked from the inside. It was the cat that attracted attention and one of the neighbours called the local police. Apparently, she had been reported missing from her place of work this morning…'

'How sad,' Abby sighed. She sat next to Edward on the sofa, leaning against him. Tonight, he was not distracted by her proximity. He had come to the decision that he wouldn't let Abby get hurt. She must be warned of the dangerous situation they were in; to leave her unprotected would be unthinkable.

He turned towards her. 'Abby, it's more than a sad case. I don't think she died of natural causes. I suspect she may have been murdered, and it's got something to do with Judith Mulholland.' She opened her mouth to speak, but he hushed her. 'Listen, I know what I'm talking about. This is serious. There are people out there willing to go to any lengths to protect this country's security, and I think the poor woman somehow got mixed up in something that made her a threat.'

Abby looked shocked, Edward thought. Perhaps he shouldn't have been so blunt.

She put her hand on his arm. 'Edward, do they know she contacted us?'

He frowned, thinking it through. It was possible, but he thought the odds were low. Unless she had left something in her house that implicated him, they should be safe.

'You didn't call that number, did you?'

'No; if you remember, you were most insistent that I left it to you.'

'Then we should be okay. The unknown factor is Judith; she's the key to this. Until I know where she is and who she's been talking to, we can't be sure. Abby, would it be a terrible inconvenience for you to stay here, with me?'

'Edward, I'm shocked! What are you proposing?' She fluttered her eyelashes, a smile curving at the corner of her lips.

He realised she was teasing him and smiled. 'How can you be so flippant at a time like this? You are a very naughty girl.'

'I seem to remember you said that before...' she leaned in and kissed him, '... and look where that got you.'

Edward put his arm around her and said, 'Seriously, though, we must be very careful until we know more. I'd much rather be safe than sorry afterwards. I'll be a lot happier knowing you're under my roof.' He hesitated, not knowing what to say next, 'Abby, the sleeping arrangement—'

'Don't go old-fashioned on me now. We're both grown-ups. If you have a special reason to sleep alone, that's fine by me, I do understand. Not all people can share a bed. Otherwise...'

'I would love to spend every hour of the day and night with you, lovely girl...' he paused again.

'But? There is a definite "but" there, Edward.'

'I suppose I am a bit old-fashioned. I don't want us to rush into something we may regret later. It feels almost as if we're running headfirst into this, out of some sort of convenience rather than—'

'Rather than what, exactly? We're not teenagers. We've both got history. We've both had relationships before. I don't feel we're rushing into anything. It's fine if you want to sleep alone but don't use my feelings as an excuse.' She sounded angry. The flirtatiousness had disappeared.

He was baffled. All he wanted to do was protect her. Couldn't she see that?

'Abby, I'm not suggesting anything other than it matters a lot to me what you think. I wouldn't do anything to upset you. I just didn't want you to feel pressured or that I'm making assumptions that you want to share my bed.'

'My God, Edward! You can be such an idiot.' She leapt into his lap and kissed him, throwing both arms round his neck so that he was pinned to the sofa. He thought, *She's strong for such a slim girl*, before pulling her close and kissing her back.

'You're an impossible woman,' he said when she let him breathe again.

In the early hours, as dawn was casting its first glimmer of light, Edward lay staring at the ceiling. He could feel Abby's soft hair on his shoulder, listened to her quiet breathing and thought about Judith Mulholland. It seemed fair to assume she was a resident at the exclusive home in the countryside north of Bath. His instincts told him the Trent woman had died as a result of her interaction with Judith. It would be dangerous to blunder into the home without knowing more. If he could gain access to Miss Trent's house there was a slim chance that he might find something. Whoever had killed her may have missed a clue, a piece in the jigsaw.

Carefully slipping out of bed, Edward left Abby sleeping, her face covered by a curtain of dark hair. He smiled, remembering last night and how natural it had felt to fall asleep next to her. Pulling on his old joggers and a dark blue sweat top, he slowly crept from the room, avoiding the creaky boards. She slept on as he pulled the bedroom door shut behind him.

Downstairs he put the kettle on the hotplate and pushed his feet into his trainers. A quick run down through the fields and back up the bridle path would blow the mental cobwebs away. When Edward left the house by the side door, he spotted a van parked a hundred metres down the lane. It was in the shadow of the old stone wall, with dark tinted windows and grubby paintwork. He felt his heartbeat rise before he had taken a step.

If the van was occupied, he thought he mustn't reveal he'd noticed it, and behave naturally. If not, it didn't matter and he was being paranoid. Edward jogged slowly past, bending to tie his shoelace as he drew alongside so he could get a good look, and spotted a fresh cigarette butt on the ground next to the van. He continued up the lane, turned left into the woods and carried on for twenty metres or so before diving into the undergrowth. From here he could see the vehicle without being seen. He waited, his breath forming clouds of mist, his fingers chilled from inactivity. There was no movement from the van.

He looked at his watch. Another ten minutes then he would jog back down. There was a musty smell in the woods, damp undergrowth littered with last autumn's mouldering leaves as yet unaffected by new growth. Edward waited and watched. He checked the time and was just about to move when the driver's door opened.

He saw a cigarette flicked to the ground, the nub still glowing. The driver got out, stretched and looked around as if waiting for someone. He was well built, tall and dressed in nondescript dark trousers and jacket. Edward didn't recognise him. The man reached into the van, spoke to someone inside and then strolled in the direction of Edward's house. Knowing Abby was inside, sleeping innocently, gave Edward only one choice of action. He had to go back down. Taking a deep breath, he stepped back onto the track and jogged down the slope between the trees.

As he broke cover, he saw the van twitch as if someone inside had moved quickly. The driver was walking away and didn't hear him coming. Edward loped towards the vehicle and watched the driver put his hand to his ear and stop briefly before continuing at a leisurely pace. Edward passed the van, his body tense as he approached the walking man.

He reached him, jogged past with a friendly good morning, and turned down his path. Without looking back, he went inside, closing the outer door before running through the house to the front door where he peered through the peephole. He watched the man stroll by without looking at the house, noting he was talking into an earpiece. Without taking his muddy shoes off he raced upstairs into the small front bedroom. From behind the lace curtain he could see the driver standing in the lane, still not taking any interest in Edward's house but talking quietly. The van appeared beside him and he jumped into the passenger seat, casting a quick glance at the house, before it drove away up the lane.

Edward cursed. He knew his link to Judith must matter to someone and was sure now he was under surveillance. Abby stirred in the other bedroom, calling his name, and he went to her. She looked tousled, sleepily smiling up at him. He felt that overwhelming urge again to protect her, keep her safe.

She said, 'I woke up, and you'd gone. Where did you disappear off to at this time of the morning?'

'I went for a run through the woods. Thought I'd stretch my legs before getting you breakfast.' He bent to kiss her head and she grabbed him, bringing him down on top of her.

'You're not very sweaty.'

'I didn't go far; it's still quite cold out there.' Edward tried to disentangle himself, but she clung on. 'You'll have to let go or forgo breakfast.'

Abby grinned, 'There's plenty of time for breakfast. Why don't you come back to bed?'

'You are a greedy girl.' He gently extricated himself, kissing her again as he sat up. How could he tell her he was scared that their relationship put her at risk; that they were being watched; and whilst jumping back into bed with her was hugely tempting, he was too unsettled? He said, 'I need a shower. Stay where you are.'

Abby stretched her arms above her head, revealing a hint of pink nipple as the bedclothes dropped down. 'Okay, but don't be long.'

Edward threw his clothes on the bathroom floor and jumped under the shower. The hot water soothed him as he thought things through. Keeping Abby with him had seemed the best thing to do. Now he questioned his motives. She would have been safer at home. He doubted they knew who she was or where she lived. He realised he'd dug a hole for himself; sending her home now without an explanation would be heartless. They'd crossed the line between friend and lover.

He stepped out of the shower and reached for a towel. As he rubbed his hair dry, he felt a presence in the room. Someone had silently entered behind him. He reacted quickly, spinning round, towel raised to wrap against the intruder. As he raised his arm to strike, he realised it was Abby, naked and startled, who was standing in front of him.

'Shit! Abby, I'm so sorry. You surprised me. Oh God, I'm sorry.'

She looked shocked. He put his wet arms around her, felt her tense. 'Abby…'

'Edward, it's okay. You just gave me a fright. It was my fault. I shouldn't have crept up on you.' She still felt stiff in his arms. He kissed her hair, apologising again until he felt her relax.

'What happened out there, Edward?' She was staring into his eyes.

'What do you mean? I just went for a short run—'

'… and came back edgy. You left a trail of mud through the house, into the front bedroom, and you didn't raise a sweat. Then you nearly jump on me. What's going on?' She wasn't going to let him off the hook.

He sighed. She was stunning in every way, but her intelligence worried him. It meant he couldn't hide things from her. He knew he had to trust her to listen to him, act on his guidance and keep safe.

'Let's go back to the bedroom. I feel a bit self-conscious standing here dripping.'

'Tell me what's wrong, then.' She released him and turned away. He watched her pale skin tremble as she moved and thought how much he wanted to take her back to bed.

'I will. Let's go back to bed.'

Chapter 5

E dward watched the countryside rushing past the window. The green fields would soon be replaced by grey London suburbs. He worried about Abby, hoped she would be sensible while he was away.

It had been an eventful few days. He'd been surprised at how well she had taken what he told her about his past life and the current risk that it presented to both of them. He'd glossed over his days in Defence Intelligence and, before that, Special Projects. Too much information could endanger her. He remembered the look of concern on her face when he said he thought he was under surveillance. She appreciated what that meant. Edward was convinced Judith Mulholland was at the heart of it.

The train slowed as they approached Clapham Junction. Passengers were getting up, reaching for bags, coats and umbrellas as it jolted and creaked its way into the station. Was one of these fellow travellers a shadow, following his every move? Edward wondered. He considered it likely. Since he went to the station to buy his ticket, he thought it possible he'd be followed. At this point in time, he reasoned he would be a low priority and the tail would be relatively inexperienced so easy to throw off.

At Waterloo Station Edward strode through the crowds towards exit three, pushing his way past groups of giggling Japanese and old ladies with trolley bags. He didn't pause to look back, just walked quickly past the coffee shop and into the street. Outside the station he headed for the taxi rank.

Jumping in the first taxi in the queue, he asked the driver to take him to the British Museum. As they pulled away, he saw an agitated young man running to the next cab and thought, *That will be my tail*. The traffic was heavy as they edged towards Waterloo Bridge. Edward chatted to the driver about trivial things; they exchanged views on the latest government U-turn, how England needed a new manager, and the dire state of television. If asked later he would say his fare had been a nice bloke, very ordinary but decent.

They crossed the bridge. Edward looked back. The taxi following them was stuck behind a bus on the bridge. He leaned forward to speak to the driver.

'I want you to drop me off on the next corner. There's fifty quid in it for you. But it's important you continue to the museum.'

'Whatever you say, mate. You in a spot of bother, then?' The driver seemed unfazed. Edward thought that London cabbies faced all sorts of unusual requests, some much more bizarre than this one.

'Yes, you could say that. Got in the wrong bed and now the husband is after me. He's a bit of a City whizz-kid so tons of money...'

'Ha ha, you want to keep your trousers zipped in future, mate. No problem. I'll play along for you.' The cabbie chuckled.

They were off the bridge now and heading for the Strand. There was still no sign of the following taxi. Edward imagined the anxiety of the young man following him, and he was just about to make it worse. He pulled a fifty pound note out of his pocket.

'Just here will be fine. Thanks for the help. If anyone asks later, you dropped me at the museum, okay?'

'Yeah, no problem. It's not the first time I've done this. Good luck, mate. I hope she was worth it.'

Edward laughed, 'Oh yeah, definitely.' Then he jumped out of the taxi and strode away into the crowded street.

St James's Park was green, damp and quiet. The lunchtime crowd would probably be thin on the ground today, Edward thought, as the drizzle settled in. He pulled the collar of his padded jacket up to cover his neck. His hair was sticking to his head.

At twelve fifteen he saw a tall figure, hidden under a large umbrella, striding across the park from the direction of Horse Guards Road. He recognised the gait and knew it was his old friend Sebastian Darrow. Dressed in the regulation long trench coat, black leather shoes shiny from the rain, the man stopped in front of him. Sebastian stretched out his hand.

'Good to see you, Edward. It's been a long time.'

'Yes, it has. How are things, Sebastian?'

'Same old shit. *Plus ça change, plus c'est la même chose.* You know the score.'

'Indeed.' Edward smiled. Sebastian hadn't changed at all. He chose his friends well. 'I guess it will have to be the bandstand if we want to get out of this rain.'

Sebastian gave a wry laugh. 'Not the Inn on the Park, then?'

Edward laughed too. They walked together along the edge of the lake and over the bridge to the bandstand. The park seemed deserted now that the rain had gotten heavier. Under the shelter of the canopy they shook hands again. Sebastian rested his umbrella against the railing and pulled a brown envelope from his pocket.

'I don't have long,' he said. 'I'm on my way to the dentist – conveniently true. This is everything you asked for. Judith retired three years ago but there were rumours at the time she had been offered a deal she couldn't refuse. It happened quickly. This is a list of the operations she was overseeing.' He pulled out a wedge of papers. 'And this is a list of the people working for her at the time. There are a few familiar names. Also, there was some talk about her becoming ill after she left but no one seemed to know what it was or where she was being treated. I heard whispers of cancer or a stroke. Anyway, she disappeared from view. I've also managed to get a list of her previous work. Maybe there's a clue there?'

'I'm very grateful for this, Sebastian, and hope you've been careful. I don't want to get you involved as I have no idea what's going on or how big this is. All I know is Judith tried to get some information to me and the contact is now dead.'

'Sounds like pretty heavy shit, then. I'm low on the radar so I should be fine, but you take care, Edward, you're on the outside now.' Sebastian frowned.

Edward was grateful for his old friend's help but still concerned he may have put him in a difficult position. Sebastian seemed to read his mind.

He patted Edward on the back and said, 'Look, old man, I've been in this game long enough to know how to look after myself. Don't worry about me. I know what I'm doing. If you need to reach me, I've put my phone number in there too.' He smiled, and before Edward could speak added, 'It's a pay-as-you-go mobile and nobody knows I've got it.'

'Sounds like you've got it covered, then. I guess this is the parting of the ways. Take care, my friend. I'll be in touch.'

'You too, Edward. Keep safe.'

They shook hands and Sebastian unfurled his umbrella and stepped down from the bandstand. Edward watched him walk away into the rain. He thought this may be their last meeting and felt a twinge of sadness. He folded the envelope and put it inside his jacket before leaving the shelter of the stand. Now he must get to the museum as quickly as possible to maintain his cover.

At the museum Edward headed for the toilet. He needed to dry off, so he looked as if he had been there a while. There was no sign of the young man from the station, but someone was sure to be looking for him, assuming the cabbie had played his part. He rubbed his hair dry and took off his jacket.

He'd spent many happy hours here so decided to enjoy the rest of the day by revisiting his favourite galleries. If his trail caught up with him, it would look like a genuine day out. The Egyptian mummies were always top of his list and, as he peered into the brightly lit cabinets with the gold reflecting in the faces of the visitors, he kept his eyes open for the young man. Eventually, towards the end of room sixty-three, he saw him studying the contents of a cabinet containing papyrus documents.

Edward glanced at his watch. He would need to leave soon if he wanted to get out of the city before the commuters left work. The young man was leaning against a pillar trying to show an interest in the nearest exhibit. Edward guessed his tail must be new to this. That meant he was still considered a low priority, but how long would that last?

The rain had stopped, allowing a watery sun to filter through the clouds. Edward strode down the museum steps and headed for Holborn underground station. He wanted to get back to Waterloo and out of London as quickly as possible. It held no magic for him anymore. Walking quickly, he caught a glimpse of his shadow in the crowds behind him as he reached the tube station.

At Waterloo, Edward made his way through the throngs to platform six. He couldn't see the young man from the museum. Either he'd reported back and been told to stand down or someone else had taken over. It didn't matter. Edward had what he wanted and was heading home.

Chapter 6

E dward put his bag on the table. There was no sign that anyone had been in his house, but he needed to carry out a few checks before he could be sure. He went into his living room, took his phone from his pocket and clicked on photos. Comparing shots of his heap of newspapers, the magazines on the stool and the mantelpiece showed nothing had been moved.

In his study, the story was the same, no sign of any disturbance in the dust or the contents of his drawers. He felt confident his home was secure. Not for the first time he wondered whether he was being paranoid.

The living room was cold. Chilly weather seemed to invade the house and keep the cold in. Edward rubbed his hands together, watched his breath forming a mist in front of his face, and decided to light a fire. The logs were ready; all it needed was a match to ignite the firelighters placed within the kindling. He reached for the matches and knelt in front of the hearth.

As he struck the match, he saw it. Next to the logs, almost under the fire grate, was a small piece of pale blue paper. He leaned forward to pull it out as the flame reached his fingers; swearing, he dropped the hot match on the slate. The paper was a crumpled receipt from a sandwich shop in Whitehall dated three days earlier. The owner must have dropped it when reaching over the mantelpiece. It couldn't be seen from above.

Suddenly the room felt colder. Edward shivered. Putting the paper in his pocket he struck another match. He kept himself occupied for the next few minutes getting the fire to light. As it began to burn, he stood over it deep in thought. His house was no longer a haven. It seemed fair to assume he was under closer surveillance than he had thought. All his carefulness had got him nowhere.

As the fire crackled into life, he thought nothing could be taken for granted. He needed to behave as if every move was being watched, every call recorded, and every keystroke monitored. He pulled the thick curtains shut and turned on his television and table lamp. As far as anyone out there knew, he was settling in for an evening at home.

Abby opened her door to find Edward standing on the doorstep. He wore a dark close-fitting jacket and joggers, almost blending into the shadows in her porch.

'Edward! I didn't expect you. I thought you'd ring first. Are you okay?'

He said, 'Can I come in or are you going to keep me on the doorstep?'

'Of course, come in. I'm pleased to see you. How did it go today?'

Edward stepped into her hallway and shut the door behind him. He pulled off his trainers and jacket. Damp patches were visible on his sweat top. He felt hot and sticky.

'Sorry, I'm probably not very savoury. I ran over.' He pulled a folded envelope from his pocket. 'Things have moved on a bit, Abby.'

She looked concerned. 'Come through to the kitchen and I'll get you a drink while you tell me what's happened.'

He followed her into her large bright kitchen, gleaming with stainless steel and polished marble worktops. She went to a huge fridge and dropped some ice into a tumbler before adding cranberry juice.

'Your favourite,' she said, 'unless you want something stronger?'

'Not right now, thanks.' He downed it in one.

She stood leaning against the marble top, waiting for him to speak. He looked at the way her leggings clung to her legs, wished he could take her upstairs, forget about Judith Mulholland, but he knew he couldn't.

'Well, I met up with my old friend. He gave me some names to check but didn't know much so I went to the British Museum for a while then came home.'

'And?'

'And what?'

'Don't be so infuriating, Edward. I know damn well this unexpected visit isn't just because you couldn't wait to see me. What else happened today to spook you?'

An apt turn of phrase, Edward thought, then said, 'I'm being watched. I was followed in London and someone has been in the house while I was out today.' He knew it was best not to hide anything from her.

Abby stared at him. She frowned slightly then said, 'Shit. I was really hoping we were overreacting, and everything would be fine. I guess that's not the case. How did you get here tonight without being followed?'

'I'm sure they're overconfident and don't know I've sussed them. If they bother checking on me, they'll think I'm watching the TV in front of the fire or, if the surveillance is good enough, they'll think I'm out for a run.'

'Sounds a bit James Bond. Are they likely to be watching me?'

'I don't think so. They have no reason to.' Even as he said it, he wondered if he really meant it.

Abby looked unsure. Edward went to her, put his arms round her and said, 'I won't do anything to put you at risk. You know that.'

She rested her cheek against his chest. 'I know.'

He kissed the top of her head and asked if she still had her old laptop.

Abby said yes and took him through to her office. It was warm and cosy, tucked away at the back of the house behind the dining room. She found the laptop in the bottom drawer of her filing cabinet. After searching for the connection cable, she started it up for Edward.

He glanced through the list Sebastian had given him. The names were in no particular order but seemed to be batched chronologically by project work. He recognised some projects, but most were new, since he'd left the service.

Abby asked, 'Are you hungry? Would you like some pasta? My culinary skills aren't as good as yours, but I can do pasta.'

He turned to look at her. 'Sorry? Oh yes, that will be fine. Actually, I'm starving.'

'Okay, no problem. Pasta it is, then. I'll leave you in peace and give you a shout when it's done.'

She left him, closing the door behind her, and he turned back to the list. He flicked through the pages then stopped with a start. There was a name he couldn't believe, hadn't expected to see. He thought it must be a coincidence, just someone else with the same name.

Edward turned to the computer and brought up the search engine. When Abby called, he was reading through death records and scribbling notes on the list. She stuck her head round the door. He shuffled the papers, pushed the chair back and smiled at her.

'Anything helpful? You look... I don't know... a bit shell shocked. Seen a ghost?'

'There's a list full of ghosts here. It just brought back some memories I'd rather forget.' Edward stood up, careful to put the list back in his pocket. She noticed, he was sure, but said nothing. He closed the webpage, cleared the memory and turned off her laptop.

They sat together in the brightly lit kitchen, eating creamy pasta and drinking wine. He felt she was waiting for him to tell her everything, so he gave her some selected snippets of information, nothing too harmful.

'So, where does that leave us now? If you're being watched how can we...' she seemed lost for words. Edward took her hand and kissed it.

'You mustn't worry. I'll sort it. Once I find out what's going on, I'll know what to do. In the meantime, we need to behave as normal, though I think it would be a good idea if you didn't stay with me. Don't frown. We just need to assume everything in my house is being recorded. Everything.' He added emphasis on the "everything", and watched Abby realise what he meant. She coloured a little.

'Oh! That's horrible, Edward. You think they would watch it all?'

'Depends how closely they're monitoring me, but they could if they wanted. Which means, sweet girl, I must get back and give them something to stare at.' He stood up and stretched.

Abby stood up too and wrapped her arms round him as if she wouldn't let him go. He held her close, stroked her hair. She had no experience of his world; he realised she was probably afraid.

He lifted her face, kissed her and said, 'Abby, don't be scared. They will leave you alone. Just remember we're friends, it's a new relationship and you know very little about me. Stick with that and you'll be fine. Also remember, if you ring me they will be listening and, most important of all, I'm just a few minutes away if you need me. I'll see you tomorrow.'

'I'll be alright. It's a bit scary but I trust you to do the right thing. I just don't want to be alone, but I'll cope. Don't look so worried. I'll be fine.'

'Abby, we could end it. Just walk away and pretend nothing happened, then this will stop in a few weeks. They will give up...'

'But we can't be sure of that and your old boss wanted you to find something. It's obviously important, Edward...' she paused, '... so I think you should carry on.'

Back at the house Edward took off his sweaty jogging clothes and took a shower. The fire had burned down to a few glowing embers, but the room was still warm. *Newsnight* was on TV, with two red-faced politicians arguing over the economy. He sat in his armchair and let the screen flicker in front of him without registering a thing they said. Even his fleece robe couldn't warm him. The list had given him a chill that a hot shower had had no impact on.

He decided not to share with Abby what he'd learned. Watching the last sparks die in the fireplace, he clutched his tumbler of malt whisky and wondered what to do next. The single most shocking thing about today had not been the number of unexplained deaths, but one in particular. Hidden on the last page was a name that shocked him. The young man had entered the department as he left, which was why he couldn't remember meeting him.

Edward already knew the story of his death. The incident on the unmanned railway crossing had resulted in his car being destroyed by the train carrying tons of stone from the local quarry. Robert Rayner had been killed instantly, although nobody knew why he'd been there, least of all his wife, Abby.

Chapter 7

E dward woke to the sound of heavy rain beating against
the bedroom window. He felt tired and his head ached.
Then he remembered the full tumbler of whisky. Hauling
himself upright he muttered, 'idiot' and headed for the
bathroom.

Breakfast was a cup of strong coffee and two pieces of
toast. He watched the water streaming down the window
and thought about ringing Abby. The list, neatly folded,
was hidden in his trouser pocket. It would go wherever he
went; there mustn't be any mistakes.

He felt trapped in the house. Knowing that his every
move was being scrutinised restricted what he could do. The
internet was out of the question, as were any phone calls.
There was little he could do to progress his investigation
without giving his watchers the slip. Edward paced up and
down the living room, ran upstairs for a magazine but
couldn't settle to read it. The post dropped through the
door, but that only consisted of bills and flyers. By eleven
he had to get out.

He picked up the phone and called Abby. She answered
almost straight away, as if she'd been waiting for him to
ring.

'Hi, Abby. How are you today? I guess the weather stopped you walking this morning?'

'Oh hello, Edward. I was just thinking of ringing you.' Her voice sounded natural.

He thought, *Good girl* and said, 'Beat you to it. I'm going into Bath to do some shopping. Do you want to come with me?'

'I'd love to. Shall we catch the train in? The parking will be dreadful. It's half term week.'

'Good idea. I think it's easing off a bit. Do you want to meet me at the station?' He knew she would say yes. She was playing it just right.

On the train, they chatted about the weather. She told him she needed to spend some time catching up with her fitness programme ready to start dance teaching again in the autumn. He told her he needed to get some articles finished for the history magazine he wrote pieces for. Anyone listening in would have heard a pleasant if boring conversation.

They left the station, crossed the road, and dodged through the crowds into the shopping centre. Edward hoped the surrounding noise would drown out anything they said to each other.

He leant over her head and said softly, 'You're doing brilliantly. Are you sure you're not a spy?'

Abby laughed. 'I always thought it would be glamorous, all furs and diamonds, like Mata Hari. When I was young, I wanted to be Greta Garbo after my mum showed me one of her films.'

'You're far too lively. She was a cool Swede. Seriously, I think you're doing great.'

'So are you. But I suppose you've had far more experience than me?' She made it sound like a question, as if she wasn't sure exactly what Edward was.

He gave her a small smile. 'Unfortunately I have but I'm not saying any more than that, and certainly not today.'

'Edward, I won't ask if you don't want to tell me but… I do appreciate who you are. It makes me feel safe.'

He gave her arm a squeeze as they walked into Marks and Spencer. They spent some time choosing some sweat tops and T-shirts. Abby amused herself trying to guess who their tail was as Edward did his shopping. He didn't have the heart to tell her he'd already spotted the young man from London. It irritated him how sloppy the department had become, sending the same man out, especially as he wasn't very good. He was so tempted to go right up to him and say, hello, didn't I see you the other day?

Instead he said to Abby, 'Let's go for lunch without our tail.'

'How?' She looked surprised.

'Just follow my lead and be prepared to move quickly.'

He paid for his purchase and they ambled through the racks towards the down escalator. As they approached it Edward linked arms with Abby and pointed to something in the furniture section. They walked slightly past the escalator as if they were going to look at the sofas. As a crowd of tourists moved towards them, Edward suddenly turned and pulled Abby with him. They were going down with a group of people behind them. He caught sight of the startled face of his shadow as they descended and resisted the temptation to wave.

Abby held his arm tightly. As they reached the bottom he said, 'We need to move quickly now. Head for the back door, through the food department.' Then he gave her a gentle push and they almost ran past the card display and into the food aisles. Before he let her stop for breath, they were in Abbey Green.

Abby was laughing, her eyes sparkled. 'Wow! I didn't know you could move that quick, Edward.'

'We're not done yet. He's young and could soon catch up if he realises which way we've gone. Come on, my girl. Keep moving.'

Edward knew the crowds were their best defence and headed past the Abbey and up towards Bond Street.

'I know a nice little pub where we can get some food and a beer in peace with a bit of luck.'

Abby was struggling to keep up. 'I'm out of breath. How do you keep so fit?'

'What, at my age?'

'Don't start that again. You know that's not what I meant.'

'Only teasing. We're nearly there, just up here.' He took her arm and steered her down some steps to an old passageway, then through a glass door into a small bar. 'I'll be very impressed if he finds us here. In fact, I'll buy him a pint.'

Inside the dim interior of the old pub they settled in a corner where Edward could keep an eye on the door. The regulars clustered round the bar, laughing and joking. The noise they made drowned out any conversation. They leaned towards each other to talk.

'So, what next?' Abby asked.

Edward stared into his drink. 'I think I have only one choice. I've got to find Judith and talk to her. Find out why she sent me that picture. It doesn't make sense. What concerns me is the death of that woman. Why kill her?'

Abby leaned closer and whispered, 'Because she knew something important.'

'Yes, but what?'

'Where's the picture now?'

It was a simple question, but it made Edward nearly drop his pint. He had completely overlooked the photo since the day they returned from visiting the archivist. It had been in his car then... What had he done with it? Abby watched his face and touched his arm.

'You don't know where it is?'

Edward gripped his glass, almost hissed through his teeth, 'No, I don't. Christ, what a complete idiot. No wonder I've been under such close surveillance. I've been giving clues away. They probably think I know much more than I do.'

Abby moved closer on the bench. 'Edward, don't be so hard on yourself. Could it still be in the car? Does it really matter if they have it?'

He carefully thought through events. The photo had been in the glovebox with the notes. He had left them there. Then a few days later, he'd moved them. They were in a file in his office, surrounded by receipts and invoices. Maybe, if their search of his house was as shoddy as their surveillance, it was still safely hidden.

He told Abby. She looked relieved.

'But what do we do next?'

He took her hand, kissed it and said, '*We* do nothing. *I* will go to see Judith. And I think it must be as soon as possible.'

Abby ignored the obvious attempt to exclude her, 'Why not today? You've lost our shadow. Why not go straight home and get the car? I'm assuming you think she's in that home?'

He thought it over. Abby was right to think of using shock tactics, but that would undoubtedly escalate things. She was smiling at him. Then she dropped her bombshell.

'Anyway, I have an interview there this afternoon at four.'

'What?' He spluttered beer across the table. 'Are you mad? When were you planning to tell me?' He was angry with her. How could she be so naïve?

'Calm down; people are looking.' Abby gripped his arm. He saw she was right; several of the men at the bar were looking curious. She kissed him, wrapped her arm round his neck and they went back to their drinks.

Edward hissed in her ear, 'This is not some Girl Guide challenge. You could get yourself killed, Abby.'

'I think I might survive an interview—'

'This is no joke.' He was thinking of her husband, an experienced officer, killed on a level crossing. How would she feel if she knew that? 'These are dangerous people. I want you to ring and cancel.'

Abby stared at her drink then raised her eyes to his and said quietly, 'I thought it would give you cover, provide a diversion for you to speak to Judith. When I'm being interviewed the decision makers will be with me, not watching who comes and goes.'

He was surprised. She had really given this some thought. Worse still, she was right.

'But what about what happens afterwards? Did you think of that?'

'Not really; that will depend on what you find out, won't it?' She gave him a half smile. 'We might have to move in together, go live on an island somewhere.'

Edward was exasperated but impressed. 'Oh, Abby. I don't know what to do with you.'

She looked at her watch. 'It's one thirty. I think we should go back to mine. I'll go off for the interview early so we can stake it out.'

'There's no stopping you, is there? Just one last question: how did you intend to lose me, and the tail, so you could go off to the home?'

'I didn't need to lose the tail. He's following you not me.'

They reached the station and made the journey home without seeing the young man again. Edward thought it possible someone else had taken over but didn't say so to Abby.

As she got ready, he watched the road from her bedroom window for any activity and grilled her about the interview. She'd found out which agency supplied the home with temporary staff and approached them. They were recruiting for a temporary employee to cover Miss Trent's job, which turned out to be the administrator role. Edward had to admire her guts. He was praying that the organisation hadn't put two and two together. If only he had some way of knowing whether they saw Abby as a problem.

He watched her dress in a smart grey suit. Her hair was pulled back and tied up. Suddenly, the bubbly girl he loved had become a serious looking administrator. She caught him watching her and smiled.

'Do I look the part?'

'You look… completely different. I'm impressed.'

'Good. I have some glasses too.'

Edward was amazed. She'd thought of everything.

Then she said, 'There is one last thing I didn't tell you. I'm not going as Abby Rayner. I stole a friend's identity. I'm Sarah Mitchell, recently moved into the area with my husband, who's in the army, and just want a temping job till we move on again. Impressed?'

'How the hell…?'

She waved her hand in the air. 'Oh, don't ask! She owed me a favour from long ago. We look similar enough for the passport to match up. So… are you a bit happier now?'

'Happy? I'm completely overwhelmed by your ingenuity. As I've said before, you're a very clever girl.' But something was bothering Edward. She'd hidden all this from him; the decision making, the planning had all been her idea and completed without his help or support. What else might she hide from him – something that might endanger her or both of them? She might be clever, but she wasn't aware of how treacherous a game this was.

Chapter 8

Westwick Manor stood in twelve acres of parkland and manicured gardens. The sweeping drive, lined by ancient horse chestnuts, led the visitor to the grand entrance. Abby stopped outside the tall iron gates. Edward got into the back and lowered himself between the seats so that he would be invisible as they approached the house. He was nervous, more for Abby than for himself.

She chatted as she pulled onto the drive. 'Apparently, it's late Elizabethan with a Georgian façade and bits added by the Victorians. Typical English country house, large and rambling. Like me; rambling that is, not large.'

'Abby, keep calm. You'll be fine. They'll expect some nerves – this is an interview. When it's over, come back to the car. If I don't come out within five minutes, drive away. It will look suspicious if you hang around. I'll meet you back at that layby up the road. If I don't appear within twenty minutes you are to leave without me. Promise me you will.'

There was a pause. Then she said, 'Okay. I promise, but it'll be fine. Right, we've reached the house. There's a car park around the side of the building. I'm going to park by the wall. There are some large bushes the other side of the car parking area. We're only visible from what looks like the dining room so you should be able to get out without being seen.'

Abby turned off the engine. He heard birds singing in the shrubbery and the gentle rain on the car roof. She turned to reach for her handbag and gripped his hand tightly. He squeezed it and she let go.

They said in unison, 'Don't do anything silly', and she laughed.

Abby looked at her watch. 'I'm going to go in now. I want to seem eager and it will give me a chance to check things out. I'll leave the car unlocked. See you in a while, Crocodile.'

'See you later, Alligator.' It was on the tip of his tongue to add an endearment, but she'd already gone.

The silence in the car felt almost overpowering. Edward waited, checked the time, and adjusted his position so he could see out across the car park. He had to get his timing right and enter reception just after Abby had gone through for her interview. This was the tricky part. He hoped they'd be punctual.

At five past four he got out of the car and stretched his stiff limbs before walking briskly around the side of the building to the front door. Daylight was fading due to the persistent drizzle. The front of the house, with its Bath stone façade, looked very grand, even in the gloom. He walked up the well-worn shallow steps to the large oak door.

He thought luck was with him as he entered the entrance hall. The welcome desk stood empty, and he guessed the receptionist had probably taken Abby through to her interview. He moved quickly, knowing he would have just a few minutes before the receptionist returned.

There was no one about. He slipped behind the desk and searched for a plan of the building and, hopefully, a list of residents. A pile of leaflets and welcome packs for potential clients lay on a shelf beneath the desk. He grabbed one. It included a map of the site, but he couldn't find a record of the occupants. That would make his search more difficult. He didn't want to ask for her by name. His instincts told him they would be prepared for any unknown visitors.

He heard the sound of a door closing. Edward cut his losses and moved swiftly away from the desk. He headed away from the direction of the sound and into a long corridor. He saw a sign for visitor toilets and headed for it. Inside the marble-clad convenience, he flicked through the brochure.

There was more to this place than just the main house. Behind the grand old building were some purpose-built single-storey blocks, nicely faced in Bath stone and prettily landscaped. The bushes would provide cover if he needed it, he thought. Reading through the brochure, he realised that one block hardly merited a mention, other than it housed terminally ill residents. This seemed the logical place to start.

Edward cautiously opened the outer door. The corridor was empty; distant voices came from rooms further along, accompanied by occasional laughter. He slipped out and strode purposefully towards the glass doors leading to the rear courtyard. As he left the building, he passed a woman in a carer's uniform. She gave him a quizzical look, so he smiled and commented on the awful weather before slipping out into the rain. He turned to see if she looked back, but she moved on without a backward glance.

The courtyard opened out into landscaped walkways leading to the four blocks; each had a sign with a name relating to a local place. He passed Dyrham and Hinton before turning a corner to find the last block standing slightly apart, surrounded by low hedging.

As he approached, he saw a door lock on the main entrance. *This might pose a problem*, he thought. The path led to the front door and continued around the side of the building. He followed it. At the rear was another entrance with a path leading to an area of paving under a wooden structure. There were cigarette ends on the floor. This was his way in.

He waited under the shelter. Picking up a half-smoked cigarette from the ground, he watched the door. Within a minute, a young nurse backed out, struggling to light a cigarette. He flicked the end across the paving, said, 'thanks' and slipped in before she could register who he was. Chances were, she would be agency staff, he thought, as he walked briskly down the corridor. No shouts of challenge followed him, so he reckoned he'd guessed right.

It was eerily quiet. This building had a clinical quality about it, more hospital than residential home. He looked at each sign he passed and noted the storerooms. The building had four spurs, with one corridor running the length of the block. Peering into the side rooms as he passed, all he saw was an occasional nurse or nursing assistant. There seemed to be no visitors. He would raise an alarm if he was spotted. He needed a cover.

Edward tried several storerooms before he found what he was looking for. Five minutes later, dressed in a white coat, he continued his search. It would work from a distance, but he had no security badge.

Judith had to be here somewhere. He began checking each room he passed. Some rooms had four beds, some two and some single. None had names on the door. He was surprised at how young some occupants seemed to be. He had expected elderly residents but most of them looked no more than forty. He worried he may not recognise her if she was terminally ill.

Towards the end of the final corridor he found a single room with an old lady in a hospital bed. He peered through the glass panel. She turned her head and, seeing him, waved a frail arm in his direction. He paused but she gestured again, more urgently, and he realised he was looking at Judith Mulholland.

Edward was shocked at how emaciated she looked. He remembered her thick glossy hair, now thinly framing her shrunken features. She gave him a tiny smile as he approached the bed. He saw a drip connected to her arm. She mouthed, 'morphine' and coughed slightly.

Edward took her hand. 'Judith, I'm so sorry to see you like this.'

Her eyes retained their startling blue directness, but her voice was faint.

'Edward. I knew you would come.' Speaking seemed an effort for her. He leaned closer.

'I don't have long, Judith. If they find me here…'

'I know.'

'Why did you send me that picture?'

'It was all I had left. They don't let us have paper. The girl was very helpful. Did they get her? She stopped coming to see me...' She struggled for breath.

'I'm afraid so, Judith. She was found dead in her house; waiting on a coroner's report.'

'That's regrettable.'

Same old Judith, Edward thought, *no real attachment or emotion*. Judith coughed. Edward guessed she must be in a lot of pain.

'Edward, listen to me. I'll be brief. I can't be anything else...' she coughed again, '... I've been a prisoner here for over three years. They brought me here after the Tennyson project fell apart. I asked too many questions. I was told to retire.' She paused, gestured towards a jug of water, and he poured some into a plastic mug. She sipped it and then continued, 'This place is full of "retired" spooks. They keep them sedated. It looks like dementia to anyone who checks. Some have been disposed of...' She paused again. 'Sebastian kept a list.'

'I know. He gave it to me. Can I trust him?'

'Absolutely.'

'How come you're not sedated now?'

'They don't need to, Edward. I'm dying. Cancer.' She stared at him. 'You must stop this, Edward. Some of my best people are rotting here or have been killed. I chose you because I know I can trust you and it's a long time since we worked together. They wouldn't think...'

Edward held her hand. He said, 'I'll do my best, Judith. I need evidence to pin on them. Does Sebastian have anything else?'

'He was American. The one who came to see me...'

'American? Who was he, Judith? From Washington?'

'You need to find the link between all the projects.' She coughed again, a rattling, body shaking cough that affected her speech. Edward leaned close but all he caught was what sounded like 'muffin' and 'Warminster' but the rest escaped him. She gestured to the water jug and he offered her a glass, lifting it to her dry lips.

'Is there anything else, Judith?'

Judith looked confused. She put her hand to her head. 'They took everything from me, you know? All my belongings, my lovely pearls.' A tear rolled down her ashen cheek. 'Everything. All gone. All gone.'

'Judith…' Edward leaned over her and touched her arm, '… what else should I look for?'

But she'd slipped back into a state of semi-consciousness. He couldn't reach her. She looked tiny, shrivelled, a shadow of the powerful woman she'd been. He watched the tear trickle onto the pillow and stroked her cool forehead. This would be the last time he saw her, he thought.

Sighing, he straightened up. Now he must get out of here before he was discovered. If they found him, he might end up in one of the beds.

Leaving Judith without a backward glance he slipped out of the room. The corridor was still quiet. Edward listened closely to every sound; the slightest noise made his neck prickle as he made his way quietly towards the central corridor. He passed a storeroom where he heard voices on the other side of the door and hurried on.

Abby was here in this hellish place. That worried him more than his own safety, but he knew that his discovery might endanger her too. He reached the outer door to the smoking shelter without being seen and slipped out into the dusk. The rain fell steadily now, and the darkness offered him some protection. He decided to ditch the white coat and dropped it into a waste bin.

Checking his watch, he wondered if her car would still be there. He almost hoped it wouldn't be as that would mean she'd left safely. He took the path around the old house, keeping close to the shelter of the bushes. Crossing what looked like the old stable yard he came out into the car park. It was four forty-five, and Abby's car was still parked where she'd left it.

He was about to cross the gravel when he saw her walk around the corner, and she wasn't alone. A tall, severe looking woman and a broad, grey-haired man walked beside her. Edward dropped back behind the bushes. He heard their voices as they reached the car.

'Well, thank you very much for coming today, Mrs Mitchell. We'll be in touch shortly with the details. Congratulations. Have a safe journey home.'

Abby's clear voice floated across to him, 'Thank you so much. I can't wait to tell my husband.'

He listened to their receding footsteps crunch across the gravel and the car door slam. The rain was running down the back of his neck. He waited for a minute then dashed across the car park and jumped into the car. Abby gave a little shriek then clapped her hand to her mouth.

'Sorry, you made me jump.'

'Get out of here, Abby. Don't hang around.' Edward slipped behind the seat as Abby started the engine and turned on the lights. 'And lock the doors. I don't want anyone climbing in.' He held his breath as she reversed and pulled out of the car park. He half expected alarms and running people pursuing them down the drive. The place had made him nervous.

They reached the end of the drive and she pulled out onto the road. Edward lifted himself back onto the seat.

Abby said, 'Are you going to tell me what happened back there? I'm shaking.'

'I'm sorry if I came over a bit paranoid. Let's put some miles between us and that place and we can stop.'

'Okay.'

They stopped at a supermarket on the outskirts of Bath. Edward bought some food and they sat in the car eating sandwiches while he told her what he'd found. Abby was horrified. He could see she now understood the seriousness of their situation.

'Nobody saw you?'

'Nobody other than the nurse and the care assistant; they looked like agency staff. But we can't assume anything. I think we were lucky to get in and out without being detected but that doesn't mean they won't put two and two together. Your identity theft is only as good as your car. I'm sorry, Abby, but that might be why they walked you back to it. There's the possibility they're checking the ownership right now.'

'You're scaring me, Edward.' Her face looked pale under the yellow lights of the supermarket car park.

He said, 'I'm sorry, Abby. I've got to be honest with you.'

'What are we going to do?'

Edward frowned and ran his hand through his hair. 'I don't know. I need to talk to Sebastian again. Do you have anywhere you can go? Any friend who might put you up for a while?'

'I'm not leaving you.' She said it forcefully.

'You're not safe with me, Abby,' he said quietly.

'Neither of us is safe now. I'd rather be unsafe *with* you than without you.'

Chapter 9

As they drove back, they argued about what to do. Abby was adamant she wouldn't leave Edward. He tried to convince her, but she wouldn't budge. As they got near to home, he watched for any signs they were being followed. She pulled onto her drive and turned to face him.

'Do you think they're out there in the shadows?' she said as she turned off the engine.

'Possibly.' He felt a creeping sense of fatigue, the type of tiredness that drains a person of the ability to think straight. 'Let's go in. I need to decide what to do next.'

As Abby made tea, Edward went up the stairs into her bedroom to watch the road for signs that she was under surveillance. The streetlights lit the road for several hundred metres in each direction. There was no one to be seen. Abby came in with a mug of tea.

'Do you think I should contact the home and tell them I'm not interested after all? They may not check my vehicle if I don't accept the job.'

'Well, you definitely can't take it so there's nothing to lose by turning it down, but we can't be sure they haven't already run checks on you.'

Abby put her hand to her mouth and cried, 'Oh my God! What about Sarah? I've implicated her in this.'

Edward smiled and pulled her onto the bed beside him. 'It will be obvious she's a victim of identity theft. If they visit her at all, they would quickly rule her out. They're not fools. Don't worry about her.'

He didn't want to worry Abby any more than necessary, but he couldn't decide what to do. He took one last look outside and suggested they go back downstairs.

Edward paced about the kitchen; he couldn't settle. How much did they know? What was fact and what was theory? After a few minutes of watching him pace, Abby almost shouted, 'Edward, will you please talk to me?'

'Sorry, I'm just trying to get things straight, work out what the risks are.'

'And?'

Edward stopped walking and stood in front of her. He wanted to wrap his arms around her and tell her it was all going to be fine.

'The truth is I can't be sure that whatever I do next will be the right thing. Any action I take now carries a risk. What do we know? The only thing I'm sure of is that I'm being observed and listened to. That's a given. So they must be aware that Judith contacted me. They've probably worked out that I think I'm under surveillance after we shook our tail in Bath today. What we don't know is whether they're watching you too. I can't be one hundred percent sure I got in and out today without being spotted. I can't be sure they haven't linked you to the home either...' Edward paused, frowning slightly. 'The thing is, Abby, they have an arrogant belief that they're invincible. Judith has definitely rattled them, but they might still think it's a storm in a teacup. If that's the case and I overreact we could be in more danger than by doing nothing.'

Abby opened her mouth to argue but Edward stopped her, 'But – and this is the big one – if I do nothing and I'm wrong, we'll get no second chance. There will be no warning.'

'So what do we do now?'

'I have to make up my mind which is the lesser evil.'

Abby phoned the agency and told them she'd discussed the job with her husband and decided not to take it. Edward thought it gave her comfort that she had somehow reduced the risk. He let her believe that to be true. As she was talking on the phone, he decided to ask her to stay the night with him. He wanted to keep her close. She jumped at the idea and went to pack an overnight bag.

Outside the street was quiet. The rain had stopped but there was no one about. They drove across town and she parked by the wall where the van had been two days before. There was no sign of any unusual vehicles in the lane. Before they left the car, Edward reminded Abby that every word they spoke was possibly listened to. She nodded but said nothing.

He hugged her and whispered in her ear, 'Sorry, I didn't mean to patronise you.'

Inside everything looked the same. Edward thought it would be easy to reason he was being paranoid. They went through to the living room. It smelled of burnt wood; the hearth was covered in ash from the last fire.

'Sorry, I left this morning without clearing it. I'll get rid of this and light a fresh fire. It won't take long.'

Abby said, 'I'll take my bag upstairs.'

Edward cast his eye around the place. It all looked as if nothing had been touched, but then he remembered how he'd been fooled before. He remembered the photo and thought he'd see if it was still where he'd left it. Abby came back into the room and he smiled at her.

'I'm just going to check some paperwork. Would you like to put the kettle on?'

'Yes, of course. Tea or coffee?'

'Tea please.'

Edward opened the door to his office and thought everything looked just the same, but that was no guarantee. He lifted down the file of bills and found the photo exactly where he expected it to be. Slipping it into his pocket he closed the door and went back into the living room.

He cleared the grate and got a fire started while Abby made a pot of tea. They'd decided not to drink anything stronger; he wanted to stay alert. She put the TV on and watched the news as he searched for something to cook.

'Actually, Edward, I'm not that hungry. Cheese on toast would do me.' She followed him into the kitchen. He looked at her pale face and strode across the floor to give her a hug.

'Cheese on toast it is, then.'

As the bread toasted, Edward pulled a notepad and pen from a kitchen drawer. He put it on the table in front of Abby and wrote *This is how we communicate*. She smiled and took the pen from him.

Sitting in front of the fire they scribbled notes to each other, throwing them into the flames afterwards.

Abby said, 'I'd like to see that film. What's it called? Ah yes, *Burn after Reading* with George Clooney. I think maybe you look a bit like him.'

Edward wrote, *Don't be naughty*, and said, 'It's a comedy, isn't it? And I don't look anything like him. Wish I had his money though.'

'Me too.' *What next? Have you got a plan yet?*

'Shall we go to bed? The fire's dying down and it's not worth putting more logs on.' *I'm going to contact Sebastian tomorrow.*

'Yes, okay. I'm feeling a bit tired.'

Edward poked the fire, making sure the notes were completely burned. He wasn't sure how much sleep he'd get but Abby needed to rest. She looked worn out.

While Abby slept, her head on his shoulder and an arm across his chest, Edward thought it all through. He couldn't make the connections. Judith had been too ill to give him much to go on and he wasn't sure how much faith he had in what she'd said. Sebastian seemed his only hope of getting to the bottom of it all. Judith said to trust him, and her judgement had always been sound. Then he remembered the morphine drip. What if her judgement was impaired? He thought he had to trust his own instinct; after all, Sebastian was an old friend.

By the early morning, after hours of wakefulness, Edward decided to take Abby to a safe house. He had a friend with a cottage on Dartmoor that he hardly used. He was currently working in America so it would be empty. They could stay there as long as they liked. But first he needed to see Sebastian and make a few phone calls.

Abby shifted slightly, and he slipped out of bed. Dawn was breaking. He went into the guest room and looked down the lane. There was still nobody there.

Chapter 10

Edward put the shopping bags on the back seat of Abby's car. The supermarket had been quiet: too early for most people. He cursed, having cut his finger on the sharp plastic edges of the pay-as-you-go SIM card packaging. A new mobile phone lay on his lap. Sucking the blood from his finger he fitted the card and closed the phone cover.

He checked the rear-view mirror again. There was no one in sight. It didn't feel right; convinced something was wrong he tapped out a brief text message to Sebastian before turning on the engine. *This is my PAYG number. Ok to text. Edward.*

Why weren't they following him? He thought it probable the car was tagged; they didn't need to follow him if they knew where he was. He thought about Abby alone in his house as he drove back. She'd been sleepy when he left and happy to stay in bed while he went shopping. He hadn't told her yet about the cottage.

By the time he reached his lane it was drizzling again, a fine mist of rain on the screen. He parked carefully next to the wall, leaving enough room for cars to squeeze past. Pulling his collar up against the damp breeze, he pulled out the shopping bags and walked the short distance to the house. He could see the kitchen light on as he made his way up the path.

Edward dropped the shopping on the table. There was no sign of Abby. He called out that he was putting the kettle on. As he began to unpack, he felt the phone vibrate in his pocket. It was a text from Sebastian. He read the screen – *Contact me soonest. We need to meet urgently. I can travel out as far as Newbury.* He thought, *What the hell?*

Why hadn't Abby come down? Edward went to call up the stairs. As he entered the hall, he saw the white sheet of paper on the side table. It was a note, neatly written in green ink. He felt his heart pound as he picked it up and read it. Throwing it on the floor he ran up the staircase, two steps at a time. Flinging open his bedroom door he saw the overturned chair, the bedclothes pulled across the floor and the broken glass tumbler. Abby's night bag lay in the corner, upended, its contents strewn around.

Edward slumped on the bed and swore repeatedly. He'd lost her, after telling her he would keep her safe. Why hadn't he acted quicker? If they'd gone yesterday instead of dithering – why hadn't he been more decisive?

He went back downstairs and read the note again. It said, *We have her, Edward. You won't see her again. Take this as a warning. You do NOT interfere. You do NOT take an interest in our affairs. Judith Mulholland is dead. She was a confused and unreliable old woman and you should not take any communication from her as anything other than the ramblings of a sick mind. You will NOT try to find us or your friend, or else you will join Judith. We will be watching. Mrs Rayner's life depends on it.*

It made no sense. Why take Abby? Why be so obtuse? It only made sense if they weren't sure what he knew, how much he knew. They hadn't killed Abby because they intended to keep her as a bargaining tool if it turned out he knew enough to damage the organisation. This was a shot across the bow. Edward put his head in his hands and took a deep breath. He felt utterly helpless. He had no knowledge worth bartering. He was fumbling in the dark. One thing he was certain about: he would get Abby back if it was the last thing he did. They'd declared war, and this was a battle he had experience in.

Sebastian must have some answers. Edward sent a text suggesting a meeting as soon as possible. He would catch a train to Newbury, but first he had preparations to make and a false trail to lay.

The train pulled out of the station. Edward was the last to get off. The other passengers left the station; not one looked back. He decided he wasn't being followed and walked out of the station to the car park as arranged with Sebastian.

A dark blue Citroen drove slowly past him and the passenger door opened. A familiar voice shouted, 'Jump in!' Edward clambered in and shook Sebastian's hand.

'Good to see you, Sebastian.'

'And you, Edward. How's things?' Sebastian drove quickly away. Turning right he headed out of the town.

'Not good. They've got Abby; took her this morning. I presume they intend to keep her as a hostage. I saw Judith yesterday. Is it true she's dead? She was in a pretty bad way when I was with her.'

'Is that what they told you? It could well be true. I heard she was dying. I wasn't sure whether that was just a rumour. So you found her? Do you think that's what triggered things?'

'Possibly but I don't think so. The security was pretty lax. I got in and out without being challenged. I think what did it was Abby going for a job interview there.'

'What? You let an amateur do the dirty work?' Sebastian sounded shocked.

'Not exactly. She organised it all herself, but I should have stopped her. Instead I used it as a way in and now I regret it bitterly.'

'Do I take it, Edward, that there's some attachment? How many rules did you break here?'

Edward resented Sebastian's tone, wanted to tell him to fuck off but held his tongue. 'Yes, there is an attachment, as you so quaintly put it, but we formed our relationship before all this shit took off. I had no way of knowing what I was walking into because nobody warned me.'

Sebastian smiled, 'Okay, point taken. Don't get arsy with me. I'm sorry about the girl. Listen, Edward, this is seriously deep shit we're in. I've dug around as much as I can but I daren't go any deeper or else I'll be joining your girlfriend.'

'How safe are we today?'

'Well, my car is in the garage having a service and this is a courtesy car so we should be alright. I've only got my private mobile on me and I swept it all before I set off. What about you?'

'I left my phone at home, switched on. I don't seem to have a tail at the moment. They stopped following me about two days ago. I know they were in my house, so I've assumed I'm well bugged, probably the car as well. I don't have any way of testing it as I'm an outsider now.'

'Yes, that's a distinct disadvantage for you, and potentially dangerous for me too, so I've bought you some things.' He gestured to the back seat. 'We'll go through everything when we get there.'

'Where are we going, by the way?'

'My sister's place. I'm staying for a couple of days, to look after her dog while she has a break in London.'

'That's convenient.'

'Yes, very. Here we are.' Sebastian drove up a winding driveway and stopped in front of a neoclassical red-brick house. 'My brother-in-law's in the financial services sector – all new money and no taste.' He chuckled as he climbed out of the car.

They entered through the side door into a large glossy white kitchen. Sebastian let the dog out of the utility room and into the garden. He took Edward through the polished hallway to a family room overlooking the expansive garden. They stood watching the old Labrador ambling about in the flower beds. Sebastian put a small holdall on the coffee table in front of them.

'Your goodies. Don't say I never give you anything.'

Edward unzipped the bag and looked in. He pulled out a glasses case, watch, several small boxes and a handgun.

'Let's go through it.' Sebastian sat down and Edward sat opposite him in one of the leather armchairs. 'I managed to get my hands on this lot bit by bit. It's untraceable. The glasses have infra-red and built-in camera. The watch is both camera and audio – you have up to four hours' storage. This...' he opened one of the boxes '... is another camera but works perfectly well as a clock radio too. This other box contains a working Samsung phone, with a difference of course. It will record all conversations within a range of twenty-five metres. You can put your SIM in it and use it as your phone. Programme it to call me automatically if you need help. Then there's...' he pulled out the handgun, '... the gun. Remember how to use one of them, Edward?'

'Hah, hah, Sebastian.' Edward picked it up, felt its smooth cold surface and put it down again. He wanted to wipe his hand on something. 'I thought I'd finished with all this. So, what do you know? Why are they going to so much trouble?'

Sebastian sat back in his chair and chewed his lip. 'That's the thing, Edward. It's complicated. I'm not sure what's going on, but I know it involves several UK departments, including the MoD, and the US have a stake, a fairly big one too. I've come across a few communications but no detail whatsoever. I think Judith stumbled onto something by accident but not enough to get herself killed. They just played safe by removing her from the arena. All I can tell you is that she knew the people on that list had some involvement in it.'

'In what, though? What could be so big that it's worth removing or disabling all those people? What did they have in common?'

'That, old boy, is the million-dollar question. Once you crack that you've got your bargaining chip, but also,' he leaned forward, 'possibly your death sentence. Be careful, Edward. I won't be able to protect you. I can't even be sure I can protect myself.'

'I think the answer is in that list. I have to find the common factor between them all. Are you able to get your hands on their service histories, where they worked, what projects, et cetera?'

'I'll do my best.'

'Thing is, Sebastian, I'm not even sure who's following me – who I've upset.'

'Well, old friend, it seems to be headed up by our old department but with input from Defence Intelligence too. I told you, this is serious shit. I hope you have a good plan and a good hiding place.'

'I think the hiding place is sound. As for a plan...' Edward paused, '... it's pretty fluid at the moment. Until I know more about these guys, I can't plan a course of action.'

He ran his hands through his hair and stared at the things on the table. Where was Abby and what were they doing to her? Sebastian seemed to guess his thoughts. He leaned over, patted Edward's knee and stood up.

'Can I get you a drink? Something to sooth the pain?'

'Usually I'd say no but, to be honest, I think today I'll make an exception. What have you got?'

'Let's raid Jeffery's bar and find out.'

Chapter 11

Edward left the railway station on foot. He checked and double checked but nobody was tailing him; perhaps they thought they'd got him where they wanted him. Abby's car was still in the car park, if anyone cared to check. As he made his way up the narrow streets to the Bath side of town, the rain became heavier and the sky darkened.

Before leaving Sebastian, he gave him the grid reference for the cottage, as a final resort in case he needed an emergency bolthole. Edward told him to get himself out if things got tough.

It was a five-mile walk to his friend's house. He knew how to get in, where the keys for the cottage and his car would be. Ben would not be a problem. They knew each other through the sports centre when Edward had been serious about keeping fit, but he hadn't been in a while. Ben had said, on numerous occasions, to use the cottage if ever Edward felt the need for a break. There was only one rule – 'Just leave it as you found it.'

The bag hung heavy on Edward's shoulder, the rain soaked through his jacket and his head ached slightly from the brandy they'd found in the bar. He shook himself and trudged on. Abby filled his thoughts, and how the hell he was going to get her back.

Ben's neat stone house stood at the end of a narrow lane. Luckily it wasn't overlooked, but Edward doubted anyone would be out in this awful weather. As he passed the other houses all the curtains had been pulled shut. He reached the house, slipped around the side to the back garden and switched on his small flashlight. In its thin beam he could just make out the old owl statue sitting on the rockery – Ben's chosen key safe. He found the spare back door key tucked under the stone.

There was no alarm system; Edward silently thanked his friend for his slapdash approach to security. He let himself in and dropped the bag on the slate floor, followed by his dripping coat and shoes. There was no need to make a mess; stealing was enough.

In the cold, dark silence of his friend's kitchen the enormity of his situation finally hit Edward. The loss of Abby gnawed at him, an ache that wouldn't leave. He felt helpless and vulnerable; if he allowed it, he could actually cry with frustration. Instead he shook himself, rubbed his hands together to bring back some warmth into his fingers and searched for the keys to the cottage. It didn't take long to find them in one of the kitchen drawers.

While creeping around in his damp socks he had an idea. Ben was roughly the same size as Edward, slightly taller and bulkier but his clothes would fit. Why not borrow some? He would be dry and more difficult to spot if anyone was looking.

The man who drove the old Land Rover down Shepherd's Drove Lane would have passed for Ben. He wore the same dark blue waxed jacket and checked cap. None of the neighbours would have looked twice. In Ben's kitchen amongst his pile of post lay a sealed envelope containing a note from Edward telling him not to worry – his car was safe and would come back in one piece.

Edward's house was in darkness and the lane deserted; no white van with blacked-out windows parked by the wall. He seethed at the thought of Abby in their hands, these arrogant faceless spooks.

He parked the Land Rover right outside the front gate. It wouldn't take him long to get his things out. Inside, he switched on lights, the radio and the kettle – all homely familiar sounds for the bugs to pick up. Then he shoved some clothes into a large holdall, grabbed a few pairs of boots and his toilet bag. A box of food stood waiting by the door. He looked back at his homely kitchen and sighed slightly as he turned off the lights and locked the door.

In less than five minutes he'd loaded the car and was driving down the lane. He stopped by the post office in town to post a small padded bag to a hotel in Scotland, addressed to him. He'd phoned to make a reservation for two nights' time; it wouldn't throw them off for long but gave him breathing space. The packet contained his mobile, which he knew they would track. A clever spook would spot what he'd done but they were using inexperienced personnel and that might give him breathing space.

The frantic activity had stopped him thinking about Abby, kept his hands and his brain occupied. As he drove along the quiet roads, wind buffeting the car and rain beating on the screen, he considered his next move. The keen loss of her company almost overwhelmed his ability to think clearly. He realised he was very tired and switched on the radio in an attempt to keep himself focused. It failed to retain a signal and the white noise hiss irritated him.

Fighting drowsiness he drove on, leaving the A38 and heading through the dark tree-lined road towards Bovey Tracey. He pulled over outside the town and used the torch on his phone to check the map and directions he'd jotted down. Satnav was hopeless here. He knew he hadn't far to go now, another fifteen minutes and he'd be there, left towards the high moor and then right at the bottom of the hill.

Twelve minutes later he pulled up in the narrow lane beside a high, thick hedge broken by two stone gateposts with an old wooden gate wedged between them, tied with wire to hold it closed. He got out of the car and walked along the hedge, using his flashlight to find the small garden gate almost covered by an arch of ivy. Beyond the gate was a small white-washed cottage barely visible in the darkness. This was it.

Edward untied the gate, wedged it open and edged the old Land Rover cautiously between the stone posts and into the meadow behind the hedge. He swung the car around and parked next to the wood store before closing the gate. There was a mowed track leading to the cobbled garden path. The old cottage had a red tin roof, which had replaced the thatch after a chimney fire in the last century. Its thick walls and small, latched windows let draughts in but kept the rain out and had done so for nearly two hundred years.

He remembered Ben saying he would never change a thing about the place, but after two winters he'd succumbed to the warm charms of a large wood burner. Inside the air was cold and a smell of damp permeated the place. Edward flicked the light switch and the lights came on. He walked through to the small kitchen, dumped his box of food and turned on the electric wall heater. This would be home for the foreseeable future.

Checking his watch, he realised it was past midnight. Too tired to make up a bed, he grabbed some blankets and put them on one of the two sofas. The rest of his stuff he left piled in the hall and made sure the front door was locked and bolted. He just managed to get his shoes off before crawling under the blankets and falling asleep.

A slant of light fell across the dark room. It took Edward a second or two to remember where he was, then to realise the darkness was because the wooden shutters were still in place. Once he pulled the retaining bar off, and opened them up, sunlight filled the room. The rain had stopped in the night and warmth flooded in with the bright daylight.

He yawned, looked at his watch and stood up, stretching before heading for the kitchen. Behind it a utility room had been added years before and that housed the shower and loo. Beyond that was the back door opening into the garden a few feet from the fast-running stream that formed the boundary.

Before Ben bought the old cottage, it had been a holiday let. One wall of the kitchen was covered by a large plastic-coated map of the local area. Ben liked it and kept it. Edward decided to use it as his planning wall. As he sat drinking coffee and eating toast, he replayed the last few days and what he should do next. The loss of Abby had thrown him, but he knew he had to focus if he was to rescue her and solve the mystery. He knew he had to find out *why* she'd been snatched before anything else.

He taped sheets of white paper over the map, found a thick marker pen and wrote across the top left "people" and in the top right "projects/links?". Then he put the names from Judith's list down the sheet. Those who had died were at the top, seven in total, then the three unaccounted for, followed by the terminally ill and mentally unstable. He stood back and looked at the list. Rayner jumped out at him. Why had he died? Perhaps he should start with him.

Chapter 12

It was two days since Edward had arrived at the cottage. He'd set up an old laptop on the kitchen table and covered the wall with lots of scribbled notes. The internet had delivered death records, and Sebastian had supplied some potted service records, but none of it joined up. There were more question marks than before.

Edward had given up shaving and now sported a three-day stubble that aged him, making him appear tired and thin. He kept Ben's hat, hoping he would fit in amongst the local rural community and not raise any interest. At this time of year there were few tourists.

In the local supermarket, a small affair with three aisles of basic provisions, he bought milk, bread and frozen meals. The fair-haired girl behind the counter stared at him as he put the basket in front of her. He smiled.

She smiled back, revealing pearly white teeth. 'Sorry if I was staring but you look just like that bloke they're looking for.'

'Do I? Which bloke is that?'

'That murderer the police are after. Mind you, they reckon he's gone to Scotland.' She carried on putting his stuff through the scanner, beep, beep, as he stood stock still in front of her. 'Yeah, but he looks younger than you. It's all over the papers.'

'Really? I've been busy working so haven't had a paper for a few days.' He calmly walked to the newspaper rack and pulled down a tabloid. Giving it to the girl he said, 'I'd better have a read, so I know what's going on.'

She looked up and grinned. 'Yeah, then you'll know why people stare at you. That'll be twenty-two pounds ten, please. I haven't seen you before; are you staying local?'

'Yes, with some friends up in Bovey for a few days. The missus is in hospital and I can't cook so they offered to feed me. Just doing some shopping for them.'

'That's nice. Well, take care and watch out for the cops.' She laughed and he laughed back, waving goodbye as he left the shop. He was glad he'd parked out of the line of sight, further down the street, and that there was nobody else in the shop.

Flinging the shopping onto the back seat he jumped in, flicking through the pages of the newspaper. It took less than a second to find the story and a large picture of him, obviously CCTV footage from his trip to London. He was looking at the camera, frowning, but it was a good clear shot. The story was that he'd killed the woman from the care home and should be considered dangerous. The public were not to approach him but to phone a hotline if they saw him. He threw the paper onto the passenger seat and started the engine. His hands trembled slightly as he gripped the wheel.

Edward drove steadily out of town and back towards the moor. He swore to himself. This would make things difficult. Lucky for him he'd taken to wearing Ben's hat and let his beard grow. Without that, the girl may not have found it amusing but just phoned the police instead. He was angry with himself for not anticipating their next move. But he decided it meant they still considered him a threat and Abby a good hostage. If they knew where he was it might be a different story.

The microwaved beef casserole did not live up to the packaging's claims. Edward chewed the tasteless meat and washed it down with strong tea while flicking through his notes. He wondered what the connection might be between these people. Rob Rayner was definitely an important piece of the jigsaw, but his last project didn't warrant his permanent removal, did it? Everything on his record suggested him heading for a promotion. The last thing he'd been involved with was a low-value collaborative project bringing a sonar application into service. It seemed to go well, and he'd been earmarked for a bonus, then put on secondment to a company in Cumbria and a month later he was dead.

Edward thought that perhaps he wasn't asking himself the right question. As he was staring at the list of names, another thought struck him. He stood up, ran his hand through his hair and swore. Abby! They thought Abby knew something; that Rayner had talked. He'd got it wrong; it wasn't the interview that had spurred them into acting, it was Judith's contact with him *and* Abby. They considered Abby a potential threat too.

He had to find her as quickly as possible. Sebastian would need to call in favours and use his contacts to trace her. He grabbed his phone and tapped in a text message – *Contact me soon as poss, Bill*. They'd agreed to use pseudonyms, although Edward thought it a waste of time. Then he looked through his phone contacts and sent another short message. Now all he could do was wait.

The biting wind crept into the car and chilled Edward's hands as he sat in the car park waiting for the train to pull into the station. It was eleven o'clock and too dark to see past the trees and into the park. Newton Abbot was quiet; all he could hear was the wind and the occasional vehicle driving up Queen Street towards the town centre. Had he been a smoker still, now would have been a good time to light up.

At exactly five past eleven the Plymouth train pulled into the station. The two other cars in the car park started their engines and switched on their lights to welcome home weary travellers. Edward waited, watching people hurry to their vehicles and leave. Then three figures, muffled against the cold, came out of the grand entrance and made their way towards him. He switched on the engine and opened the passenger door. A blast of cold air rushed in.

'Over here, guys,' he called to them and they waved back.

Sebastian was first to reach the car, throwing his bag into the back and pulling the passenger seat forward for his companions. The other two clambered into the back, cursing the cold. Sebastian jumped in and slammed the door against the wind, rubbing his hands together before blowing into them.

Edward turned to greet them, 'Good to see you, guys. I guess you three have had a chance to get to know each other?'

'Not at all,' Sebastian said. 'We decided discretion was the better part of valour. I'm Sebastian.' He held his hand across the seat to the other two and shook their hands.

'I'm Buzz and this is Kip.' The taller, thinner young man spoke first. His face was half obscured by glasses and a woollen beanie hat. His companion, also well wrapped up, nodded and made a grunting sound that passed for a greeting.

Edward drove out of the car park and headed towards the town centre. He nodded at Sebastian, 'These two are the best hackers in the business. They've helped me in the past. When I told Buzz what I needed, he jumped at the chance of helping.'

'Too true, mate.' Buzz sounded enthusiastic. 'And the same goes for Kip.'

Sebastian grinned and turned to Edward. 'Where are we going then, my friend? It's a bit out in the sticks, isn't it?'

'You wait till you see it. Ben always calls it his Snow White house. We even have our own water supply and back-up generator.'

'Cool,' said a voice from the back seat.

The lanes were deserted as Edward drove back towards the moor. They drove through Bovey Tracey without passing another vehicle and were soon heading down the narrow track to the cottage.

Edward parked the Land Rover next to the wood stack again and went to turn on the outside light so the others could find their way down the path without tripping over the low dry-stone walls. He showed Buzz and Kip into the ground floor bedroom, with its two single beds, and

Sebastian was given the twin room upstairs. Once everyone had dumped their bags Edward offered a drink.

'I want to say thank you to all three of you for coming to my aid. I really appreciate it. We're up against some ruthless people so it could be dangerous.'

Sebastian said, 'Less of the speeches, Edward, just pour us a drink.'

Buzz nodded agreement. 'Yeah, man, we know what these spooks are capable of. That's part of the fun, beating them at their own game.'

Kit mumbled, 'Yeah.' He still had his hat pulled down level to his eyes, which made him look incredibly young, Edward thought. What had he got these kids into?

'Well, here we are. There's beer, local cider or whisky. Pick your poison.'

Buzz and Kit enthusiastically poured cider for themselves. Edward poured a large scotch for himself and Sebastian. He raised his glass. 'Here's to success!'

They sat in front of the fire for a while and Edward told them an abridged version of what had happened so far, about Abby's kidnap and the press, which they already knew. Sebastian explained that, officially, he was on holiday. Luckily, he'd booked three weeks off months ago so this would not raise suspicion. The boys kept under the radar and their activities were as clandestine as the organisations they hacked into. Buzz said it didn't matter where they operated from, they couldn't be traced. Edward hoped that that was true.

After the two young men had stumbled off to bed, Edward and Sebastian sat by the fire, too weary to move and too tense for sleep. Edward watched the fire burn down, sipped his whisky and stirred the embers with the poker.

'I can't stop thinking about Abby and what she's going through. Buzz and Kip are top of their tree so I'm hoping they'll throw something up that will give us a lead.'

'I hope so too. Do they know what they're getting into, though? They're very young.'

Edward chuckled. 'They're the same age as us when we joined. They know their stuff. They'll be fine.'

'Christ! They look so young. I guess I must be getting old.'

'You and me both.'

'I think I need to hit the sack. I'm absolutely buggered. See you in the morning.'

'Yeah, I won't be long myself. Sleep well.'

'You too, Edward.' Sebastian got to his feet, stretched and headed for the stairs, yawning as he went.

Edward prodded the glowing embers. There was no heat left in the fire and no chance of it escaping the grate, so he replaced the poker and stood up. The house was quiet. He heard the gentle sound of heavy breathing from the ground floor bedroom and slight creaks from above as Sebastian crossed his bedroom floor. He sighed, yawned and padded towards the door, switching off the light before going upstairs to bed.

Chapter 13

He found it difficult to sleep. Every time he drifted off, Abby's frightened face appeared. She screamed, shouted and cried through his troubled dreams. Eventually, as the first pale glimpse of daylight crept through the parting in the curtains, he got out of bed. He pulled on his clothes, old trousers and a thick sweater, and went downstairs.

The past few days had been spent in the safety of the old cottage but being indoors had driven him mad. He longed for fresh air and to stretch his legs. He pulled on his boots and coat then slipped out of the house, locking the door behind him. It was damp underfoot but not raining. He paused beside the gate, listening to the early birdsong echoing through the high hedges in the lane.

As Edward strode up the narrow lane towards the trail, overhanging branches brushed his head. By the time he reached the gate his hair was damp. He put his hand on the cool, smooth lever to pull it open and stepped through into the field. The stream was flowing fast, splashing and gurgling noisily over the stones as it rushed to meet the river further down the meadow.

There was nobody to be seen, no dog walkers or postal vans. It was too early. Edward took in a deep breath of clean country air and sighed. He felt better for being outdoors. The fresh air loaded with country scents revitalised him. The unsettling effects of last night's imaginings were swept away by a walk along the riverbank. By the time he got back to the cottage he was ready and keen to take up the challenges ahead.

The smell of bacon cooking brought the other three from their beds. Sleepy eyed, they groggily took mugs out of the cupboard and poured coffee. Edward served up breakfast, watching them come to life as they greedily devoured everything he put in front of them.

Buzz and Kip looked even younger this morning. Both had gone to bed in boxer shorts and T-shirts. Hair sticking up and yet still managing to half cover their faces, Edward found it difficult to tell one from the other. Sebastian, by contrast, was clean shaven and dressed in a checked shirt and cord trousers. He sat, one leg elegantly crossed over the other, sipping black coffee. Edward thought, *Chalk and cheese*, as he put more toast on the table.

'Edward, old man, you'll make someone a lovely husband.'

'Breakfast is my speciality. Just don't expect fancy dinners.' Edward sat down next to Sebastian and poured a mug of coffee.

Buzz smiled. 'Yep, that was great, man. Just what I needed. I was bloody starving.' He stood up and took his plate to the sink, looking out at the garden. 'This is a great hideaway. I can see why you chose it.'

'Let's hope you boys know your stuff,' Edward said.

Kip said, 'We're better than good. We'll hack them and they won't even know they've been had.' His voice was quiet but surprisingly deep. It was the first time Edward had heard him speak. Kip stared at the floor. He seemed to have a problem with making eye contact.

Edward said, 'I hope you're right about that, Kip. That would give us a huge advantage.'

Kip just said, 'Yeah,' and took his plate to the sink before sauntering out of the kitchen. Buzz followed him, muttering something about throwing on some threads.

Sebastian turned to Edward and raised an eyebrow. 'They're a rum pair. Let's hope they're as good as we think they are.'

'I *know* they are. I've used Buzz's services before, and he's never let me down. Kip is...' Edward hesitated, 'I suspect Kip is possibly autistic or maybe Asperger's. He has a problem with personal contact, but in front of a computer he's absolutely brilliant.'

Sebastian got to his feet, brushing crumbs from his crumpled trousers. He dropped his mug in the sink. 'I reckon your assessment is probably right. I'll be interested to see him in action. Before we get started, I must go and put a sweater on; this place is freezing.'

By eleven o'clock the living room had been converted into an office. The boys had set up their laptops and were busy checking their security. Edward watched as they went through their rituals before declaring the cottage impenetrable to cyberspace attack. He felt as if he were a medieval baron protecting his castle from invasion.

Buzz looked up from the flickering screen. 'Right. We're ready, man. Where do you want us to go?'

Edward turned to Sebastian, who gave him the list of their chosen targets. He passed it to Buzz.

'These are the targets. We're looking for references to myself, a woman called Judith Mulholland or any of these people.' Edward gave him the list of names that he had been working through. 'It could be all coded, in which case we'll think again, but let's try this first.'

Buzz and Kip hunched over their screens, fingers flying over the keyboards. Edward watched rows of numbers rolling down the display, then databases appearing. The boys worked quickly; speed was essential to ensure they were one step ahead of the security systems. Edward had no idea how they did it and reasoned he didn't need to know. All he wanted was the information.

Sebastian had settled himself in an armchair by the window and appeared to be reading a book he'd taken from the shelf. Edward knew his old friend's casual demeanour had been honed from years of practice. He would be closely monitoring the action.

Kip scribbled notes as he worked through the lists, while Buzz was studying a database intently. He called Edward over.

'I've found something. All these people on your list had a project in common. Well, I'm assuming it's a project; does Cradle mean anything to you?'

'Cradle? No, not at all...'

'Well, Cradle appears somewhere in each of their records. It's not mentioned in the personnel files but each one is linked to it in some way. Mostly payment records. They got paid extra for working on or in Cradle. This Rayner guy received a large payment before his service ended.'

Edward leaned over Buzz's shoulder. He thought of Abby and wondered what Rayner had done in those last few months before his death.

'Can you track Cradle anywhere else in their records? How about emails? Have you had a look at Controller's emails?'

Buzz grinned. He looked up at Edward. 'Whoa there! One thing at a time. Let me just close the door on this one. I've saved you a copy of all this stuff.'

'I know I won't understand the answer... but is this safe? They can't track it back to you?'

Buzz leaned back in his chair. He swivelled to face Edward and said, 'I could give you a highly technical answer to that but let's just say no they can't. If you imagine I'm a burglar, very good at what I do. I've got a key from somewhere and gained access to their office. I'm wearing gloves so there're no prints, no DNA. I open the filing cabinets, take a photo of each record and put it back *exactly* as it was. Then I leave the room, lock the door and I'm gone without a trace. That's what we do.' He swivelled back to the screen and carried on typing, fingers hammering on the keys.

Edward felt relieved. He decided to trust them. They seemed to know what they were doing but he worried about what they would find. He was sure it would go beyond top secret. They could all be compromised.

The light level in the room dropped. He turned to find Sebastian standing at the small window, gazing into the garden.

'Oh, sorry. Am I blocking the light? It's a bit dark in here. I need some fresh air; feeling a bit stir crazy. Shall I go and get some shopping? I know it's difficult for you now with this murder story hanging over your head. I could go into Newton Abbot and bring back a month's supply.'

'Good idea, Sebastian. I'm running a bit low. I'll draw up a list of stuff. Until this beard grows…' he rubbed his chin, 'I daren't venture out.'

'Yeah, that was a mean call. Do you have any idea why that poor woman died?'

'I guess it was because they thought she knew too much. Judith had spoken to her, but I don't think it would have been anything substantial. I'm not convinced that Judith had much information herself. Can you bring some papers back? It'll be interesting to see how much coverage I'm getting in the press.'

'No problem. Let's go draw up a shopping list. I guess it's okay for me to take the car?'

'I stole it anyway so go ahead. I'm sure Ben wouldn't mind!' Edward laughed at the bemused looks the two boys gave him. Buzz grinned and Kip just shrugged.

Sebastian had been gone nearly two hours. Edward and Buzz spent the time trawling through emails looking for Cradle. They drew a blank. Kip continued to tap away at his keyboard. After an hour or so he suddenly stopped working and sat back, flexing his hands. Edward looked up.

Kip spoke quietly. 'I've found some stuff. You might be interested…' his voice tailed off. He seemed unsure of what else to say. Buzz gave Edward a nod.

Edward said, 'Okay if I take a look, Kip?'

Kip shrugged. 'Yeah, sure.' He pushed his chair back and stood up. Edward took that as a sign he could sit in front of the screen. He sat down on the warm seat.

'What am I looking for, Kip?'

'Cradle. You're looking at some US files…' he paused, 'from the Pentagon. Defence Intelligence.'

He had Edward's attention. 'American Intelligence? Shit.'

Kip gave an odd little laugh. 'Yeah, deep shit.'

'Where is it? What am I…?' He saw the words on the screen. *This is top secret, code word Gaia. British Ministry of Defense officials are to attend next briefing. They will bring us up to speed with progress on service date for Cradle. It is anticipated we will be running test trials early next fall, possibly October, at the plant in Cumbria, UK. Presidential approval will be forthcoming.* Edward looked up at Kip, who was staring at the floor. Buzz had come over and was reading the screen over his shoulder.

'Well, boys. It looks like we've stumbled onto something big. I really hope your security is good.'

'Don't worry. We're sound. What is it?'

'Don't know yet but thanks to Kip we're a step closer to finding out.' He turned back to the screen. The document was a memo sent to just a few names. He only recognised one who had been copied in. It was Rayner.

'Kip, can you carry on looking through their files? Look for references to Rayner as well. He seems to be at the centre of things.'

'Yeah, no problem.'

'And link it to Gaia, can you? I think we've found what we're looking for. This is why I'm being hunted.'

Chapter 14

Sebastian crashed through the front door, armed with shopping bags. Edward looked at his watch.

'I was getting worried. You've been gone over two hours.' He took some bags from Sebastian and kicked the door shut. He noticed it was raining again.

'Sorry about that. The traffic in Newton Abbott was awful. I had a bit of a wander round – not worth the effort to be honest – then the queues in the supermarket...' He tripped over a cable as he navigated the living room and nearly dropped a bag on Buzz. 'Sorry, Buzz. Anyway, I got loads of stuff. We'll eat well tonight.'

Edward started putting things in cupboards while Sebastian put the kettle on. He pulled a pack of cigarettes out of his pocket. 'I'm just going out by the stream for a smoke.'

'When did you start smoking again? I thought you'd given up.'

Sebastian grinned. 'I did. For about two years, then the department cuts started to bite, and I started again. Couldn't take the stress.' He opened the back door, grimaced at the rain and slipped outside. Edward thought it strange that his friend hadn't mentioned it before or that he hadn't smoked since he got to the cottage. Something felt wrong, but he shrugged it off, deciding his nerves were getting the better of his common sense.

Buzz called from the living room, 'We've found some more memos!'

Edward walked through and stood behind them. Buzz and Kip were hunched together over one of the laptops. He leaned over and read the document on the screen. It was another Defense Department memo from the Pentagon files.

The Cradle trial date has been fixed for 24 October. We have requested that Rayner attend on behalf of DI15. Professor Stephens will lead the trial. Once the results have been analysed, there will be a further trial of Cradle-enhanced systems before a combined services report is produced. Gaia to be maintained at all times. This includes the President and the UK Prime Minister's office. Under no circumstances pass any information relating to Cradle to any person without Gaia authority.

Edward straightened up. He frowned. 'I'm very surprised you found this. It's obviously an ultra-sensitive project.'

Buzz looked up. 'We're the best. Haven't you got that yet? This wasn't easy to find, man.' He sounded annoyed.

Edward patted his shoulder. 'No offence meant, Buzz. I'm surprised they kept an electronic copy, that's all. This is as heavy as it gets. You realise the significance, don't you? This is saying that the President and the Prime Minister have been excluded. They didn't know about it.'

'Oh, we had to dig deep. It wasn't easy to find. They thought they'd deleted it, but someone hadn't done their job properly.'

'Have you looked through British records? Is there anything of ours to give us more of a picture?'

'Not so far.'

'Okay. Thanks, you two. Really good work. I appreciate it.' Edward thought that sounded lame, but what else could he say? He was a bit dumbfounded by the memo. October 24th was the day before Rob Rayner had died. His death was no accident. He had obviously seen or heard something that was too sensitive, or they thought he might talk. Edward paced up and down, rubbing his stubbly chin.

'Guys, we need to change tactics. Buzz, I want you to continue looking for Cradle. Kip, I need you to find Abby. I don't know how you're going to do that, to be honest, but we need to try. If she's still alive, they'll be holding her somewhere. You need to find that somewhere for me. Do you think you can do that? I know it's a big ask.'

Kip nodded without looking up. He said, 'I'll try.'

'And one more thing, boys, keep whatever you find to yourselves. If Sebastian asks, tell him you're making slow progress – only lists. Okay? It's for his safety and ours. The fewer people know about this, the better. You both okay with that?'

They both looked up from their screens and nodded as if he'd just asked them if they wanted tea or coffee. He thought, *Good lads*.

Edward heard Sebastian slam the kitchen door and went through the narrow passage to join him. He was shaking the rain from his jacket before placing it over one of the chairs.

'It's bloody horrible out there again. Shall I make tea? How are the boys doing? Anything new?'

'We've found references to some project they all seem to be involved in but nothing new. I've decided Abby is the priority. I've asked Kip to look for anything that might suggest where she is.'

'And then what, Edward? We go in guns blazing and rescue her?'

'Yes.' Edward held his friend's gaze. 'Yes, that's right.'

Sebastian laughed, raising his eyebrows as he did so. 'You're serious, aren't you? My God, you really think you can just pull her out without getting yourself killed, or her too, come to that?'

Edward glared at him. 'Actually, Sebastian, I do think exactly that. Don't forget what I've done. I may be older now but I'm sure as hell wiser. It's all in the planning. I will get her back.'

'I admire your tenacity. Don't let's fall out over this. You know I'll do all I can to help.'

He had no intention of falling out with Sebastian as he needed his help. Leaning over, he patted his friend's shoulder and said, 'Sorry. I'm a bit tense. Let's have that tea. I'll see if the boys want some.'

Chapter 15

Edward found Kip, head on the table, arms spread over his laptop. He was snoring gently; his dark fringe covered half his face. It was five in the morning. Edward had woken from another disturbing dream and had seen the light on in the living room. He hesitated. Should he wake the boy and send him to bed? Deciding against it, he went into the kitchen and put the kettle on. It was too late to return to sleep, too early to be up and about.

As he opened the cupboard to find a mug, he heard movement behind him and turned to see Kip standing in the doorway. His hair covered his face and his T-shirt stuck to his body; he yawned, eyes squinting against the artificial light.

'Sorry, Kip. Did I wake you? I couldn't sleep. I'm making tea. Do you want one?'

Kip yawned again. 'Yeah, thanks. That would be nice.' He flopped onto a chair and pushed his hair back from his face. He still resembled a grumpy porcupine but at least his eyes were open now. Edward thought how vulnerable this young man looked, and what he'd asked him to do seemed unreasonable. He kept his thoughts to himself and passed a mug of tea to Kip.

'I may have found your… umm… girlfriend.' Kip sipped his tea and studied his socks.

'Really? That's good news.' Edward kept his voice calm. He'd learned it was better to avoid emotional responses with Kip. He tried to sound neutral. 'When you've drunk your tea, perhaps you can show me what you found?'

'Yeah, sure.' Kip carried on drinking. Outside, the birds were waking and starting their early chatter. Inside, if he listened carefully, Edward could just hear Buzz snoring in the ground floor bedroom. He peered through the kitchen window to see if there was any sign of the dawn breaking.

Kit stood up. He put his mug in the sink and ambled off to the living room. Edward took it as a sign he was ready to show him what he had discovered and followed him.

The laptop illuminated the corner of the room. Kip sat in front of it, waiting for Edward.

'Shall I show you?'

'Yes please, Kip.'

Kip opened the various files he had come across that seemed to him to suggest Abby's continuing detention. There were references to a special delivery and movements to and fro. Edward recognised the modus operandi of the intelligence department and knew that Kip was right. She was still alive and being passed from one safe house to another. The last file Kip showed him had a date stamp of two days ago.

Edward read the screen. *The packet must be delivered Tuesday at 10.00. Make sure someone is at home to receive it. We think the actor may have some friends helping him. We need to keep one step ahead.*

'Kip, can you go back to the last email please?' Edward knew the packet was Abby, but where were they holding her?

They read the emails again, but nothing jumped out. Some text was nonsense and seemed to be a mixture of languages. It frustrated him. Field work was his speciality, not code-breaking, and he realised that these messages were coded. He would need Sebastian's help.

Buzz wandered into the room wearing an all in one fleece decorated with snowflakes and polar bears, rubbed his eyes and yawned. He saw Edward's surprised expression and grinned.

'Present from the girlfriend. It's really warm. What are you guys doing up so early?'

'Kip didn't make it to bed,' Edward said.

'Ah, I thought it was quiet.' Buzz teased. 'Have you found something then, Kip?'

They showed Buzz the emails and Edward explained about the code. Buzz frowned and asked Kip to print them off.

'Any chance of a strong coffee? If it's coded, it might take me a while to work it out.'

'I was going to get Sebastian on the case, but if you reckon you can break it…'

'I'll give it a go. They seem to be using something simple. Think about it, Edward. The best way to hide something is to put it right under the seeker's nose. Same with codes. You guys live by them so the most effective is the simplest. Maybe something old that no one uses anymore.'

Edward stared at Buzz. Something old! He swore, and Kip looked up. How stupid of him. Of course, the best way to hide something – use an outdated code that hasn't been used for years.

'I think I know what code they've used. It will be one that Judith designed. She used to send messages to her brother when they were young. It's very easy once you know how to read it, but we need a Latin dictionary. She used a mixture of Latin, French and English. Her mother was French, so she spoke it fluently.'

'Latin? I don't know any Latin,' Buzz said.

'I did it for four years at school but I'm really rusty.' Edward stood up. 'We'll have to wake up Sebastian. He's a Classics scholar. He'll be able to help.'

'Right, I'll make a pot of coffee, then. You can wake Sebastian.' Buzz headed for the kitchen. Edward grinned. He knew Sebastian could be a bear in the morning, and this was an early morning wake-up.

Sebastian swigged his half-cold coffee and asked for a fresh cup. He frowned over his scribbled notes. Edward had a few pages of his own as well as a half-drunk cup of coffee.

'I'm nearly there but it's the French that's giving me trouble. It looks like she used quite out-of-date terms.'

'If I remember right, her mother was quite old when she had Judith so it's probably formal language, no modern idioms.'

'That would make sense. I think my schoolboy French is just about up to the job.' Sebastian leaned back in his chair and stared at Edward. He looked as if he wanted to ask a question but didn't know how to phrase it.

'What is it? You've got that I'm-not-sure-if-I-should-ask-this look.'

'Something strikes me about this. Don't you think it's odd they're using one of Judith's ciphers? It's almost as if they're sending the message to you. As if they expect you to decode it.'

'I know. The same thought struck me too. But I'm hoping it's just a coincidence they chose that one. Would they even be aware it was Judith's own? It's old; maybe that was why they chose it?'

Sebastian pulled a face. 'You might be right. I sincerely hope so; otherwise we could walk into a trap.'

'I hope so too. I really don't want to have to shoot one of our own.'

Edward laughed at the look of horror on Sebastian's face before he realised Edward was joking.

'You git! I believed you for a second. You wouldn't though; seriously, tell me you won't shoot one of them?'

'Only if they fire first; that's the best I can offer.' Edward was serious now. 'Let's get back to the code-breaking. We've nearly cracked it.'

Buzz and Kip came through from the kitchen with plates of bacon sandwiches and slumped on the sofa. They watched as Edward and Sebastian compared notes.

Buzz asked, 'How's it going?'

Edward spoke without taking his eyes off his pad, 'Pretty good. We've got the code. Now we just need to find the pattern and we'll have the message.'

'Cool.' Buzz munched on his sandwich.

The smell of bacon made Edward's stomach rumble, and he remembered he hadn't eaten. He was jolted back to the task by Sebastian whooping.

'I've got it! I've found the pattern. It's the first letter of every third word and "A" forms the full stop. Right, here we go!'

He circled the letters and Edward wrote them down. It was a random mixture of Latin, French and English words but it didn't take them long to get the message which had been spread over three messages. Once they'd translated it Edward read it out to the boys.

'It says – the woman is untrustworthy. Move her one more time. If she does not deliver dispose of her. He is the one we need to find. He will be working hard to find answers. We must stop him before he finds the truth. Move her to number twelve. I will tell you when we are ready. Then close ten and clean thoroughly. The actor may be in on this so be wary.'

Edward looked up to see them all staring at him. Buzz spoke first, 'Is that helpful? Do you know where she is?'

Kip said, 'Who's the actor?'

Sebastian smiled. 'I think that might be me. I used to do amateur dramatics when I was younger. And yes, I know where these places are.'

Edward was quiet. He had tried to avoid thinking of Abby, viewed now as being disposable, but now the ache of her loss had returned. He looked at Sebastian.

'What do you think they mean by "untrustworthy"?'

'It could be my translation. It might be "unreliable" or "devious". I suspect she's been playing a game, and they sussed it. Look on the bright side, Edward; at least you're sure now she's still alive.' He added, 'And she doesn't know enough to compromise you or lead them to us. You told me she's clever. She's alive and that's what matters.'

'I'm sorry. It looks as if they suspect you're involved as well. What will you do?'

'Phone a friend and see if any questions have been asked.'

'Then what?'

'I believe that's your call, Edward. I suppose you want to go get her, and I can't say I blame you. But how do you plan to achieve it? Knowing where she is and recovering her are two different things. They'll be on full alert.'

'Perhaps we should start by staking it out. Maybe the best way to rescue Abby will be whilst they're transporting her. I need to think about it.'

Sebastian said, 'Don't forget you're Britain's number one wanted man. You've got the police on your case too.'

'Yeah, I know. This won't be easy.'

Chapter 16

The street was empty. Dawn was yet to break, and the streetlights cast a yellowy glow over the parked cars, rendering them all the same sickly orange colour. A light drizzle sparkled in the pools of light under each lamp.

Sebastian blew smoke through the cracked window. Each time he drew breath Edward saw his profile lit by the red glow of the cigarette. They sat together in silence, waiting and watching. Number ten, St John's Road looked just the same as the other houses in this suburban street. The red front door and lace curtains hid a secret world its neighbours knew nothing about.

Edward checked his watch. It was five thirty. He felt Sebastian shift his weight as the car moved slightly. It was a long time since either of them had been active in-the-field operatives; their nerves were on edge.

'Nearly time. Are you ready?'

Sebastian coughed. 'Yes, absolutely.' He sounded hoarse in the early morning cold air, and his breath misted the screen as he spoke. Stubbing out his cigarette in the ashtray, he turned his collar up to cover his ears.

At exactly five thirty-five a group of men came into sight. They were shouting and singing loudly. Edward muttered,

'Here we go,' to Sebastian. They slipped out of the car and headed towards number ten. As the men drew closer, they upped the volume. Edward saw lights coming on in the house windows opposite. He pulled his woollen balaclava over his face and, motioning Sebastian to follow him, went through the side gate of the house and into the back garden.

They flattened themselves against the wall and waited, listening to the noises coming from the street. It sounded as if a full-scale fight had broken out, and he heard voices shouting from nearby houses.

Lights came on, narrowing the shadows across the lawn. The back door opened, and Edward braced himself. Although they stood hidden by a small shed, he was ready for detection. A large man ran past them, out into the street. He heard the front door open and steps crunching across the front garden path.

'Two down,' he whispered to Sebastian. They waited in the darkness, listening closely. The noise in the street had reached crescendo level. It was only a matter of time before the police turned up.

Edward took a deep breath and motioned to Sebastian. They crept across the space between the shed and the back door. There was nobody in the kitchen. Closing the door softly, Edward turned the lock and signalled he intended to move forward into the house. There were faint sounds from an upstairs room as they crept up the staircase. His one hand clutched a small canister of pepper spray and the other his gun. Sebastian was two steps behind him as they climbed the stairs.

Outside, the battle continued with no sign of the two men returning. They reached the top of the stairs and paused, listening for sounds from the bedrooms. There was a light under the door of the front room overlooking the street; muffled voices came from within. Edward followed his instincts and moved to the rear bedroom; placing his hand on the door handle, he pushed gently. It was locked.

He turned to look at Sebastian, who crouched at the top of the stairs with a canister in each hand. He nodded to Edward as he turned the key and opened the door, slipping into the dark bedroom. From the light outside he could see the figure in the bed. Praying he'd got this right, he reached the bed in three strides and in one motion pulled back the bedclothes and clamped his hand over the mouth of the occupant.

He didn't need a light to tell him it was Abby. She struggled weakly. He bent and whispered in her ear.

'Abby, it's me. It's Edward. I've come to get you out of here.'

'Edward?' Her voice sounded weak, groggy, as she struggled to raise herself.

He'd guessed they would drug her. They wouldn't leave her alone without incapacitating her. She fell back on the pillow, groaning softly. He bent over her, stroked her face and lifted her from the bed. She was dressed in pyjamas. Her head fell against his chest, dark hair obscuring her face.

Back on the landing Sebastian crouched in the same position, anxiously watching the other door. Edward motioned to him to close the door behind him and carried Abby down the stairs. Her hair partly covered her face, but he saw marks on her arms where she'd been restrained. A wave of anger swept through him and he struggled to keep focused on getting them out safely. The need to keep her safe overwhelmed his desire to go back up and crack open a few heads.

Sebastian caught up with him in the hallway and stepped ahead into the kitchen, opening the door and slipping out into the darkness.

'It's all clear. I'll shut the door.'

Edward eased past Sebastian and headed for the cover of the shed. Abby shivered in his arms. He wrapped his coat around them both as he waited for Sebastian.

The commotion in the street was tremendous. He caught glimpses of figures racing past and angry shouting from houses up and down the street. Sebastian appeared by his side.

'I'll go and get the car. Are you sure you're okay?'

'Yes, you go ahead. She's no weight. I'll manage. See you in five.'

Edward knew this would be the most challenging part of the operation: to get away undetected. Sebastian hopped over the next-door neighbour's fence and headed off down their drive into the street. He folded his balaclava up onto his head to make a hat, looking like a man off to work.

As soon as he'd gone, Edward lifted Abby over his shoulder, muttering an apology, and clambered over the fence into the rear garden of the house next door. Luckily, no lights illuminated him as he crept through the flower beds to the end of their garden.

Before planning the escape route he'd carefully gone over the layout of the area using online maps to plot their way out. He knew he had only to get over the fence and through the garden behind and he'd be out into Tenby Road where Sebastian would be waiting.

Abby mumbled something into his ear, and he whispered to her. She felt lifeless over his back as he struggled to climb over the fence. His heart was pounding from the exertion and an adrenalin rush. The noise from the street had died down. There was the sound of running footsteps as the men scattered and the distant wail of police cars.

Heaving himself over the fence, Edward crashed heavily to the ground, nearly dropping Abby as he landed. The drop had been further than he'd anticipated. The garden he landed in was several feet lower than the one he'd left. He silently cursed as pain stabbed through his left ankle. Abby groaned on his shoulder.

Edward caught his breath, wincing at the pain in his foot. Looking up the lawn, he saw lights on in the house and figures in the kitchen. He hoped it was dark enough to hide him as he made his way cautiously towards the side gate. As he moved forward, the light went out, and he sighed with relief. He knew he had little time now to get away before their escape was discovered. He limped unsteadily towards the gate on full alert for sounds of pursuit. The latch on the gate was stiff and squeaked as he drew it across. He pulled it open and strode as quickly as he could manage along the drive towards the road. He limped but managed to put some weight on his foot. Abby felt heavy on his shoulder, her head bouncing against his back. Reaching the pavement, he looked up the street and saw the car parked twenty feet or so up the road, under the shady cover of a tree. He stumbled to it and wrenched open the back door, tumbling Abby's semi-conscious body onto the back seat. She whimpered in protest, but he was already climbing into the passenger seat.

Sebastian cast a quick glance at Edward as he drove away. They crossed the junction behind two police cars rushing towards St John's Road.

'You okay, Edward? You look a bit pale...'

'Yeah, I'm okay. I've just twisted my ankle. There was a bloody drop on the other side of the fence.'

'How's Abby?'

Sebastian concentrated on driving, following the route they had drawn up to get them quickly out of town avoiding any CCTV cameras.

'I think she's okay. I haven't had a chance to check her. Let's get some distance between us and them, then we can pull over.'

They had hours of driving in front of them to get back to the cottage. Buzz and Kip had coordinated the rent-a-mob and would be keen to hear how things had gone. Edward hoped all the lads had got safely away from the street before the spooks or the police grabbed any of them.

Abby had been held on the outskirts of Coventry and they'd planned a route south using the old Fosse Way. There was little traffic and they would be able to make good progress before the roads became busy. Joining the M5 south of Bristol should get them quickly to Exeter. Edward worried they might raise a roadblock, but Sebastian thought it unlikely they would organise one that quickly, and the route they'd followed was not an obvious choice.

Edward said, 'It ran too smoothly for my liking. It doesn't feel right. I can't believe they were that sloppy. What happened to the two who went outside?'

'They were taken care of. Still sleeping it off now I expect. Those lads were good, really impressive. I hope they all got away."

'I hope so too.'

Edward looked over his shoulder to the back seat where Abby lay slumped. He turned back to Sebastian.

'Can we pull over? I want to check Abby.'

'I think that's a good idea. Something has just occurred to me. It was you saying it all went too easily...' Sebastian pulled the car over into a pub car park. 'I wonder if they've tagged her? We need to make sure otherwise we're in a heap of trouble.'

Edward swore. Of course, that's exactly what he would have done in their shoes. He hobbled out of the car and opened the rear door. Abby lay draped across the seat, apparently sleeping. She was wearing thin pyjamas which had ridden up slightly, exposing her back; her skin looked blue.

He gently lifted her fully onto the seat and covered her with a blanket, then ran his fingers over her arms feeling for the tell-tale sign of an invasive tracker, stopping over an area of skin on her upper arm. There was a slight red mark and raised bump under the skin.

'I think I've found it, Sebastian. I really hoped you were wrong.'

'So did I. Shall I deal with it or do you want to do it?'

Edward frowned and said, 'You do it and I'll hold her still. I'm glad she's medicated. Do we have any clean tissues?'

'Don't worry. There's a whole medical kit under the seat; I found it in the boot. We'd better be quick. They might be on our case right now and we're still too close for comfort.'

'Yes, you're right. Get on with it, then.'

Edward climbed into the back of the car and cradled Abby's head in his lap. Sebastian pulled a folding penknife from his pocket and put the medical kit on the floor next to him. He rolled Abby's sleeve up and carefully felt for the slight lump. As Edward watched, he made a small incision and flipped a tiny object, a little bigger than a pea, from Abby's arm. Abby moaned and stirred but still seemed sedated. Sebastian dropped the tracker on the ground and stamped on it before cleaning the small wound and putting a dressing around her arm.

Edward stroked her face and tucked the blanket around her before climbing back into the passenger seat beside Sebastian. They drove through the streets and out into the countryside. It was getting light now and early commuters were beginning their daily treks to work.

Sebastian said, 'I'm sure she'll be fine, Edward. Hopefully they're not on our tail.'

'I've been watching. If they are, they're bloody good. I've seen nothing.'

'Let's get some miles behind us then we can stop for a coffee. You'll have to stay in the car while I go and get it.'

'Don't you feel a tad nervous driving a murderer around?' Edward teased.

'I've always known you were a dodgy character.' Sebastian laughed and suddenly the tension in the car seemed to lift. Edward experienced a surge of relief despite the nagging pain in his ankle. He looked at Abby who lay wrapped up like a mummy, sleeping soundly. They'd done it. He had her back. Then the enormity of their situation hit him, and the euphoria washed away. What had she been through, his lovely bubbly girl? And what future awaited them now he'd come out into the open?

Buzz was making coffee when Edward limped into the kitchen. It was nearly midday, but Kip was nowhere to be seen, sleeping off the excitement of the past few days. Buzz looked up and said hi.

'Did it all go off okay? What happened to your foot?'

'It went okay. Sebastian's bringing Abby in. The boys were great. Please thank them for me. I twisted my ankle dropping over a fence; bloody silly really.'

Edward winced as he stepped into the kitchen. Sebastian appeared behind him.

'Abby's asking for you. I've left her on the sofa. Shall I make some coffee? I'm parched.'

Edward said yes to the drink and hobbled back down the passage into the living room. He found Abby propped on the sofa, still wrapped in blankets, looking like a small child far from home. She gave him a weary smile.

'Edward, I knew you'd come for me.' Her voice was little more than a whisper. She looked exhausted. He sat beside her and put his arm round her shoulder.

'There was no way I'd leave you in their hands. You're safe now. I'm not letting you out of my sight.'

'Quite right too,' she said and leaned her head on his shoulder.

'Abby…' he hesitated, not knowing what to say to her, 'did they hurt you? I know they kept you sedated but…'

'Edward, I'm happy to be out of there and back with you. I'm too tired to talk about it but I will when I'm ready.'

'Of course, I wasn't… I just want to know you're okay.' He couldn't think what to say to her.

Abby smiled and snuggled up to him. They sat together in silence until Sebastian brought two mugs of coffee in and they persuaded Abby to drink. She managed half of it before falling asleep against Edward.

Sebastian said, 'Shall I carry her upstairs for you? I don't think your ankle would take the strain.'

They put Abby in Edward's bed and pulled the curtains against the bright daylight. Edward sat in an armchair and watched her sleep. He didn't want to leave her to wake up in a strange house alone.

He worried about the damage to her psychological state. An encounter with the dark side of the state was never a pleasant one, especially for a civilian. As if reading his thoughts, she gave a moan, and then cried out in her sleep. Anger welled up in him. They would pay for what they'd done. He'd get to the bottom of their dirty secrets and expose them all.

Chapter 17

Abby sat on the bed propped up by pillows. She was wearing one of Edward's T-shirts. Buzz and Kip had volunteered to go shopping for clothes. Buzz said that he often bought clothes for his sister so wasn't bothered by it. Sebastian drove them to Newton Abbot, so Edward and Abby had the cottage to themselves.

It was three days since the rescue operation, and so far Abby had kept the experience to herself. Edward didn't want to push her on the subject. She seemed to sleep better now and was more alert during the day. He noticed that the bruises and needle marks had faded too.

'I think I'll have a shower while the boys are out. I'm still feeling grubby.' Abby smiled at Edward as he lay on the bed beside her.

'I expect you'll be glad to get out of my old clothes,' he said, stroking her arm.

'Yes and no. I love the smell of your T-shirts. It's comforting.'

'Really? Comforting, eh? I'll remember that next time I've been running, and you complain,' he joked, but she didn't smile.

'Edward, you can't know how much it means to me,' she waved her arm in the air, 'all this. I hoped you'd rescue me, but it was more to keep myself sane. I didn't think you'd manage it. I thought...' she paused. He could see tears in her eyes.

'Abby, it's okay. I understand. Few people get to experience what you've been through. I've had training. You haven't.' It sounded stupid but he wanted her to know it was alright to be scared.

She turned to look into his eyes. 'They said horrible things about you. And they kept asking me about Rob. What did I know about his work? I told them I knew nothing, but they wouldn't accept it. That's when they injected me with stuff.' She laughed. 'Apparently I drove them nuts because I kept talking about you. I remember, vaguely, that I kept saying I was going to marry you. One of them said they'd overdone the dose. Then they started asking about you.'

Edward put his arm around her. He said softly, 'What did they want to know?'

'Had you seen Judith? What had she told you and were you in touch with some people? I can't remember the names. I think Sebastian might have been one of them.'

'Do you remember what you said?

She frowned then said, 'I'm sorry. I told them you'd spoken to Judith and you had a list of names. I don't think I told them about Sebastian.'

'Abby, it's okay. They gave you a truth drug. You would have told them anything they asked. There's no way you'd be able to stop yourself.'

Abby reached for Edward's hand and burst into tears. He held her close, her head buried in his chest. She sobbed, clinging to him, till eventually with a shuddering sigh she pulled away and wiped her hand across her face.

'I'm sorry. I didn't mean that to happen...' her voice was quiet, 'I just couldn't hold it in.'

'Don't be silly. Stop being so hard on yourself.'

Her lower lip trembled as she smiled at him. Edward leaned in and kissed her gently. She responded instantly and put her arms round his back to stop him pulling away.

Edward heard himself say, 'I missed you so much.'

Abby pressed her face to his and whispered in his ear, 'I was scared I'd never see you again.'

They lay on the bed together, holding each other close, and talked quietly about what they'd do after this was over; then they heard the front door slam. Buzz called up the stairs before charging up to present Abby with two bags full of clothes. She excitedly pulled out jeans, a white shirt, trainers and a sweat top from one, before flinging her arms round his neck and kissing him on the cheek. Buzz grinned and pulled away.

'You haven't seen the rest yet. You might change your mind.'

'I doubt it.' Abby laughed at him and investigated the contents of the other bag, revealing some T-shirts and underwear. She held up a white lacy bra and pants set, laughing at the men's faces.

'Right, off you go while I get showered and changed. I'm desperate to get dressed properly again.'

Edward and Buzz obliged, leaving her to it. They went downstairs to join the other two in the kitchen. Sebastian was making tea; Kip was hunched over his laptop as they entered the room.

'How's Abby?' Sebastian said as he handed a mug to Edward.

'She's surprisingly okay. At the moment she's transforming herself back into an ordinary girl.'

'That's good.' Sebastian looked distracted. He handed Edward a newspaper he'd picked up at the supermarket. 'You need to see this. Bad news I'm afraid.'

Edward put his mug on the table and looked at the paper. Two pages in, he saw what had upset Sebastian. The headline jumped off the page at him. *Police seek woman in care worker murder case.* He read the article with growing anger. It was aimed at him, he knew that. He read enough to see how it would affect Abby if she knew about it. *Police would like to question a local woman about the murder. They believe she can help them with their enquiries. Anyone who knows her whereabouts or has seen her recently should contact them as soon as possible.* There was a photo of Abby, slightly grainy, standing in the rain looking miserable.

Edward dropped the paper on the table and swore. Kip looked up, blinked and went back to his screen. Sebastian sipped his tea, waiting for Edward's response to the story.

'The bastards! Haven't they done enough to her?' Edward was fuming, pacing the small kitchen. 'It's to get at me. This is a shot across the bow. A warning of what they might do next.'

'I'm afraid that's exactly what it is.' Sebastian spoke quietly, his eyes on Edward as he paced up and down the quarry tiled floor. 'The thing is, are you going to tell Abby?'

'That's the big question, isn't it?' Edward stopped and ran his fingers through his thick hair. 'What do I say, if anything?'

Sebastian pulled a pack of cigarettes from his pocket and searched for his lighter. Edward folded the paper and dropped it into the kitchen bin.

'I think we need a plan, Sebastian. I've been dancing to their tune. It's time to put pressure on them. In the meantime, we'll keep this away from Abby.'

'That might be difficult. She can't go out now. What if she wants to get more clothes?'

'Leave that with me. Let's focus on our next move.'

Sebastian frowned slightly. He had his lighter in his hand and was heading for the back door. Before he reached it Abby bounced into the kitchen, smiling broadly. She wore the dark, close-fitting jeans and a white T-shirt. Edward could see both fitted exactly as they should. She twirled in front of them.

'What do you think? Didn't Buzz do well?'

'Of course I did. My sister taught me well.' Buzz had slipped in behind her and was admiring the view from behind. Edward thought he probably had a crush on Abby. He caught Kip's entranced expression and knew he wasn't the only one.

'You look great. Much better than you did in my old shirt.'

'I feel more like me now. Is there some tea? I'm dying for a drink.' Abby smiled at Sebastian who waved his cigarettes in the air before disappearing into the garden.

'Guess I must make my own, then.'

Later, Abby volunteered to cook dinner. The men eagerly agreed. She raided the larder and freezer before suggesting chicken and pasta. As she cooked, Edward leaned against the kitchen cupboard watching her chop onions. Her hair was tied back on her swan-like neck, falling in a glossy ponytail across one shoulder.

'You're watching me.' She said it without turning around.

'Yes,' he said, 'do you mind?'

'No. I could just feel your eyes boring into my back…' she turned to smile at him, 'in a nice way. I'm okay, you know? I can handle it.'

'If you say so, but I'll still watch over you.'

'Like a guardian angel?'

'More like a security guard.' Edward laughed.

Abby stopped chopping and dropped the onions into the pan. She took a swig of the wine Edward had poured her.

'Who does Sebastian talk to?'

'Sorry?'

'When he goes out for his smoke, he chats on the phone to someone. I saw him from the bathroom window earlier.'

Edward felt his skin prickle. His long-forgotten training rose to the surface, along with the mantra – trust no one, ever. Abby watched his face change. She stopped stirring.

'You didn't know, did you? Who could he be talking to, Edward?'

'I don't know. Don't say anything to him. It could be innocent, family or somebody.'

'Or it might not?' Abby's voice rose a pitch, and her eyes fixed on Edward.

He forced a smile, hoped it was convincing. He needed to find out quickly who his old friend was communicating with. Why would he keep the phone calls secret if they were just personal? Worse still, if the people who had taken Abby had connected Sebastian to him, they already knew where he was. He needed to know and prepare to move.

Edward opened the fridge and pulled out the bottle of Italian wine. He casually poured another glass for Abby.

'Don't worry. I'm sure it's nothing.' He leaned over the stove and sniffed. 'That smells delicious. We're all sick of pies and spaghetti Bolognese. Buzz makes a mean chilli, but this looks lovely.'

'You don't fool me, you know, changing the subject. Just let me know if I need to worry.'

Edward smiled and hugged her tightly. He kissed the back of her neck, savouring the sweet scent of her pale skin.

'Will do,' he whispered into her ear and then, patting her on the back, he left the kitchen in search of Sebastian.

Sebastian sat on the stone bench with his back to the house; a curl of blue smoke hovered in the air above him. Edward trod gently on the long grass but was four steps away when his friend turned to greet him.

'I heard you coming. There's no need to tiptoe.' He appeared relaxed, legs crossed and cigarettes on the bench beside him.

'I wasn't tiptoeing. The grass is wet. Having a quiet moment? Do you mind if I join you?'

'Not at all,' Sebastian patted the bench; 'plenty of room for two. I was just admiring the view.'

'Yes, it's lovely here. So peaceful. I just wonder how long it'll stay that way.'

'What do you mean?'

'I think we'll have to move on soon. I can't believe they haven't traced us yet.'

Edward watched Sebastian's face for any sign of concern. He pulled on his cigarette and threw it on the ground, grinding the life out of it on the grass under his leather boot. His fingers lingered over the packet as if he were considering lighting another one. Then he popped them in his pocket.

'Why do you think they would trace us here? Everyone's been very careful.'

Did Edward imagine the stress he heard on "everyone"? He looked at the man beside him and wondered how far he could trust him. Was he becoming paranoid now or did he have a reason?

'I'm not suggesting anyone would compromise us. It's just I don't want to underestimate their capability.'

'I agree with you. We mustn't do that. The thing is, Edward, where else is there that's safe? This place is unknown to anyone in the service. It's unconnected to any of us, except you.'

'Yes. But what if they made that connection? I even left a note for Ben telling him what I'd done. It wouldn't take a genius to find out where his cottage was.'

'If you're asking me what level of risk I think this is, I would say low. They would have to know all your friends and go through them all to find Ben, who I believe is overseas? Why would they make that connection?'

'I guess you're right. What about the boys; can we be sure they haven't spoken to anyone?'

'What if they did? Their voiceprints aren't recorded. They never use the phone. They communicate online or by text. And, by God, they cover their tracks.'

Edward wondered how Sebastian would know that. Was he exercising his sharp intellect, or did he have information he wasn't sharing? He decided to push his friend on the subject.

'What about you? They'd have yours and mine.'

'Yes, for sure. Why are you asking me? If I didn't know you better, I would think you were suggesting something.'

'Such as secret phone calls?'

Sebastian swivelled to face Edward. He showed no emotion as he produced his phone and put in on the bench beside them.

'Do you really think I would be so stupid as to use my phone here? Even if they still believe me to be on holiday, which is possible, I'm not going to pinpoint my whereabouts. If I were in their shoes, I'd be listening to anyone you'd ever worked with.'

'So, you haven't made or received any calls since we've been here?'

'Absolutely not,' Sebastian spoke calmly. 'If this has come from Abby, you can reassure her I wasn't talking to anyone, just listening to messages.'

'It hasn't come from Abby. I saw you with your phone, that's all.'

Edward lied smoothly. His friend's explanation sounded unconvincing, but he had no intention of revealing his suspicions. They both knew that a phone could be tracked whether it was used or not, so why lie?

'No hard feelings? I'm just doing my job.'

'Of course, I understand. The training never leaves; we just look as if we're normal people.'

Edward thought it was a good attempt at humour. He said, 'Any chance of a smoke?'

Sebastian pulled a face at him, pulling the packet from his pocket.

'I thought you'd given up?'

'So did I.'

Abby lay on the bed, her pale legs draped elegantly across the old eiderdown matching the colour of the cream sheets. She was reading a book she'd found on one of Ben's bookshelves – *The Art of Ancient Byzantium* – which she seemed engrossed in. Edward wasn't sure if she was genuinely interested or just distracting herself. He sat on the end of the bed.

She looked up and smiled. He noticed the dark smudges under her brown eyes; he thought how beautiful she still looked even when tired.

'What are you thinking? You have that look again.'

'What look?' Edward leaned on his elbow. 'I don't have a look.'

'You do. That look that says I'm keeping something back and I'm not sure if I'm going to share it.'

'That's one hell of a look.'

Abby sighed. She put the book down and sat up. Edward moved to sit beside her as she leaned forward to kiss him.

'Tell me, Edward.' She kissed him again. 'Tell me what you're thinking.'

'I'm thinking how beautiful you are, how much I love you...' he kissed her hand, 'and what the hell are we going to do next?'

'Ah hah, well, I love you too, and if you don't know I'm sure I don't. No further to finding out about the mysterious phone calls, then?'

Edward frowned. He leaned back on his elbow and reached out to stroke her hair.

'I'm afraid not. Sebastian wasn't giving anything away. I shall have to resort to subterfuge. We need to know. It's possible he's playing a double indemnity game and that leaves us vulnerable if he gets it wrong.'

'How do you mean?'

'Like a double agent, he feeds them duff info while squeezing them for their plans.'

Abby sat up and put her book on the bedspread. She looked concerned.

'So, what can we do? We're no further forward and we're stuck here in the middle of Dartmoor just waiting.'

Edward reached for her hand. What could he say to ease her frustration? He felt it too. She was absolutely right. They were no further forward, and she didn't yet know the true extent of their situation.

Chapter 18

Sebastian stood in the shadows. It was cold and his breath rose in clouds around his face as he spoke. His cigarette lit his features each time he raised it to his mouth. The wind took half of his words, but snatches of the conversation floated over the garden. He held his phone close to his left ear.

'What do you mean? How many?' There was a pause while the other party spoke, then Sebastian replied, 'I can't be seen to be involved with this. Are you sure there isn't another way of getting him in?'

He dropped the cigarette stub, still glowing, onto the grass and reached for the pack, shaking another one into his free hand. Putting it between his lips he struggled to light it; the wind caught the flame each time until he turned his back to it, leaning against the wall of the old privy. The cigarette took the flame, catching alight with a bright brief spark.

'Okay. Okay. Friday it is, then. What about the others? We'll have to take the girl as well but the boys...' there was a pause; he sucked on the cigarette. 'Yes. I don't think they've found anything of significance. He had them locating the girl. They are untraceable as far as I can see. Let them go? I can get them back to London. What do I tell Covington to keep him off my back? I think he's getting suspicious. We don't want him on the loose again, like a bloody mobile rocket launcher.'

Sebastian laughed then looked around him into the darkness. He leaned back against the wall, drew hard on the cigarette and held the phone close to his ear.

'So, we're no closer to finding them? What happened to the lead on Maxwell? I thought you'd found him?' There was a pause as Sebastian listened to whoever was on the line. 'I don't buy the accidental death story. He's out there somewhere. Just keep looking.' A gust of wind took his next words, and then he was finished. Putting his phone back in his jacket he finished his cigarette, flicked it across the path towards the stream and turned back to the house.

Edward heard the back door close and slipped out of his hiding place behind the wood pile. He made his way quickly to the front door, into the hall and up the stairs to the bedroom before Sebastian reached the living room. Abby was in the bath. He could hear her singing to herself and the sound of water splashing. The boys were watching some documentary on the TV.

Sebastian was asking one of them if they'd seen Edward. He didn't catch the muffled reply but knew what it would be – that he was in his bedroom waiting for Abby to come out of the bathroom. That would satisfy Sebastian.

What should he make of what he'd just heard? He thought his instincts not to trust his old colleague were justified. But what of Maxwell, and more importantly what the hell was he going to do next? It was obvious that Sebastian was, at the very least, playing a double game and he and Abby were to be snatched on Friday. Two days to plan an escape route and find another safe house.

Edward lay on the bed and stared at the cracks in the ceiling. Maxwell was on the list. He was supposed to have died in a fire in Birmingham. His body had been identified by dental records. Because he'd died Edward had discounted him from the investigation, despite his having worked alongside Rayner. He realised the others, whoever they were, had done the same, giving Maxwell time to disappear.

Maxwell had been a very promising operative when Edward met him several years ago. News of his death had shocked him; it seemed such a waste, and he'd had no reason to think it anything other than a sad accident at the time. Now it all made sense that Maxwell had faked his own demise to escape the dangerous situation his knowledge had placed him in. Edward thought he was no nearer to knowing what it was that was causing such alarm amongst the spooks.

Noises from the bathroom indicated Abby would soon be joining him. She was his main concern: how to keep her safe while he worked out what the hell was going on. He stared at the ceiling and frowned. What to tell Abby was uppermost in his mind.

Abby leaned into the small fridge, calling to Buzz over her shoulder. She moved things around, pulling an empty orange juice carton from the door.

'Who is it that keeps putting empty cartons back in the fridge? Don't you know how frustrating that is? We need juice, milk and more bacon. Got that? Oh, and some coffee as well. I think that will do.'

She straightened up, nearly bumping into Sebastian as he entered the kitchen. He apologised and sidestepped her as he reached for the kettle.

'Are you going, Sebastian?'

'Going where?'

'Shopping. We've made a list. If you don't want to, then Edward and I can—'

Sebastian interrupted her, 'No, that's okay. I'll do it. I don't mind; it will give me a chance to get some more cigarettes.'

Edward came into the kitchen. He noticed Buzz was watching Abby again.

'We need some more fuel for the banger. Can you fill her up, Sebastian? Every round trip to the supermarket is the best part of half a tank in that thing.'

Sebastian frowned. He poured hot water into his mug, stirring the coffee granules vigorously. Edward waited for the response.

'Fill her up? Are you sure? That seems a bit unnecessary.'

'I just thought it would save making too many trips to the petrol station, keep our heads low, and I saw on the news that the fuel prices are rocketing again, threats of strikes and public unrest.'

Sebastian seemed to accept Edward's explanation and just shrugged his shoulders. He took his coffee out of the kitchen, leaving them to finish the shopping list.

Edward sat down next to Buzz, who was jotting down the last few items on Abby's list. He leaned across the table and spoke quietly to him.

'I need you and Kip to find as much as you can on Gareth Maxwell, one of the names on the list. I want to know everything about him, however insignificant; anything relating to his childhood, friends, relatives, all his jobs, girlfriends, boyfriends, any clubs he joined. And one last thing – don't tell Sebastian anything about it. I'll explain later. Okay?'

Buzz turned his eyes away from Abby, smiled at Edward and said, 'Yeah sure. No problem. We'll start when Seb goes shopping.'

Edward wondered how these two naïve young men survived in such a cut-throat world. Had he just heard Buzz say Seb? He worried about what might happen to them after Friday, but he had to make sure he and Abby were safe. The boys would have to look after themselves.

They stood together under the old tree. The clouds had lifted but the light rain persisted, and the tree offered some protection.

'It's really important we behave as normal.'

Abby made a sound like a laugh, but her eyes didn't smile. Edward raised his eyebrows.

'Don't look at me like that,' she said. 'Normal you say, but what is normal anymore? I don't know how to act normal.'

Edward sighed. She was upset and he knew she was right to be. He had spoken without thinking, been patronising and now she was annoyed with him. He put his hands in the air and apologised.

'I didn't mean to sound so—'

'Stuffy and overbearing?'

'Okay, okay. I'm sorry. I just worry about being able to keep you safe after what happened…'

Abby stood in front of him. Her dark eyes were inches from his. She shrugged.

'Edward, I'm sorry too. I overreacted. I know you worry but please don't. As long as we're together we can work our way through this.'

They stood facing the cottage. He could see a face in the window of the living room watching them, but from this distance wasn't sure who it was. The old apple tree offered shelter from the drizzle and obscured the view back to the house. As far as the others were concerned, he and Abby had come outside for a private conversation.

'Kiss me,' he said, taking her arm.

'What?'

'We're being watched. Let's kiss and make up.'

'I see, kisses on demand now, is it?'

He could see the old sparkle back in her eyes. She was joking, and before he could say another word she wrapped her arms around his neck, whispering in his ear, 'Aren't you going to resist?'

'Are you mad?'

They held each other tightly. Edward thought if Sebastian was watching it would look like two lovers enjoying a bit of privacy. Abby kissed him as if nothing else in the world mattered.

'That's better,' she said simply when they pulled apart.

'As it should be.'

'I still find it hard to believe Sebastian would do anything to hurt us.'

'I might be wrong. He could just be playing the other side, but in this game you can't take any risks. We have to plan for the worst-case scenario.'

'And have you? Do you know what you're doing next? Where we're going?'

'Yes and no. There's one piece of the jigsaw left to find. Are you all packed and ready?'

'Well, yes. I don't have much to pack.'

'Oh, yes. Sorry, I forgot.'

'Edward, don't worry. I'm fine. In a strange way it's quite liberating to be free of all those material things. It focuses the mind on what really matters.'

'Oh God, don't go all New Age on me!'

Edward laughed, and Abby poked him in the ribs. They were still laughing when they reached the house.

Sebastian was sitting by the fire reading a newspaper. He looked up, smiled and carried on reading. Buzz winked from behind his laptop screen. Kip, as usual, was staring intently at his and didn't acknowledge their presence.

Abby said, 'I'll start the dinner.'

She went through to the kitchen. Edward sat in the armchair next to Buzz's table. He could just make out the screen. Buzz angled it slightly so Edward could read what he was doing. He typed onto a blank document – *Got lots of stuff on GM. Will go through it with you on S next fag break. GM went to a school not far from where I used to live.* Then he deleted it and switched to another document with a list of places and names. Edward glanced at Sebastian, who seemed engrossed in his paper. He could hear Abby moving around, pulling pans from the cupboard.

He stretched and said, 'I'm going stir crazy stuck in this cottage. Sebastian, do you mind if I take the boys to the station when they go? You can stay with Abby.'

Sebastian looked up. 'What?'

'When the boys leave, I'll drive them. I'm not going to attract attention with this beard,' he stroked his stubbly chin, 'and I don't intend to stop anywhere. Anyway, when you go home, I'll need to take you back to the station.'

Sebastian folded his newspaper and crossed his legs. He looked calm and relaxed. Edward thought it was a very good act.

'Are you sure?'

'I think the risk is very low. I need some different scenery.'

'Will Abby be okay with that?'

'Of course. If we can't trust you who can we trust? She knows you would protect her.'

'I'm flattered. When are you two boys going?'

Buzz stopped typing and sat up, peering over the top of his screen.

'We thought we'd catch the late afternoon train tomorrow. There's nothing more we can do here that we can't do at home. Kip needs to get back to his studies and I'm like Edward; I'm feeling a bit cooped up.'

'Have you found any more? Anything that would help us find out why Edward is public enemy number one?'

Buzz hesitated then said, 'No, nothing. It's puzzling. I think the answer lies with one of those people on the list, but nothing has jumped out at us.'

Edward watched Sebastian's reaction, but he just shrugged.

'Puzzling indeed. And what about you, Edward? What are you going to do now?'

Sebastian was watching him closely. Edward could see the sharp mind at work behind his steely grey eyes.

'Do you know, I'm really not sure? We'll have to have a chat about it after the boys go home. See what we can come up with.'

Edward saw a muscle twitch in Sebastian's jaw, then it was gone as he leaned back in his chair and smiled.

'I think I need a cigarette. Do you want to join me?'

'No, I'd better not. I promised Abby I'd help with dinner. And she doesn't know I started smoking again.' He stood up and turned towards the kitchen.

Sebastian said, 'Okay. Catch up later.'

Sebastian stood in the garden smoking. Edward had asked Abby to call for help with opening a bottle when he came back through the kitchen door. He reckoned he had five minutes to go through things with Buzz.

'Right, Buzz. What did you find on Maxwell?'

'Okay, I'll be quick. I've saved what we came across with his name on and...' he passed Edward a small memory stick, 'this is everything I've found so far. All the files we've accessed are on that stick so be very careful with it. As far as Maxwell goes, it seems he led a very dull life. Not many friends, few relatives and no lasting relationships.'

Edward interrupted, 'No lasting relationships? Did he have *any*?'

'There seem to have been two girlfriends. The first was in his twenties, a girl from university who he dated for two years, and the second was when he joined the service. She transferred to the Middle East after six months and married a diplomat. They live in UAE. He had several friends, male friends that is, from playing cricket. They're all married with kids and came to his funeral. His parents both died years ago and his sister lives in Australia. She didn't come to the funeral. Seems they weren't close. Work colleagues spoke about his dedication and hard work. All sounds very dull. None of them used any "caring" words about him.'

'That first girlfriend, do you have any more information about her?'

'Only that she lives or lived in Worcestershire, near the border with Gloucestershire. She married but divorced a few years ago. No kids and she works in adult education.'

'No sign of contact between the two of them?'

'None whatsoever.'

'How old is the info on her? Could she have moved?'

'Possibly but she was there on the electoral roll last year and the one before so it's unlikely.'

'Okay. So, no close friends in London that we know of. What did he do in his spare time apart from playing cricket?'

'He belonged to a film club, all European films. His account shows regular purchases for that. No income other than his salary. No outgoings other than standard bills: gas, electricity, food shopping, car repairs and all the usual stuff.'

'Any savings anywhere?'

'Nope. Not in his own name anyway. There were regular cash withdrawals every month but nothing major, just a hundred quid here and there. He wouldn't save much if he had invested that.'

'So, all things considered, a very ordinary life.'

'Yep, very. Everything's on the stick. Good luck.'

Edward patted Buzz on the back and put the memory stick in his pocket. He heard Abby call for help to open the wine bottle. He stood up.

'Thanks, Buzz.'

Sebastian stepped aside for him in the passageway as he went through to the kitchen. They smiled at each other. Edward was reminded of circling sharks, wary of each other's teeth.

Chapter 19

Thursday morning brought more rain, not the drizzle of previous days but heavy, road-washing downpours. The cottage echoed to the thunderous deluge as it beat on the tin roof and battered the windows. Buzz and Kip watched nervously as the water rushed down the cobbled path.

'Geez, do you think we'll be able to get to the station in this?'

Edward looked through the window. He turned back to speak to Buzz.

'Yes, we'll be fine in the Land Rover. She's built for difficult days. You'll get soaked getting your bags to her though. Tell you what, I'll move and park outside the cottage gate. Once you've got the bags in, I'll move her across the lane onto the bank so that any cars can get through.'

Abby was curled up on the sofa in one of Edward's baggy sweat tops. She looked pale and tired. Sebastian sat reading in his favoured armchair by the window and looked up as Edward offered to help the boys with their bags.

He put his newspaper down, stood up and stretched. 'Does anyone mind if I smoke out back with the door open? I don't fancy going outside in this.' Nobody objected, so he sauntered off through the kitchen into the utility area and opened the door.

Edward signalled to Abby to be watchful. He turned to Buzz.

'I'll bring our bags down and put them on the road. You get yours while I move the car.'

Abby said, 'I'll distract him if he comes back.'

When Sebastian walked back into the living room five minutes later, he found them deliberating on whether to have a cup of tea before they left. Abby offered to make it, but Edward said no.

'You're not feeling well. Why don't you say your goodbyes and go have a sleep while I take them to the station? I'll bring you a cup of tea up before we leave. Sebastian will be here, so you'll be perfectly safe.'

'If you don't mind? I think it's a migraine. I've taken some tablets so I should be okay in a few hours.'

Buzz and Kip hugged her and said their goodbyes. Abby smiled and told them she'd see them soon and went upstairs to bed. As the boys gathered their belongings Sebastian volunteered to make tea and Edward followed him into the kitchen.

'We'll have a chat later. Catch up on how things are and what to do next. I just want to get the boys safely back to London.'

'Yes, I think we should talk things through. I need to go back soon as well or else tongues will wag.'

'Yes, of course. You've been very helpful, Sebastian. I really appreciate you putting yourself at risk for me.'

'Isn't that what friends do? I'm sure you'd do the same for me. Anyway, I haven't done a great deal, really.'

Edward gave Sebastian a pat on the back and said, 'If nothing else you've stopped me starving and, more importantly, you helped me get Abby back.'

'Yes, true. How is she?'

'Not too bad. A decent sleep will do her good. She hasn't been sleeping well. I'll take her tea up to her.'

When it was time for the boys to leave, Sebastian waved them off, standing at the gate under the arching beech hedge. Edward watched him in the rear mirror as he drove away. The cottage was soon out of sight. Would he go straight up to Edward's room to check on Abby or did he believe the story they'd presented? That was the question that would affect the success of their flight. He needed several hours to disappear.

As the car weaved its way down the narrow lane, the commotion caused by Abby's appearance from under a pile of coats made Edward smile. Buzz knew she had slipped into the car, but Kip had been kept out of the plan. Soon they shared the back seat, laughing like children on a trip to the seaside.

Edward imagined Sebastian's reaction when he found the shape in the bed wasn't Abby, turned and found Edward's note on the chest. *Sorry. I believe I'm better on my own. Watch your back. Edward.* He'd decided not to reveal he knew his friend had turned. He was experienced enough to know things can change overnight and he may need his help again. Hopefully they had at least two hours before Sebastian realised he'd been tricked.

Edward spoke over his shoulder, 'Change of plan, boys. I'll be dropping you at Tiverton station. If Sebastian checks on Abby, Newton Abbot would be the first place they'd look for us.'

Buzz said, 'That's okay. As long as we can get back to London I don't care where you drop us.'

'If anyone asks, tell them we're heading to Scotland. I mentioned a hotel booking. And remember, you found nothing. Take care, both of you, you know the score.'

'Sure, no problem.'

Tiverton was quiet. Abby hugged Buzz and Kip then they said goodbye to Edward, shaking his hand and wishing him good luck. Edward told them to get out at the first hint of trouble. Buzz had his PAYG number and promised he would text if he needed Edward's help or if he found anything useful. Then they disappeared into the station, waving cheerfully.

'Are you sure they're safe, Edward?' Abby was chewing her lip as she watched them go.

'I can't promise but I think they'll be okay. Sebastian assumes they found little more than a list of names and your location. They don't pose the threat that I do. Judith is the key.'

They headed north on the old A38. Abby sat in the front seat with a map on her lap.

'Where are we going, Edward?'

'Good question, well presented.'

'And the answer is…?'

Edward turned his head slightly to look at her. She had that quizzical expression that he had grown to know well. He couldn't begin to understand what it must be like to be Abby, having to trust him so completely, to put her future in his hands without really knowing why.

'We need to make a phone call and hopefully that will decide where we go next. We have to ditch this car. Sebastian has the number and description, so we'd be easy to pick up.'

Edward glanced at his watch. It was an hour since they'd left the cottage. By his reckoning he had maybe twenty minutes, possibly thirty maximum, before Sebastian wondered why he was taking so long and checked on Abby. He wanted to get as much distance between them as possible but organising the next move was equally important.

The rain had stopped, and the cloud cover seemed less dense as Edward pulled over into a layby edged by trees. They sat facing the open countryside, strangely peaceful after the stressful drive through the storm. Abby sighed and reached for Edward's hand. He squeezed it before leaning over into the back of the car to open his bag.

Abby got out of the car and stretched. Edward followed her.

'Are you okay?'

'Yeah, just tired.'

'Abby, this phone call… I can't speak to anyone. They'll have my voiceprint. I need you to do it for me. I'll tell you what to say and you just repeat it and tell me what he says. Is that okay? I know it's a weird thing to ask—'

'Of course, I did wonder about it. Are you sure they won't have mine as well?'

'No, to be honest I can't be sure, but it's a risk we have to take. We'll keep it brief and then move on straightaway.'

Edward handed his phone to Abby, telling her the man they were calling was an old colleague from years ago who owed him a favour.

'If he doesn't want to play ball, then no problem, we'll just have to go to Plan B.'

'Which is…?'

'I'll tell you after. Let's try this first.'

Abby made a face at him and, leaning against the car, put the phone to her ear. It rang three times before a male voice answered. With Edward talking quietly beside her she said, 'Mr Sidmouth, I am calling on behalf of an old friend who can't speak at the moment. Mr Wise wants to send you his best wishes and asks if you are well?'

The voice at the other end expressed surprise at hearing from Mr Wise and asked after his health. Abby said he was well, just slightly incapacitated at the moment.

'I'm phoning to ask if you would like to see him. He's very keen to meet you again.'

'When? I'm rather busy at the moment.'

'He said to tell you his leg is much better now and asks how your back is these days?'

'Goddamn it! Tell him he's always been a pain in the backside. I'll be here all day if he wants to ring back later and arrange something.'

'We're having a bit of car trouble so bear with us. Mr Wise says it will have to go in the garage, but he'll definitely speak with you later. In an hour or so.'

'Good. Please tell him my back is fine and I look forward to meeting up with him again. Goodbye.'

Abby handed the phone back to Edward, who was grinning broadly. He knew Marcus would come good.

'What was that all about?'

'I told you he owed me a favour. We've just arranged a car drop and hopefully new wheels.'

'Have we?'

'Yes, lovely girl. Now he's expecting us, and we need to get a move on. We have another fifty miles to go, and I suspect that by now they'll be on our case.'

Edward opened the car door for Abby. It was drizzling again. He didn't mind the dull greyness. He hoped it would make them less visible.

'So, what was all that about his bad back? Is that code for something? And I'm guessing his name isn't Sidmouth?'

Edward smiled. 'More of a reminder of the favour he owes me...' he paused, swinging the old vehicle out into the traffic, 'from when we were active together. We were both young and a bit rash at times. His name is Marcus McKellen and he was known as "Mad Marcus" because he took so many risks. Well, one time he took one too many. Lucky for him I was his partner. He took a bullet in his back and I got hit in the leg. We'd been dropped behind enemy lines and were on our own. I got him to a safe place where he could be recovered. He was in hospital for six months. They said he might never walk again but he had other ideas.'

'And you? What about your leg?'

'Oh, it was only a flesh wound – lots of blood but no lasting damage.'

'There's so much I don't know about you.'

Edward gave her a sideways glance. He smiled and thought, *There's much more I can't tell you.* As they drove through the dull drizzle, he told her about Marcus, how they met and the three years they had been teamed up. It was over twenty years ago, he realised with a shock. It must be fifteen years since he had seen him face to face. Abby jolted him back to the present.

'So, where are we going?'

'Almondsbury. It's a small place just off the M5, and once we get rid of this old beast we can use the motorway.'

'Edward,' Abby swivelled to look at him, 'what was Plan B?'

'Plan B was to take this back to Ben's house and steal his other car.'

'Thank God Plan A worked.'

'Quite.'

Chapter 20

Edward pulled the Land Rover down a narrow track beside a cream-coloured cottage. It stood alone on the country lane on a ridge overlooking the Severn Valley. They could see the new Severn crossing clearly, even in the misty gloom. They bounced to a halt outside a metal farm gate. A tall figure was walking towards them, limping slightly. He had two large black dogs running at his heels.

'I saw you coming,' the man called out. His voice was deep, booming across the space between them. He shouted at the dogs to keep back then pulled the gate open for Edward to drive into the yard.

Slamming the gate shut behind them he waited for Edward to climb out of the vehicle before moving forward to give him a rib-crushing hug. The dogs jumped at them, barking excitedly.

'Edward! Great to see you! Get down, Nelson! Sit, Winston!' Marcus let go of Edward and tried to get the dogs in check, but they were too excited to listen and continued to bounce around the two men.

'It's good of you to help, Marcus. I know it's a big ask.'

'Don't be bloody silly! I wondered if I'd hear from you when I saw your ugly mug all over the papers. Knew something was badly wrong. And I guess this is your accomplice, the mysterious woman?'

Edward winced. He hadn't told Abby yet about her notoriety. He signalled to Marcus before turning to open the door for her. She hung back, unsure of the dogs.

Marcus called to her, 'Don't be scared of them, my dear. They're all bark and no bite. Bit like their owner.' He moved forward to take her hand, bending stiffly to kiss it.

Abby smiled. He grinned back at her then bellowed at no one in particular.

'Let's get inside! Out of this bloody rain. Come on, Nelson, come on, Winston.'

They followed him into his kitchen. It was warm and welcoming. A large range threw out the heat. There was a kettle bubbling on the hob, and two dog baskets occupied the area immediately in front of the stove. The dogs flopped into them on command and lay, heads on paws, great brown eyes on the visitors.

Marcus pulled three chairs out from under the large oak table and motioned to them to sit down. He offered tea which they gratefully accepted. Edward thought how little his old friend had changed, thicker in the body, greyer and hairier but as mad as ever. He was ten years younger than Marcus, but they had worked together well.

Marcus put three large mugs on the table before dropping heavily into his chair.

'Every time I get up in the morning, stiff and aching, I think of you and remind myself I have a lot to be grateful for. How are you, Edward? What happened?'

Edward hesitated, unsure how much to tell him. It

wasn't a case of not trusting his old partner, more that he didn't want to put him in any danger.

'Judith got in touch. She sent me a strange message which I still haven't got to the bottom of. Then she died but so did the messenger.'

'The woman care worker?'

'Yes. I guess you've seen the story put out to scare me off.'

'Couldn't miss it, old chap. Your face was everywhere for a few days. So, what did Mulholland know that got her killed?'

'To be fair, they didn't kill her; she died of cancer. But they could have helped her more. They had her incarcerated in a phoney care home because of something she found out. I'm trying to put it all together but still looking for the missing pieces.'

Marcus wrapped his large hands around his mug. He looked bemused.

'What can I do to help? I guess you need to dump the car?'

'Yeah. Sebastian knows it and I think he's been compromised.'

'Are you sure? I'd trust him with my life.' Marcus looked surprised.

Edward said, 'So would I, but it all points that way, so I have to be careful.'

'I suppose so. Who does the car belong to?'

'Friend of mine. I borrowed it while he's in the States. I need it to be kept safe.'

'No problem. I'll look after it. What about wheels? I guess you need a replacement?'

'Please, if you have anything you can live without for a while.'

Marcus laughed a rich rumbling belly laugh. He said he had just the thing. Edward knew he'd come to the right person for help. Even Abby looked brighter. Marcus's enthusiasm for life was infectious.

The dogs put their heads on their paws and closed their eyes. The warmth from the range made Edward feel drowsy too. When Marcus offered a bed for the night in return for their company, he hesitated only for a second. This place felt safe.

Abby put the cutlery on the table while Marcus stood at the stove stirring a huge cast-iron pot. He wore a striped apron and had a large glass of red wine in one hand, for all the world like an old French chef.

'So, did you ever marry, Marcus?' she asked him.

Marcus turned to look at her before returning to the pot. 'Yes, I did. We had six glorious years together.'

'What happened?'

'She died.'

Abby said, 'Oh, I'm so sorry! I shouldn't have asked.' She fidgeted with a fork.

Marcus left the pot and turned to face her. He looked sad.

'It was a long time ago. She had a car accident on the motorway. It was foggy. A lorry had jack-knifed and several cars ran into it. Suse got caught up in it.'

Edward spoke from the doorway. He had come in from the yard and caught the conversation.

'I'm really sorry, Marcus. You should have contacted me.'

'There was nothing you could have done. There was nothing anyone could do. It's just one of life's challenges.

As I said, a long time ago and here we are – three survivors. I did my grieving and now I live each day as it comes…' he took a large swig of wine, 'and today I have excellent company! Let's eat.'

After dinner they sat around the table reminiscing while Abby washed up. The dogs lay stretched out by their master's feet, a picture of contentment. Edward could feel the wine creeping through his body, numbing his senses. He wondered briefly if he was being wise relaxing his guard, but Marcus had always made him feel secure. Very few people knew the debt they shared, and he doubted Sebastian would think of looking for him here. Tomorrow they would move on.

As they lay in bed together Edward told Abby about the newspaper story that implicated her in the fake murder. She took it well; resting her head on his chest, she just said she knew something was being held back from her.

'How?' He put his arm around her bare shoulder and pulled her closer.

Abby sighed. 'I know you so well. You have this overwhelming desire to protect me as if I'm some small child. I'm tougher than I look, you know.'

'Sorry, but you had been through a lot. I found out just after we got you back and there didn't seem a right time to tell you.'

Abby made a sound like a small elephant, a hmmph that made him laugh. She punched him in the ribs, and he groaned in mock agony.

'Shush! Marcus will wonder what we're doing! Do you think we need to disguise ourselves?'

'What, like fake noses and big glasses?'

'Ha ha. No, I mean change things a bit: hair colour and eyes maybe, and glasses would be a good idea.'

Edward looked at Abby. He thought, *She's amazing to be so positive after everything that's happened.* Perhaps before leaving Marcus they should make some minor changes, something to throw the casual observer off the scent. They would need to go shopping, buy food and fuel; maybe even stay in accommodation somewhere. He couldn't afford to attract attention.

'I'll speak to Marcus in the morning. It wouldn't hurt to be careful.'

'Where are we going next? What have you planned?'

'There's someone who might have an idea about what's going on. He faked his own death a few years ago and I think I know where he's been hiding. I'm going to try to find him…' Edward hesitated before adding, 'and I wondered if you would feel safer here with Marcus. I don't know what might happen next and I'd rather—'

Abby put her fingers on his lips. 'Don't you dare suggest I stay behind. No way, Edward! After all we've been through, I want to see this through to the end. We're in this together. Don't even think of leaving me here.'

'I thought you'd say that, but I had to ask.'

'Well, you asked, and you got your answer.'

Marcus poured more coffee and handed Edward a plate of toast. Abby had gone for a shower as, she said, she didn't know when she'd get another chance.

'So, before you take my car you want me to go shopping for you?'

'If you don't mind.'

Marcus threw a tea towel over his shoulder and turned to the sink, speaking over his shoulder, 'Do you have a list?'

'Yes, I do. It's not too long, just essentials. You know the usual stuff: hair dye, glasses, fake suntan, some clothes for Abby.'

Marcus laughed. He turned to face Edward and said, 'You're going to dye your hair and wear glasses? Don't you think they'll still recognise you?'

'I'm sure *they* would but I'm hoping the shop assistant or petrol court attendant won't.'

'Edward, old chap, there are cameras everywhere these days.'

'I know that, but we'll avoid what we can and hopefully they won't know where to look for us.'

Edward could tell Marcus was unconvinced, but he knew he would get the things on the list for him anyway. He'd refused to say where they were going next; he didn't want him arrested as an accessory. Marcus had somewhere to keep the Land Rover, away from prying eyes, so there would be no evidence to prove he had helped more than by providing a meal and a bed for an old friend if anyone paid him a visit.

By midday Edward was sporting black-framed glasses, his hair was a nondescript mid-brown and his skin was the colour of an old wardrobe. He looked like an old-style explorer or ex-pat newly returned from some African state. Abby would pass as his young assistant, hair neatly plaited and thick-rimmed glasses. She said her dark hair wouldn't take a change of colour and she'd rather wear a hat.

Marcus said it was time to reveal their new wheels. He took them out into the yard at the rear of his cottage. The dogs bounced around them, barking eagerly. At the far side of the yard he flung open the doors of a barn-like building. Inside was a vehicle covered by a tarpaulin.

'Here we are!' He pulled off the cover with a flourish to reveal a timeworn pale blue camper van.

Abby clapped her hands and said, 'Wow! It's lovely!'

Edward found himself speechless. He watched Abby dancing around it listening to Marcus enthusiastically describing its charms. They were peering into the back when he found his voice.

'Marcus, are you sure this is a good idea? I'm supposed to be covert, not driving around in the equivalent of a neon sign with an arrow pointing down at us!'

'Edward, don't be so ungrateful! It's perfect,' Abby shouted as she examined the interior.

Marcus walked over to Edward. He put his hand on his shoulder and said, 'Look, I understand what you're saying but— No, listen to me, Edward...' he put his hand up to stop Edward speaking, 'this will be just right. It means you have somewhere to sleep and you can play at being holidaymakers. There's nothing to link it to you. It's full of fuel and it's reliable. Suse and I had great fun with this old thing so look after it for me.'

'I'm sorry, I didn't mean to sound ungrateful. Are you sure you want to do this? It must mean a lot to you.'

Marcus sighed. 'We both know I owe you a huge debt. We wouldn't be standing here now having this conversation if you'd been less of a mad man. You could have left me there to die but you didn't and now it's my turn to help you. Just bring her back to me when it's over.'

Edward saw Abby inside the van, checking cupboards and sitting on the rear seat. He smiled at Marcus. It made some sort of sense so maybe he should just be gracious and accept the help.

'Okay. You're probably right. I think Abby can play at holidaymaker just fine. I promise to do my damned best to bring it back in one piece.'

'Please do.'

Chapter 21

The old van heated up quickly when the morning sun rose over the trees and stroked its roof with warmth. Abby stirred under the duvet, groaning as Edward nudged her.

'Morning. Time to stir or else I'll be driving off with you still in bed.'

Abby groaned again and made a few choice comments before revealing her crumpled face. He laughed at her and kissed her forehead.

They were two days into their road trip. The novelty of living in a camper van had already worn thin for Abby once she realised the washing facilities were basic. Last night Edward had found a small camping site on a farm with a new shower block. They were the only visitors and had the facilities to themselves. He worried about being so exposed but Abby's need to enjoy the luxury of a warm shower had persuaded him. The farmer and his family had been disinterested in them and weren't at all curious, more interested in the money the booking brought them.

Edward sat in the passenger seat with a map spread over his lap as Abby dressed and folded the bed back into a bench. Buzz had been as good as his word and had continued to work on finding Maxwell. They had kept in contact regularly over the past few days. It seemed both Buzz and Kip had been left alone, but Buzz had changed phones to be sure.

'So, what does today hold in store?' Abby asked as she pulled a sweat top over her tousled hair. He thought, *She looks beautiful even in a beanie hat.*

'We're going to pay a visit to someone who I think knows where Maxwell is hiding.'

'Okay. Are we moving on again or can we stay here for a night or two?'

Edward smiled. He knew how much that shower and the use of a laundry meant for Abby.

'I think we can stay here for a while. I told them we might stay for three nights. But be prepared to move sooner if we need to.'

After a quick breakfast of toast and honey they folded everything away and drove off the field. Edward planned to use country lanes and avoid A roads to get to the village where Maxwell's old girlfriend lived. It was a small place at the foot of Bredon Hill. There was no pub or shop, just a huddle of cottages dotted along three lanes that intersected each other before meandering off around the base of the hill. The landscape was green, dotted with trees and hedges, fields inhabited by large cows. Very few people would bother to drive up these narrow roads unless they were delivering or visiting.

Edward pulled the camper van off the lane and into a field gateway. He checked his map and the directions Buzz had given him. There was no guarantee that this woman had any contact with Gareth Maxwell, but he had to try.

He had no idea where to look next. Abby broke through his thoughts.

'It's so peaceful here and so beautiful. What a lovely place to live.'

'Let's hope Maxwell thinks so too.'

'What are the chances of finding him, Edward? Do you think she'll know where he is?'

Edward closed the map and turned to look at Abby. He said, 'I hope so because, to be honest, I don't know where else to look for him.'

Abby said, 'Oh well, fingers crossed then.'

He thought, *How like Abby to remain so pragmatic.* If they failed here, they were in serious trouble, with diminishing funds and few choices. It was only a matter of time before their luck ran out and they got caught by the police, or worse.

The track was muddy with a hump of grass growing between two well-driven ruts. The old camper van bounced and bumped its way down the slope. They reached another gate and Abby got out to open it. Edward saw a large stone cottage at the end of the track. It stood alone, surrounded by a neat stone wall and green lawns. Several cows grazed in a field next to it and a large stone building stood behind.

He pulled the van up in front of the garden gate and got out. Abby followed him. There was a large brass knocker on the old front door, and when Edward rapped it against the door it shattered the silence of their surroundings. A dog barked somewhere. After a minute or so he heard the sound of bolts being drawn back and the door opened a crack. He couldn't see who was peering out at him.

'Hello. I'm sorry to trouble you. My name is Edward Covington. I'm looking for someone called Pat Loveson.'

A female voice said, 'What do you want with her?'

'Do you know her? I'm hoping she can help me find a friend.'

The door opened another inch or so and he could see the woman's face more clearly now. He knew he had to be careful not to say anything that would make her slam the door in his face.

'I'm very sorry if this is inconvenient. I know it's rude to turn up unannounced like this. I'm hoping Pat can help me. I've been abroad and I came back to find my friend had died and I wanted to see if there was anything I could—'

'What did you say your name was?'

'Edward Covington.'

'Just wait a minute.'

The heavy door slammed shut in their faces. Abby looked at Edward and pulled a face at him. He shrugged. His instinct told him something was going on here. He felt the gun in his jacket pocket. Abby didn't know about that. Adrenalin was tickling the back of his neck and he felt the urge to kick down the door and burst in, but calm reason held him back. He took a deep slow breath and remained still, waiting.

After a few minutes the door opened again, this time fully, to reveal a slim middle-aged woman, smartly dressed, with her ash blonde hair piled up in a messy bun. She smiled at them and put out her hand in greeting.

'Please come in. Sorry for seeming rude. I live alone and you can't be too careful. I don't have many unannounced visitors.'

161

'Of course. We understand, and I can only apologise again for disturbing your peace. This is my friend Abby. We're on holiday in the area and thought we'd pay you a visit to see if you can help.'

The woman smiled and ushered them through into a farmhouse-style kitchen.

Edward said, 'Are you Pat Loveson?'

'I haven't been called that for a long time. That was my maiden name. I married over twenty years ago and kept my husband's name when we divorced. My name is Manders now. Do sit down.'

Edward and Abby sat at the table. Pat offered them a drink before joining them at the table. She seemed to be weighing them up, her bright blue eyes fixed on Edward.

'Now, please tell me what this is all about. Who is this friend you want me to help you find?'

Edward thought, *You know who*, and said, 'An old friend. Someone I used to work with a long time ago. His name is Gareth Maxwell.'

'Gareth. Yes, I remember Gareth. What happened to him?'

Edward sensed the tension beneath the smooth surface of the woman's face. He kept his voice neutral.

'I'm afraid I was told he'd died, last year it seems.' He watched her face closely as he said, 'But I don't believe it.'

Pat looked him in the eye and said quietly, 'Why don't you believe it, Mr Covington?'

He sensed Abby shuffle in her seat beside him. Ignoring her, he said, 'Because I knew him well and I also know what he was working on. He was under pressure. People under pressure sometimes do strange things.'

He leaned back in his chair, hoping he had got his pitch right. She stared at him as if trying to read his thoughts. He held her gaze.

'I'm still not sure why you think I might be able to help.'

Edward thought, *Ah, we are still playing the game.* He said, 'Oh, it was a long shot. I thought he may contact you as you were close once.'

'I'm sorry to disappoint but I'm afraid I haven't heard from him in years. We separated a long time ago. It seems you've had a wasted journey.'

Edward said, 'What a shame. I was going to offer my help but never mind. If he does get in touch, tell him I asked after him.' He turned to Abby. 'We'd better leave Mrs Manders in peace.'

Abby smiled at Pat Manders, thanking her for the drink. Edward stood up and offered his hand.

'Yes, thank you. If he does contact you, this is my phone number. Please ask him to text me. Tell him I won't answer the phone.'

She looked surprised but took the note anyway. Edward smiled and said, 'He'll understand.'

As they left the house he turned to ask, 'Has anyone else been asking for him?'

He saw a flicker behind the blue eyes, but she kept her face straight saying that no one had called. They both said goodbye and left her standing by the door.

'Is she still watching us?' Edward asked Abby as he went to open the van's door. She glanced back and waved.

'Yes, she is. Do you think she's telling the truth?'

'Not for one minute. Now we just have to wait.'

They climbed into the van and bounced their way back up the track to the gate. Abby jumped out to open it. Edward wondered if he had done enough to make Maxwell get in touch. If he were in his shoes would he trust an old colleague he hadn't seen for years? He was weighing his options when his phone buzzed in his pocket. Abby hopped back in as Edward read the text. He turned to her.

'Sorry, you'll have to open it again. We're going back.'

'What?'

He showed her the text. It read: *Come back to the house. We have things to discuss.*

Pat was waiting for them at the door. She took them through to the kitchen again.

'I'm sorry, Mr Covington. I had to be sure you weren't acting against Gareth's interests, if you know what I mean. He left me strict instructions.'

'I can imagine. Please call me Edward and this is Abby. I can assure you we are both very aware of the risk Gareth is taking. I'm sure you must know we are in the same situation.'

'Yes, I do now.' Pat smiled and reached for a sheet of paper. 'I have a list of questions Gareth wants me to ask you.'

Edward said, 'Fire away.' He thought, *This will be interesting.*

'Okay. What was Judith Mulholland's involvement and how did she die?'

'Judith was managing several projects and started to get curious about the connections between them. She had a list of people who had worked for her which she passed to me via the care worker. I'm sure Gareth knows about the care worker. Judith died from cancer. I visited her just before she died.'

'How did the care worker die?'

Edward looked Pat straight in the eyes and said, 'Apparently I murdered her. I suspect she was disposed of, but I don't know how or who did it.'

Pat looked uncomfortable. She looked back at the paper and read the next question, 'Okay, how did you find me and why did you even look?'

'That's an interesting question. The answer is I overheard a telephone conversation between Sebastian Darrow and an unknown person. It was clear they were looking for Gareth. He was on my list of names and, I must admit, I ignored him because I thought he was dead. Once I realised they thought otherwise, I knew I had to find him before they did. I have a good hacker who made the link between you and Gareth. It was a long shot, but we came anyway.'

'Last question, Edward, what do you know about Cradle?'

Pat folded the paper and sat down. Her face gave nothing away. She looked calm and composed.

'Ah, that's the one question I'm not prepared to answer. It would compromise you and I'm not going to do that, Pat. I'm quite happy to talk to Gareth but I'm not discussing Cradle with either you or Abby. I think you need to go back to Gareth on that one.'

Pat smiled; she didn't seem at all surprised by Edward's reaction. She stood up as a male voice spoke behind Edward.

'Right answer. How are you, Edward?'

Chapter 22

Gareth Maxwell had changed since Edward had last seen him. He wore a full grey beard and his hair curled over his collar. Edward wasn't deceived by the slightly dishevelled look; he could see the fit, strong man beneath the facade.

He held out his hand and said, 'How are you, Gareth? Not bad for a deceased person.'

Gareth laughed; a belly rumble muffled by a beard. He gripped Edward's hand.

'I'm doing okay considering. I see you've had a spot of bother. Let's have a drink and talk about it. Is it too early for Scotch or would you rather have coffee?'

'It's too early for me. I'll take the coffee.'

Pat put the kettle on before Gareth suggested she take Abby on a tour of the house and grounds. He kissed her on the top of her head and Edward saw a softness in his manner he didn't remember seeing in the old Gareth.

After the women left the room Gareth's demeanour changed. He poured two coffees and asked Edward to sit at the table.

'Why are you here, Covington? I've spent years planning and perfecting my departure and this could compromise everything.'

Edward said, 'I didn't look for this. I was quite happy in my retirement. Judith contacted me. She was in a poor state, not making her usual rational judgements. Then that damn woman was killed, and things got very tricky.'

'So I gather. They must be scared of what you might do, to frame you like that and then your lady friend too...'

'Her name's Abby. She got dragged into this and I'd rather she was safely in her home but there's no safe place for either of us till I get to the bottom of this.'

'Get to the bottom of it? You don't know what you've stumbled across, do you? You have no idea! Fuck me, that's rich! You've fucking risked life and limb without knowing why.'

Edward felt his neck prickle. He clenched his fist and kept his face and voice calm.

'I told you, Gareth. I didn't ask to get involved. I've had to piece this together from very little information or insider knowledge.'

'So, what exactly *do* you know?'

Edward hesitated before answering the question. He wasn't sure whether to trust Maxwell but knew it was the only chance he had of gaining the ammunition he needed to overcome the enemy. He saw the look of anger in the other man's eyes and decided to address that first.

'Gareth, I appreciate how my turning up like this has upset things. I think you need to be prepared for less friendly visits. It won't take them forever to find you. Sebastian Darrow has people working on it. We've obviously fallen foul of some ruthless operators. I'm here to help not hinder you, and if you can help me too that's great. If not, I'll clear out and leave you alone.'

It was a gamble. Edward thought, *If Gareth Maxwell tells me to fuck off, I'll be alone and no closer to finding the answers that might protect Abby.*

Gareth Maxwell frowned. He sat back in his chair and glared at Edward, then he sighed, rubbing his beard.

'This bloody beard drives me mad. Perhaps I should just shave it off?'

It sounded like a question, but Edward knew he wasn't supposed to answer. He waited.

'Okay, Edward. You're so bloody smart. You always were; it drove me up the fucking wall sometimes but I'm glad to have you onside. Tell me what you know, and I'll tell you what I know. Between us perhaps we can beat the fuckers.'

Edward said, 'I'd forgotten how colourful your language can be. The Navy has a lot to answer for.'

'Fuck it, Edward.'

'Okay, I concede defeat,' Edward laughed and leaned forward, putting his hands on the table. 'The truth is, Gareth, I know bugger all about Cradle. I know it was, is, a black project. I know they operate outside any legal restrictions. I know it's collaborative, involving the MoD, MI5 and the Pentagon. I have a list of rapidly diminishing project members. And people who knew too much have died, disappeared or been sectioned.'

'That's not enough to get you killed. I guess they think you know what Cradle *is* and what it can do. And the biggie – Gaia. That's why they're after you and why they want me so badly. Together we can take them down.'

Gareth went quiet. Edward could see he was deliberating on whether to tell everything. He'd survived the last year without detection and he was weighing up his chances if he joined up with Edward. They observed each other for a few moments, until Gareth stood up, pushing his chair back noisily on the tiled floor.

'Let's take a walk. I need to talk to you in complete privacy. The women will be back soon.'

He led Edward through the hallway to the back of the old house and out into what must have been the stable yard. Cotswold stone buildings that once housed the horses had been converted years ago into workshops and a large carport. They walked across the yard and out through a heavy wooden gate to a track running down into an orchard. At the bottom was a bench with a slate roof to protect against the elements. It was situated against a stone wall so you could sit with your back against it and see through the trees to the house beyond. It was a perfect place to watch the world or hold a private conversation. Gareth sat heavily on the bench and Edward joined him.

'I'll tell you everything. It's only fair you know what you've got yourself into and I'm a bit tired of going it alone. I'm glad of the company. You probably know my story; you obviously know about Pat or else you wouldn't have found me. I worked hard to keep her out of the official version of my life so, when the time came to disappear, she offered the perfect bolthole while the dust settled on my coffin, so to speak. Nobody else made that connection; like I said, you're a clever bastard. When I heard your voice, I knew it was trouble. At first, I thought maybe you'd joined the dark side, then I thought no, this is Edward Covington, Mr Integrity.'

'I don't know if that's a compliment or not.'

Gareth gave a short laugh before he continued speaking, 'Take it as one. I've followed your story in the press. Did you know you made the news as well? When it kept being repeated in differing forms, I knew you'd outwitted them and they couldn't find you. But it also meant they'd be looking for me. Any idea how they found out I was still alive?'

'No idea. It could be an assumption. Did you leave any evidence?'

'Not as far as I know. I was very careful to find someone with the same build. The dental records were easy to fake, and I didn't rely on anyone else to do it. I didn't kill him by the way; he was a gentleman of the street off his face on drugs. He overdosed at a convenient time for me, so I made use of his body. Just planted some personal things on him and gave him a cremation.

'Anyway, back to Cradle. That's what you really want to know about, isn't it? You're quite right to assume it's a black project, money no object and no restrictions or controls. Basically, they do whatever the hell they like and they're not accountable as long as they deliver. Like the others, I had no idea what I was getting into. Cradle isn't one project – it's lots of little programmes all beavering away at their piece of kit or software. None of them knows what the others are doing. Occasionally there'd be a meeting in the Pentagon or Whitehall where the top guys talk money and check progress. The programmes would do their bit, bring their software or equipment into service then be dispersed back into mainstream MoD or intelligence.

'It's been going on for over ten years. Nobody was supposed to be on more than one of the associated programmes but somehow or other I got drafted into a second. That's when I met Rayner and when I started making connections. I think Judith did the same thing. She had several of her people involved and she started asking questions. Suddenly she "retired" due to ill health. Everyone said she had gone into a nursing home for the terminally ill.

'I worried they might go through the records and find me. I began planning my escape before I joined her. Pat knows none of the detail, just that I was in trouble and needed her help.'

Gareth stopped talking and stared at his feet. Edward waited for him to continue but he seemed lost in thought.

'But what is Cradle? What does it do? How can it be so important that it makes us dispensable?'

'It's the single most advanced weapon in the world. With the Americans we have developed a weapon that is silent, untraceable and deadly. It can take out cities full of people without touching the infrastructure; absolute annihilation of thousands without damaging anything of value, such as oil refineries for instance. It can control a weather system, that was an unexpected by-product, and destroy the enemy's weapons. And, best of all, it's environmentally friendly.'

Gareth gave a hollow laugh, but Edward didn't join him. It was beginning to make horrible sense and it made him feel sick. He knew for sure now they were all in danger. There could be no safe haven.

'So that's what it does but what is it?'

'In simple terms it's a focused beam that can be directed at an individual person or whole cities, or even a weather system to influence climate. Its power is immense and it's portable and untraceable by the enemy. Imagine a sound wave fired from a gun that could kill or stun or change the surrounding environment. It's like something from science fiction but it's real and it's happening now. Do you understand now, Edward, just how deep the shit is?'

'Yes,' he said, 'I guessed it must be something big, but I had no idea...'

'No, how could you? As I said, I began to make connections that didn't make any sense and then Rayner died. Judith has done you no favours dropping you into this. They won't stop till they find you. There's nowhere in the Western world you can hide.'

Edward sat back against the wall and stared at the peaceful scene in front of him. The sun was hanging above the fruit trees fresh with new growth. Somewhere, cows were calling to each other. He was sitting in perfect surroundings but living a nightmare. What could they do to stop it all?

'Gareth, you said we could take them down. How do you think we can do that? What can we do to stop them?'

'Apart from selling our secret to Pakistan or some Soviet satellite state?'

'I hope that's not a serious option?'

'No, whatever I may be I'm not a traitor, but we have to expose this somehow.'

Edward looked at the green orchard, thought about Abby somewhere in that handsome stone house and said, 'Yes, we do.'

Chapter 23

Gareth offered them a bed for the night, pressed them to stay, but Edward declined. He promised he would return but said they'd booked the camping site for another three days and intended to stay as planned. Abby was puzzled but Edward stood firm.

As they drove away from the house, he replayed everything they'd discussed. Everything Gareth had told him made sense, but he was cautious. Gareth had seemed sane enough but there was an air of paranoia about him aggravated by his intake of strong whisky. What if it was all an obsessive mania brought on by his experiences and his alcohol dependency? What sane man fakes his own death? The only answer was a desperate one and that brought him back full circle.

Abby quizzed Edward about Gareth. What had they talked about that was so secretive she was excluded? He told her it was past shared experiences. They reached the farm campsite as it got dark and ate the chips they had bought from a fish and chip shop in the local town.

The van interior was chilly, and when Abby said she wanted to put the bed up Edward didn't argue. He was bone tired. They crawled under the duvet together, Abby clinging to him like a child, wrapping her arms and legs round him till they both warmed up.

'What do we do now, Edward? Did Gareth help solve the puzzle?'

He couldn't see her face in the dark. It was easier to lie if he couldn't see her eyes.

'No not really, but he may be able to help. We'll go back tomorrow and I'll see what I can find out. He's a bit shot away.'

'Yes, I noticed. Pat is very sweet. She loves him to bits.'

'Did she say anything about how he came to live with her?'

'No, not really, only that she'd expected him. She knew he would return one day, and he did, just turned up on the doorstep.'

'I had the impression he'd stayed in touch with her.'

'Really? Maybe he did but she didn't know he was coming back till he arrived with his bag. She said he claimed sanctuary and she took him in.'

'That sounds like Gareth.'

Abby rested her head on his chest. Her breath warmed his skin. She was breathing slowly as if on the edge of sleep when she said, 'I like them.'

Edward kissed the top of her head and was reminded of the same gesture he'd seen between Gareth and Pat in the kitchen of her farmhouse. He thought perhaps between them they could put things right. Then he fell asleep.

The room was dark except for a dim red glow. There were rows of men in uniform staring at a flickering screen waiting for the start of the presentation. Sebastian walked through them and up onto the small stage. He had some papers and a pointer pen in his hand.

Someone switched on the projector and the screen came to life. It showed a city full of people rushing to work. The streets were alive with thousands of commuters. It could be any city anywhere in the developed world. Sebastian said, 'Gentlemen, be prepared to be amazed.'

Suddenly the commuters began running. A deluge of hailstones the size of golf balls was raining down on the street, smashing car windows and bouncing off kiosks. Some people had put up umbrellas to fend off the onslaught; some fell to the ground under the weight of the ice falling from the sky.

The scene changed. Now they were watching a man setting up some sort of cannon. He was aiming at the sky, pressing a screen to set coordinates. The screen counted down to zero while the men retreated into a small box beside the giant gun. The picture switched to a facility somewhere in the desert. Men were screaming, falling down clutching their heads.

Then they watched a missile fall from the sky for no apparent reason and rows of rocket launchers fire their weapons randomly into the air to fall back to earth. There was snow in the desert and rain in Africa. Sebastian concluded the presentation by saying, 'Gentlemen, I give you Cradle.' Then he turned to the back of the room, asked for the lights to be turned on and said, 'Please give a round of applause for our project leader, Mr Edward Covington, without whom none of this would be possible.'

Edward woke with a start; his heart was pounding. He stared at the roof of the van; for a second, he couldn't think where he was. Taking a deep breath, he concentrated on slowing his heart rate before turning on his side towards Abby. He watched her sleep, her beautiful face smooth and calm. This was what mattered. She was what he had to protect, no matter what it took. The dream was just that and nothing more. They could be beaten; he only had to work out how.

His watch told him it was six thirty. Not too early to get up, too late to go back to sleep. Edward slipped out of the bunk and pulled on a pair of joggers and sweat top. He missed his early morning runs and decided a quick jog round the local lanes would help him think straight. Abby didn't stir as he left the van, quietly closing the door and locking it behind him.

There was just enough light to see the road. A mist hung over the hedgerows as the birds began their wake-up call. Edward's breath formed clouds of vapour as he jogged along the lane. As he ran, he thought about the last few weeks, what he had discovered. How deeply was Sebastian involved? Had he been instrumental in any of the deaths? Until a few days ago he would have trusted him with his own life. And how far could he trust Gareth, so obviously damaged by what he'd seen and done?

The lanes at the foot of Bredon Hill were alive with rabbits as they drove slowly towards the track leading to Pat's farmhouse. There was nobody to be seen; it was the perfect picture of rural tranquillity. Early spring sunshine warmed the old van as it bounced along the track.

As they rounded the bend, they found the first gate leaning open against the stone wall. Edward slowed down. Abby sensed his tension as he stopped by the gate.

'What is it? What's wrong?'

'I don't know. It doesn't feel right. Both gates were closed yesterday. I'm going to pull into this field and park behind the hedge. Stay in the van while I go take a look.'

He turned carefully into the field, avoiding the worst ruts and stopping behind the high hedge that hid them from the lane. Abby shuffled into the driver's seat.

Edward told her to stay put while he checked it was safe to go down to the house.

'It could be the farmer who owns the cows in the next field, but I want to be sure. I won't be long.'

The southern edge of the field gave a view of the front of the house through a gap in the dry-stone wall. Edward could see the porch and a neat lawn. Most importantly he could see the car parked outside the gate. It was a large black saloon. He cursed under his breath and instinctively checked his pocket for the comforting bulk of the handgun. Keeping his back beneath the top of the wall he edged his way to the corner of the field. From there he would have a better view and be able to follow the wall down the slope and get closer to the buildings.

Pat's voice carried up the hill. He caught odd words but not enough to interpret the conversation. She was speaking to two men in dark suits. They stood impassively on the path as she talked, then a third came from within the house and spoke briefly to her before walking back towards the car. The others nodded to her and followed him. She stood stock still and watched them get into the car and drive away.

Edward hoped he'd hidden the camper van well enough as he made his way back along the wall, keeping his body beneath its shelter. He saw the car drive past the gateway, bouncing and throwing up clods of mud. They didn't stop to close the gate.

He reached the van to find it empty. His heart missed a beat then Abby appeared from behind it.

'Sorry, I felt safer outside. Was there someone there? I heard a car go by.'

'Yes, there was. I think we'll leave the van here and walk down across the field.' He caught Abby's worried look and added, 'Nothing to be worried about. I'm just being careful.'

They made their way down the sloping field to the old stable yard to find Pat standing beside the workshop. She was surprised to see them.

'Did you pass them on the lane? If they saw you...' she sounded panicky.

Edward put his hand on her arm. 'It's okay, Pat. We saw them from the top track and hid the van. They didn't see us. What did they want?'

She sighed and said, 'They wanted to know if I'd seen Gareth and did I know where he was. I told them I thought he was dead; I'd read it in the paper last year. I think that threw them slightly. Then they said there was some doubt about whether it was him or not, so I said it was highly unlikely I'd hear from him as we'd parted on bad terms years ago.'

Edward smiled at her. 'That was just right. Did they seem to buy it?'

'I think so but one of them, the American, was very quiet. He watched me like a hawk, as if he were trying to read my mind.' She shuddered. 'I didn't like him at all.'

'Was he the one in the house? He came out last?'

Pat looked at Edward with a surprised expression and said, 'How do you know that?'

'I watched it all from the top field. I saw them leave in the car. Was he alone in the house?'

'Only briefly. He asked to use the loo.'

'Where's Gareth?'

'Up there.' She pointed at the room above the workshop, a storeroom only accessible by a ladder. As they looked up, Gareth's head appeared. He was covered in dust and cobwebs but grinning.

Edward called up to him, 'Gareth, I think they've probably put a bug in the house. We'll have to be careful. You keep quiet while I take a look with Pat.'

He looked less cheerful as he climbed down. Edward told him to stay with Abby in the yard while he checked the house. Pat led the way back towards the house.

'Once we're inside, I won't speak. How much time did he have? Where would he have gone?'

'I walked with him through the hall and showed him the loo. He was in the house less than a minute so couldn't have gone far. I saw him walk back through the hall, so he didn't get as far as the kitchen.'

'Okay, that's good. He might have just looked into the living room, checking for personal belongings or pictures. I'll check anyway. Does Gareth leave things lying around?'

'No, we keep all his things in the studio over the carport just in case. The story is he's my handyman if ever anyone saw him.'

Edward left Pat in the kitchen and walked through the hall. It was fairly spartan, not many places to hide a bug. He checked behind the two paintings and the vase on the hall table, ran his fingers under the table edge then went into the toilet. A clever surveillance man might hide one there when there was only a woman in the house, listening for sounds of a male. He looked behind the only cupboard and the mirror on the wall, lifted the cistern and checked the loo brush but found nothing. So far so good.

The living room was less easy, but he worked on the principle that the agent would have to move fast so would choose somewhere obvious to hide a device. Where would *he* hide a bug faced with such a large room? His eye went straight to the huge fireplace with its bread oven and copper kettles. A careful check revealed nothing, and Pat was right. There wasn't a thing to suggest that a man shared this house. They had been very careful.

He closed the door and returned to the kitchen. Pat was standing by the range looking concerned.

'Did you find anything?'

'No, nothing, but I would suggest we avoid the living room for the time being, to be safe. I'll go tell Gareth and Abby the good news.'

Edward knew from experience that the house might come under surveillance if they thought Pat's story didn't stack up, but his instincts told him they were still looking elsewhere.

Gareth agreed with Edward's assessment, but he seemed unnerved by the visit. Sitting at the kitchen table with a scotch in his hand he tried to make light of the situation, cracking jokes about spooks. Edward saw Pat frown as she moved the whisky bottle out of reach.

'So, Edward, old chum, how are we going to bring the fuckers down, then? What can we do to stop them, eh?'

Edward sat down opposite him and said calmly, 'I don't know. Any ideas, Gareth? You know them, their modus operandi, what they can do. My suggestion is we put our heads together and come up with a plan. But first...' he leaned forward and grabbed the drink from Gareth's hand, 'you stop drinking and start thinking. You're no good to me drunk.'

Gareth leapt to his feet, knocking his chair to the floor with a loud crash. Pat jumped back with a gasp. He glared at Edward, who stood up to face him.

'You bastard! You think you can walk in here and start telling me what to do... I've survived fine for the last year, haven't I? Why now? Why do they start looking for me now?'

'Because, Gareth, they're scared. Judith surprised them. They think there's the possibility of losing control of the situation. I bet you're not the only one they're looking for. And you're not the only one who's lost everything.'

Edward realised his voice had risen. He took a deep breath.

Pat stood behind Gareth, picked up the chair and said, 'Sit down, darling, and talk to Edward. He's right. We're not alone.'

Edward put his hands on the table and leaned towards Gareth. He pointed at the two women.

'There are four of us in this room. I think it's time we worked together to try to find a way out of this mess. I'm sorry if I seem harsh, Gareth, but now is not the time to fall apart. Like you said, you've survived the last year.'

'Yeah, but I still think you're a pompous fucker, Edward bloody Covington.'

'Maybe, but I'm all you've got. Would you prefer to go it alone, knowing they're closing in? We stand a better chance together than we do apart.'

Gareth ran his hands through his hair and made a sound like an animal in pain. Pat looked concerned but Edward remained impassive. He knew his words made sense.

'Any chance of a coffee, Pat? I think Gareth and I need to have a chat.'

Pat looked at Gareth, who sat with his head in his hands. She brushed his shoulder with her hand as she went to fill the kettle.

'Perhaps Abby and I can go for a walk then you two can say whatever you want without worrying about us.'

Edward looked at Abby, who nodded. Gareth didn't look up as they left the kitchen.

'Gareth, we need to clear this up. You know how deep we're in this. It's important we work together. It's not just us, there's the two women to consider—'

'For fuck's sake! Stop stating the obvious. Of course, I realise that. I'm not a complete moron, you know.'

Edward sat down opposite Gareth again. He said, 'I'm sorry. I'm not trying to get your back up. Let's have a coffee and try to decide what to do next, pool our knowledge. I'm really worried we might have a return visit before we're ready.'

Gareth sat up, sighed and said, 'You and me both. I know you're right. I'm sorry if I seemed a bit... out of it, but I didn't expect to be found so quickly.'

'You managed to hide away for a year. That's pretty good going. I found you because I followed a hunch and it was only because I overheard Sebastian say they were looking for you.'

Gareth frowned and said, 'Yeah, I wonder exactly what game Sebastian is playing? Which side is he on?'

'Until a few days ago I would have trusted him with my life. Now, I don't know. Why would he be looking for you?'

'The only thing I can think of is that I'm the only one left with a working knowledge of the programme.' He leaned over the table towards Edward. 'That's probably it. The ones with the most familiarity are dead, locked away or still working in the project. I'm the only one on the outside, still on the loose. You were right when you said they were worried about losing control. I could blow the whole thing wide open, sell to the highest bidder or expose it on the web.'

'Why haven't you?'

'For the same reason you wouldn't. I couldn't betray everything I've worked for just because some arseholes got control of the asylum.'

'Fair enough. So, let's get our heads together and work out what we can do about it.'

Chapter 24

Edward leaned against the apple tree blowing smoke rings into the crisp night air. He'd given up hiding his habit from Abby. She said she'd guessed anyway when he came back into the camper van with the slightest whiff of tobacco lingering on his clothes.

Gareth had gone to get a beer – just one he said – then they stood together in the faint light from the house in comfortable silence. They'd come to a mutual position of trust as each realised they had no choice; to go it alone would be madness. Edward stamped out the stub of his cigarette on the earth beneath the tree, the lingering bitter taste rolled around his mouth. He watched the trees in the orchard bending in the night breeze, caught the earthiness of the rotting apples in the long grass around their feet. Tomorrow might be the beginning of the end for them; or it might be the foundation of a safer future.

They'd pooled their knowledge. Gareth talked about his time on the project and how he'd come to understand what was being constructed. He compiled a file of newspaper reports and snippets from the internet that began to piece the jigsaw together. Edward read through them: stories of birds mysteriously falling from the skies, airplanes flying off course due to instrument failure, extreme weather conditions explained away by climate change. The list grew longer. There were floods in areas where no rain had fallen for seven years, drought in prosperous crop-growing regions and electrical activity wiping out telecommunications. All of these, Gareth asserted, were down to the project testing the systems.

The back door opened and one of the women stood on the doorstep. A voice carried on the still night air.

'Are you two coming in for supper?'

Gareth called, 'We'll be there in a minute.' He turned to Edward, 'How much should we tell them? They need to be prepared if things go wrong.'

'Yes, I know. Abby is pretty well clued up. She knows from personal experience what they're capable of.'

'Of course...' he hesitated, then said, 'I think we should get them out of the country. I have a place in Spain they could go to. They'd be safe there.'

'Would they? How can we be sure they'd get there safely?'

'I have people who can help. I've been planning my escape route for a while. They have no idea who I am. I've given them the impression I'm some sort of dealer who needs to stay below the radar, if you get my drift?'

Edward thought he knew what Abby would say but he kept that to himself and said, 'We can put it to them and see what they think. If you're confident we can trust these people.'

'It's not a matter of trust, more a business transaction, and they hate the authorities as much as we do.'

'No way! Edward, how could you think I'd leave you and swan off to Spain? And what if I get picked up going through passport control? You're mad!'

Abby was hopping about the kitchen. She wrapped her arms around her body as if she was cold then flung them wide as she strode up and down again; Edward had anticipated this would be her reaction. No matter how he tried to sugar-coat it she was adamant. And she was angry with him for even considering it an option.

Pat and Gareth watched in amused silence. Edward saw their faces alternate between concern and barely disguised mirth as Abby flounced about. Neither of them offered Edward any support. Eventually Abby stopped pacing and glared at Edward.

Pat said, 'Abby, I know you're mad at Edward but look at it from his point of view. How can he hope to end this if he's worrying about your safety? Our only chance is to let them do their thing and keep out of the way.'

Abby said, 'What, because they're the men and we're the little women who might get ourselves hurt?'

'No, because they're the experts, professionals who know what they're doing and we're just amateurs along for the ride.'

Edward thought, *Pat sounds cross*. Abby looked at her and seemed unsure what to say. He stepped forward and took her arm.

'Abby, of course I don't want you to go. I'll worry about you and miss you but surely you can see what Pat's saying is right? Gareth and I need to focus on putting a stop to all this. I can't do that if I'm wondering whether you've been snatched every time we leave the house. And where else can we go now? If – or rather when – they work out where Gareth is, we have to run again. Go to Spain with Pat and at least I'll know where you are.'

Abby slumped into a chair. She seemed defeated.

'But Edward...'

'No buts, Abby,' he said, bending down to face her, 'you have to go. It will be alright. You'll travel on a false passport and we have people who will get you there safely.'

'But what about you? How do I know you'll be okay?'

'Because I'll be watching his back,' Gareth said, before adding; 'you've got to trust us.'

The preparations were all in place. Gareth faked the passports and made the necessary travel arrangements – a private yacht to Gibraltar then speedboat round the coast to Estepona where a car would be waiting to take them to Gareth's hideaway.

Pat told friends she was spending a few weeks in Cornwall at a writing retreat but left no forwarding address. The house would be locked up and her nearest friend who lived three miles away would come and check everything was okay.

As dawn broke, a fine mist drifted in over the hill, quickly turning to drizzle. Edward woke early and turned to find Abby staring at him intently.

'Good morning, beautiful. How long have you been awake?'

'I don't know. It feels like hours.' She looked miserable.

Edward pulled her to him and kissed her cool cheek. She sighed and snuggled closer to him. Her skin was cool and smooth like marble. He wrapped her up in the duvet and was overcome by an irresistible urge to keep her there, safe and warm, curled against his body. This was swiftly followed by a pressing desire, and when he pulled her to him his kisses were returned with passion. He felt the heat rise through their bodies as Abby responded to his touch. They made love as if the world were ending, oblivious to their surroundings or any fear of discovery. Afterwards Abby cried softly into his shoulder, her hair masking her face, and all he could do was cling to her and make promises he wasn't sure he would keep. He wondered if Gareth was doing the same thing.

'I just want to be back in my own bed, and for all of this to be a dream that never happened,' Abby whispered into Edward's shoulder. Her words cut deeper than a knife. He thought, *If only I could take her home and forget Cradle and bloody Judith Mulholland.*

'I would give anything to be taking you home now instead of sending you away. You know that, don't you?'

'Of course I do. It's my fault as much as anyone's – I encouraged you. I just thought it would be fun, a bit of a challenge. I had no idea—'

'How could you, Abby? But I should have known better, and the fault is entirely mine.' He stopped her interrupting him. 'How could you possibly anticipate what might happen? But I should have seen the risk.'

'I don't want to go, Edward. I don't want to go to Spain.' She paused and adjusted her body so that she was staring directly into his eyes. 'It doesn't feel safe; it's not that I distrust Gareth but—'

'I know. I've been trying to come up with an alternative, somewhere you can go, but I can't think of anywhere. And I really believe you're not safe with me now.'

Abby touched his cheek and said quietly, 'If anything were to happen to you and I was in Spain...' she chewed her lip, 'I don't know what I'd do.'

He held her close, breathing in the scent of her hair. She pulled away from him.

'There is somewhere. I didn't mention it before because I hoped we'd be able to find a way out of this but...'

Edward propped himself up on one elbow and said, 'Where? Why didn't you say before?'

'I have a cousin who has a holiday let business in Cornwall. He's always said I could have a break in one of his cottages if I wanted. The only problem would be getting in touch and then explaining why I've been connected to a murder and am all over the papers.'

'It might work. And there was only the one piece about you, so you could say it was a mistake and all resolved. That was to get at me, a warning. We'll have to talk to Gareth and Pat. She might be happier staying in this country too.' He felt relieved; the thought of Abby having to go to Spain in the hands of seedy characters had bothered him. But they weren't out of the woods yet.

Abby was smiling again. She wriggled out from under the duvet and offered to make coffee. He thought, *How bizarre our life has become in such a short amount of time that choosing which bolthole to run to has become part of our routine.*

She must have sensed his mood because she turned and said, 'This is reality now, isn't it? I have to keep reminding myself I'm not in some thriller film. A few weeks ago, I was planning a holiday for us and now...'

'Abby, I know I keep saying it but I'm so sorry—'

She interrupted him, 'And I keep saying stop saying sorry! We're in this together and it's not your fault!'

'Okay, so tell me all about your cousin.'

Chapter 25

'I thought the whole idea was to get them safely out of the country? Are you mad? Cornwall, for fuck's sake – full of bloody tourists!' Gareth was shouting as he paced the kitchen. Pat rolled her eyes at him and tried to butt in, but he wasn't listening. So they let him rant for a while till he ran out of steam.

'Gareth, it's fine. I trust Abby's judgement and, to be honest, I'm happier knowing I can get to them quickly if needs be. And early March is not exactly full-on tourism time, even in Cornwall. Pat, how do you feel about this?'

Pat looked at Gareth, who was quiet now, and then at Edward. 'I'm okay with it. Gareth, I was a bit daunted by the Spanish plan I must admit. No, please listen…' She held up her hand and shushed him, 'I'll feel safer in Cornwall and it wouldn't look odd if somehow they found out I was there. That's where I told people I would be. Abby, if you contact your cousin and I'll pay any of the cost.'

Abby said, 'Oh no, Pat, I think he'll probably let us stay for free if we're not fussy about where we are, and we wouldn't be, would we?'

Gareth made a noise to show his disapproval but didn't object. Instead he said to Edward, 'And talking of money…

how are you fixed? Can't exactly stroll into a bank and use the cashpoint machine, can you?'

Edward frowned. Money was becoming an issue; he'd used up most of what he'd taken out before he left home. He knew Gareth would have worked that out and was being difficult.

'I thought I'd tap you for an unsecured loan if that's okay?'

Pat stepped in before Gareth could fire back at him. She said, 'That's enough! Stop playing games, Gareth. We're all in this together. I can look after Abby as I'm still on the outside, so to speak, so I'll withdraw enough to keep us going for a while. You can pay me back later.'

'Pat, that's very kind of you, thank you.' Abby smiled at her. 'Edward, do you think I'm okay to phone Stephen? Is it still safe?'

'I'd say it's the only way. It's still unlikely they've got your voiceprint and would be able to find it amongst all the other traffic.'

'I wouldn't bank on it,' Gareth muttered, but Edward ignored him. He was thinking hard. How could they test that without putting the women at risk?

Pat put the kettle on the Aga and offered to cook a big breakfast. Edward watched her and thought she looked more relaxed than the rest of them, but perhaps she hid it well.

Abby asked for Edward's PAYG mobile. She looked up her cousin's business number on the internet and scribbled it down.

'I'll give him a ring and see if he's willing or able to offer us something.'

'Keep it as brief as possible and try to avoid getting the address or anything that will pinpoint where you are. Tell him you'll message him later to confirm. Gareth and I will make sure you get there safely, okay?'

Edward leaned against the wall smoking. Gareth sat on the bench next to him, staring at the farmhouse in silence.

Abby had spoken to her cousin who'd been more than happy to offer a vacant cottage that was new to his business which he hadn't advertised yet. He'd seemed pleased to hear from her and made no mention of the paper article, so Abby ignored it. She said to Edward she'd tell Stephen about it when she saw him and explain that was why she felt the urge for an unplanned break with her friend. The cottage was in north Devon, so they'd be closer if they needed help quickly.

The call had taken less than ten minutes, but each minute had felt like an hour to Edward. They'd set the ball rolling and could only hope it wouldn't lead the spooks straight to them.

'Are you okay now with letting them go?' Edward exhaled a plume of grey mist into the crisp morning air.

Gareth grunted, 'Don't have much choice, do we? I'm not exactly fucking happy, but it is what it is.' He threw his cigarette end down and ground it into the grass beneath his boot. 'I'm sorry about earlier. I find it difficult...' he paused, staring at his boots, 'with Pat. This is not how I thought my later years would pan out. We've got to put an end to this, Edward. Stop the fuckers before they ruin anyone else's life.'

Edward nodded. 'We can only try. But I promise you I'll do my best to get us out of this in one piece.'

'Are you sure Sebastian is playing on the other team? And do we even know who we're up against?'

'That, my friend, is the million-dollar question and at the moment I don't have an answer.'

It was all arranged. Pat and Abby would drive down in Pat's car and take a break at the services at Taunton Deane before continuing their journey to Stephen's cottage not far from Ilfracombe. Abby told him she'd be in touch to get exact directions. Edward and Gareth would follow them and be their shadow until they were sure they were safe. *Just one more night together*, Edward thought, *then what*? Gareth, for once, stayed silent and kept his thoughts to himself.

The next morning Edward left Abby sleeping while he paid the farmer's wife for their pitch. Then he went back to the van and watched her sleep for a while. He had no idea when they might be together again after today. If anything went wrong, he'd told her to contact Marcus.

Abby yawned and opened her eyes. 'Oh, hello. How long have you been up?'

'Not long. I've paid for our stay. How are you feeling?' He knew it was a dumb question and knew she did too by the look in her eyes.

'I'm fine. What about you?'

'Yeah, me too. Coffee before we pack up?'

'Yes please. I'll get dressed.'

They sounded like any other couple on holiday, but Edward felt the tension in the air. He thought it best to say nothing, try to keep things calm. Abby turned and caught his eye.

'It really is okay, you know. I'll be fine with Pat. We can console each other, and she's right. You're better off without us; you can concentrate on what needs to be done.'

He put his arms around her. 'It'll be alright, Abby. Gareth and I will find a way of putting this right.'

'You'd better.' Her voice was muffled by his sweater. 'I don't really want to end up working for my cousin in Cornwall!'

The services at Taunton Deane were surprisingly quiet when Pat pulled into the car park. Edward and Gareth parked the old camper van at the other end under some trees and watched the other vehicles come and go. Nobody appeared to be paying the women any attention; Edward was confident they weren't being followed.

'I think we should follow them to the village then leave them to it. What do you reckon?'

Gareth grunted, 'Whatever.' He fidgeted and wound the window down a bit before saying, 'I need a drink. Do you fancy anything?'

'Coffee wouldn't go amiss if you're going in.'

'Okay. I won't be long. Keep an eye on them.'

He hopped out of the van and sauntered across the car park, hands in pockets, passing Pat's car without a backward glance. Edward hoped that neither of the women would follow him. He realised he was holding his breath and exhaled deeply without taking his eyes off the car. A few minutes later Gareth made his way back, again without looking at the car. It wasn't until he reached the van that Pat left the car and walked into the building. They were behaving just as he'd told them to, Edward thought.

Gareth clambered heavily back into his seat and passed Edward a polystyrene lidded cup smelling strongly of coffee. Then he reached in his pocket and pulled out two packs of crisps, throwing one on Edward's lap.

'Thanks.'

'You're welcome. Any sign of trouble?'

'No, nothing.' He looked at his watch. 'They'll be moving on soon, so we'll know then.'

They sat in silence. Edward noted that Gareth had bought himself a small bottle of local cider but decided to say nothing. It wasn't worth an argument, he thought. Just as he finished the coffee Pat reversed slowly and pulled away, heading for the exit. Edward started the engine but waited until they left the car park before following. No other vehicle had moved, and as they re-joined the M5 he checked his mirror and still no tail. Gareth sighed beside him and he knew he felt the same sense of relief.

The rest of the journey was uneventful and an hour and a half later they followed Pat down a narrow and twisting lane towards the small village that would be home for the two women for the foreseeable future. Parking in the tiny village hall car park they watched them pull onto the drive of a pretty cottage. Nobody was about and Edward was tempted to go to Abby and give her one last hug, but they'd agreed no contact. He was only there to make sure they were safe and hadn't been followed. He glanced at Gareth, who sat silently, giving no clue about his feelings.

'Shall we leave them to it? Are you happy they're safe here?'

Gareth grimaced and said, 'Yeah, as happy as I can be. Let's get out of here.'

Edward started the engine and pulled away. He looked in the rear-view mirror and saw Abby watching them go as she pulled bags from the boot of Pat's car. She didn't wave. It hurt and pleased Edward at the same time; she was behaving just as he'd asked.

A few hours later they bumped along the rutted track leading to Marcus's house. Edward couldn't think of anywhere else to go and, with Gareth's agreement, decided three was better than two in this battle.

As they reached the gate, the dogs rushed to challenge them, barking loudly, with Marcus a few steps behind bellowing at them to 'Shut up!' as he opened the gate. Edward drove the old van behind the barn and got out, stretching his arms and back. The dogs bounced around him, tails wagging with enthusiasm.

Marcus caught up with them and said hello to Edward, waiting for him to introduce Gareth, before giving him a bone-crunching handshake that made Gareth wince.

'Heard a lot about you, Maxwell; not all of it good.'

Edward saw Gareth bristle and expected a curt reply, but he surprised him by saying, 'Same goes for you too but we're all in this together so I guess we'll just have to get along.'

Marcus laughed, one of his deep belly rumbling guffaws. He motioned for them to follow him and turned back towards the house.

'Come on in and we'll open a bottle of something and see how we go. Edward, you can fill me in on what the hell is going on.' He turned back and said, 'And thanks for bringing the old girl back in one piece.'

'Least I could do. We really appreciated it.'

'And how is your lovely lady? Safe I hope?'

Edward frowned. 'As safe as any of us are but safer now she's away from me.'

Marcus led them into the kitchen and the dogs headed straight for their beds in front of the Aga. He told them to make themselves at home and disappeared in search of a bottle. A bottle of what, he didn't say.

Gareth looked around before pulling out a chair and hanging his jacket on the back. He warmed his hands on the range and said, 'He's a bit of a bugger, isn't he? Not quite what I expected.'

'Marcus is unique,' Edward smiled. 'He's also very loyal so – trust me – we're in safe hands.'

Chapter 26

The garden centre was quiet. A wet Thursday is obviously not a good day for gardening, Edward thought as he sat in Marcus's old Toyota watching the rain stream down the windscreen. The car park was almost empty, and he'd parked close to the entrance where Buzz would see him easily.

At twelve thirty a white van pulled up in front of the entrance and a young man hopped out, pulling a large holdall with him. He wore an oversized Parka style coat with the hood up. Edward wiped the screen so he could see better. Was it Buzz? He watched him wave goodbye to the van driver then turn and look across the car park.

Edward started the car engine and waved as Buzz ran through the rain, wrenching the car door open and flinging his bag on the back seat.

'Shitty weather! Great to see you, Edward. How's things?'

'Great to see you too, Buzz. I'll bring you up to speed as we go. I'm staying with an old friend; you'll like him, I think. Abby's...' he paused, 'elsewhere but safe. We found Maxwell and he's with us too. I want you to continue looking for anything about him, particularly his links to Rayner. Have you heard anything from Sebastian?'

'Not a thing. Have you?'

'I changed phones so he can't contact me. How's Kip?'

Buzz unzipped his coat and rubbed his hands in front of the warm air coming through the heater vents. He grinned at Edward.

'Kip's fine. He gets involved in stuff and he's currently engrossed in some UFO conspiracy, so I thought it was better to leave him behind. When he's got an idea in his head, there's no stopping him.'

Edward grinned; he could imagine Kip staring at his screen all night chasing stories about aliens.

'He's an odd one. He's probably safer doing that. I'm not sure he's got your survival instincts.'

'Yeah, you're probably right. Is it far? I could murder a mug of tea.'

Edward smiled and turned the car into the track leading to Marcus's old house. As they bumped their way down the track the rain stopped, and the Severn crossing came into view through the haze.

'Nearly there.'

Buzz leaned forward in his seat and said, 'Wow, what a view. Is this it? Is this where we're staying?'

'Yep.' Edward stopped the car and jumped out to open the gate as the two black Labs came charging around the corner, ears flapping, to greet him. He grinned at Buzz. 'I hope you like dogs.'

'Yeah, I'm fine with dogs. They look like fun.'

'They're mad like their owner and here he is…'

Marcus waved and hurried to close the gate behind them. He called the dogs as they tried to mug Buzz, checking his pockets and bag for anything edible. Edward gave Marcus his car keys back and introduced him to Buzz.

'Ah, the Boy Wonder! Pleased to meet you, young man. Come on in. Ignore these two; they'll scrounge if you let them so don't let them.'

Edward followed them into the house. The kitchen was empty.

'Where's Gareth?' he asked, frowning at Marcus. 'You haven't lost him, have you?'

Marcus grimaced. 'If only; the guy's a pain. He's gone back to his room nursing a hangover.'

'And whose fault is that?'

Marcus harrumphed and turned to Buzz. 'Tea or coffee? And are you hungry? You look as if a square meal wouldn't go amiss.'

Buzz said he'd love a tea and Edward was surprised by the way his old friend fussed around the young man. He felt a pang of sadness; Marcus had lost his wife and any chance of a family; living alone for years must take its toll. Then a very small voice in his head said, Well, you did, and you survived.

'So, what do you want me to find? Are we still working through that list, Edward?' Buzz took his mug of tea with a polite thank you to Marcus. 'Do you want me to start with this Maxwell character?'

'Might be a good idea while he's out of the way. I don't want him knowing we're delving into his life. And...' Edward paused, 'can you look at Sebastian too? We want to know if there're any projects, anything at all, to link him with Rayner or Maxwell.'

Buzz set himself up in Marcus's study and went to work armed with a pile of bacon sandwiches and a huge mug of tea. The sun had broken through the clouds and Edward decided to join Marcus on his dog walk.

They walked in amiable silence while the dogs snuffled about in rain-filled ditches and rooted around at the foot of trees. It was nice to see the back of the grey skies but even the warm sun couldn't lift Edward's mood. He missed Abby and his life back in his Wiltshire home. Marcus seemed to pick up on his mood and, when they stopped to admire the view down the valley, he turned to Edward and said, 'We will get to the bottom of all this, you know. We've been in worse scrapes before.'

'Yeah, I know. It's the not knowing that's driving me mad. What am I missing, Marcus?'

'I'm sure Buzz will turn something up. Have you heard anything from Sebastian?'

'He doesn't have my new number so no I haven't.' A thought struck him. 'Did anyone contact you after I left you? Anyone at all, old friends or colleagues you haven't seen for years, maybe...'

'Edward, I can honestly say no to that. I half expected it but nothing, no contact, no strangers making conversation in the supermarket, zilch...'

'Do you think that's good news or are we being overconfident? I do wonder what Sebastian is up to. We found Gareth fairly easily so why didn't he?'

Marcus leaned on a gate and watched his dogs charging after each other across a field. He rubbed the back of his neck and sighed.

'Edward, I keep going through this and I haven't a clue what's going on. We must be missing something, and I wonder if *they*, whoever they are, know that. If I were Sebastian, I would have gone over your past with a fine toothcomb and sent someone to see me by now. So why hasn't he?'

'The obvious answer would be he's working both sides and protecting us till we find the truth, or he genuinely hasn't worked out where I am.'

'You have to ask yourself which is most likely and get that whizz-kid to find some answers PDQ.'

'Yeah, I know. Let's get back and see how he's doing. If Gareth is about, can you distract him for me so that I can have time with Buzz?'

'Sure, no problem.' Marcus whistled for the dogs and they walked back up the track together. The sun had disappeared behind thickening clouds and a chill returned to the air.

Back at the house Buzz was still working in the study and Gareth sat reading one of Marcus's books with his feet up on the table. Edward saw Marcus stiffen but he just shut the dogs in his boot room to dry off and came back in rubbing his hands together.

'Anyone for a drink? What are you reading there, Maxwell?'

Gareth looked up from the book and had the grace to take his feet off the table. He held the book up to show them.

'Not seen this one before. Seems a fair assessment of what went on.' It was a book about the Falklands War written by one of the senior officers on the ground. Marcus nodded and said he agreed.

'I've got quite a few on the subject if you're interested. I take it you found my library.'

'Yeah. Sorry, I went for a wander, a bit rude of me I guess but I'm not known for my manners as my... as Pat keeps telling me.'

Edward listened to Gareth. Was there an angle here? He was being unusually open. Marcus put the kettle on and reached for the coffee pot.

'Coffee, Maxwell? We could take it into the library if you like. I've got a few other books you may be interested in...'

Gareth looked up from the book and said, 'Yeah okay. Got to do something to keep myself occupied while Edward's whizz-kid does his stuff.'

Edward smiled at Marcus and took a coffee through to Buzz.

'Drink for you, Buzz. How's it going?' He closed the door behind him and put the mug on the desk.

'Cool. Yeah, okay but it's hard going. Quite a few doors have closed since I went in before.'

'Hmmm. Found anything new?'

Buzz leaned back from his laptop and reached for the coffee. He frowned, an unusual expression for him, thought Edward.

'Found a few more memos, references to Cradle and strict instructions to maintain Gaia. Seems people at the top have been asking questions. This guy Rayner you're so keen on was at the heart of things. He had top-level clearance to twenty-six projects and four of them were linked to Cradle. Just before he died, he was working closely with that Professor Stephens. Remember him? The Pentagon memo? He was the scientist who seemed to be designing and testing stuff for them.'

'Anything on Maxwell? They worked together but Gareth only says he "came across him". Any sign that it was closer than that?'

'No, funnily enough he's hardly mentioned. It looks like he was on the fringe of things. He was cleared to work in Cradle but no top-level clearance for anything else, unlike Rayner.'

Edward frowned. Gareth was a man of mystery and that really bothered him.

'Okay. Can you look at this professor and see what there is on him, please?'

'Yeah, sure.' Buzz went back to his keyboard, fingers thumping across it. As Edward stood up to leave, he said, 'Kip's become obsessed with aliens. He told me we've had visits and they're still amongst us. He thinks some of our technology has come about because *they* left it here – Roswell and all that. He's gone proper gaga.' He chuckled as he carried on staring at his screen.

'Poor Kip, that boy is on the spectrum. You do know that, don't you?'

Buzz looked up. 'Yeah, course I do. He's right out there but he's good so I just let him go off on one sometimes, to get it out of his system. He'll be okay.'

'I hope so.'

Edward left Buzz to get on with things and went in search of Marcus. Kip bothered him though. If he started poking around in American Intelligence databases on his own and got caught, he'd be in deep shit.

Chapter 27

The smoke drifted slowly away in the cool evening air as Edward and Gareth stubbed out their cigarettes. They'd watched the sun set beyond Marcus's garden and the temperature was dropping swiftly now. Edward avoided telling Gareth much about what Buzz was doing but he kept pressing.

'I'd almost think you don't fucking trust me.' Gareth pulled another cigarette from the pack; it was his third since they'd come outside.

'Do you want me to be honest, Gareth? The truth is I don't know who I can trust after Sebastian.'

'You went to a great deal of trouble to find me and now you're saying you can't trust me. You're a fucking wanker, Covington.'

Edward put his hand up and said, 'Whoa! Did I say I don't trust you? I'm just trying to find out why someone is after us. You haven't exactly been forthcoming about your connections.'

Gareth glared at him. He inhaled deeply and blew clouds of smoke in Edward's direction.

'My connections? What about your friend Marcus bloody McKellen then? What are his *connections*? I've had the best part of three years keeping a low profile to avoid Rayner's fate so don't start preaching—'

'All I want to know is exactly what your role was in Cradle? Why do you think Rayner died?' He ignored the jibe about Marcus.

'Well, that's the thing, isn't it? I don't know. I wasn't close enough to the action to be cleared into it. My role – for your information – was keeping the contractors happy, sweet talking them into delivering on time. You want the truth? I was fucking glad to get out of it; it's all bullshit.'

'But I don't think it is, though. If it's just an Anglo/American bullshit project, they wouldn't be going to all this trouble and Rayner wouldn't be dead.'

Gareth finished his cigarette, grinding it into the ground at his feet. He looked less angry now.

'We've all made assumptions about Rayner, even Sebastian. What if we're wrong? There are other reasons why a man dies; he might have killed himself. We still don't know where that money came from; we *assumed* it was the project. What if it wasn't?'

'What are you saying?'

'What if Rayner had been selling secrets or was being blackmailed? Because you're so close to his widow you've discounted it; that he might have gone rogue.'

'That's nonsense.'

'Is it, Edward? Can you say, hand on heart, that you're totally impartial about Rayner or even Marcus? I bet you haven't looked into *his* background, have you? How many years was it that you lost touch? He could have been involved in one of the offshoot projects…'

Edward felt a wave of dislike for Gareth and he knew it was because he was right. He'd been blinkered. In this situation everyone, absolutely everyone, was suspect until proven otherwise. He didn't think, for one minute, that Marcus was involved in anything but maybe he needed to pay more attention to Sebastian, and he needed to find out what happened to Rayner's money and where it came from.

Marcus was cooking dinner and Gareth had gone for a shower, so Edward took advantage to have a chat with Buzz. He found himself unsure who to trust now and maybe trusting no one was the safest option. The little office was stuffy, and Buzz was hunched over his screen; he looked up when Edward came in and raised one hand in greeting.

'How's it going, Buzz?' Edward closed the door behind him and stood with his back against it.

'Yeah, good. This Rayner guy is proving really tricky. Somebody has really covered his tracks. Loads of stuff has been deleted and I mean permanently deleted...'

'But you've found something?'

Buzz stopped typing and leaned back in his chair. He squinted up at Edward.

'Well, I think so. I've been trying to track the money in and out of his account. It passed through so many accounts, most of them offshore of course, and it ended up in a Swiss bank account; it certainly didn't stay long in Rayner's account. It was definitely laundered.'

'So, Abby may not have known about it?'

'I doubt it. He had it paid into a private account in a different bank to the one where they did their personal banking. He very probably hid it from her, I'd say.'

'Okay, so where did it come from? Any names we'd recognise?'

'Nope.' Buzz paused and Edward knew there was something that bothered him.

'What is it? What have you found?'

'I don't know... I need to dive a bit deeper but...' Buzz frowned, 'I think there's a Russian connection. The company that handled the payment is a subsidiary of a much bigger organisation with a head office in Malta. The parent company is owned by personal friends of the President. It's all very murky.'

Edward felt his skin prickle. His worst fears seemed to be coming to a head – a Russian involvement?

'Any mention of Sebastian or sign of involvement in it?'

'No, not in this; his name crops up in odd documents relating to Cradle, but nothing of any real interest. Do you still want me to look for anything on him or shall I carry on with Rayner?'

Edward thought for a second. Should he ask Buzz to spread the search or pursue his current investigation?

'Focus on Rayner unless you find a link between them and – I know I don't need to say this – this is strictly between you and me.'

Buzz grinned and gave Edward the thumbs-up. He turned back to his screen and, just as Edward turned to open the door, said, 'Oh, I nearly forgot. Do you remember Rayner was working closely with an American professor? That Stephens guy? Well, I found something interesting about him; he's on the MUFON research team.'

'MUFON? Who are they?'

'Mutual UFO Network. They're based in California but have teams all over. They have a website so have a look. Just the sort of thing Kip is crawling all over at the moment.' Buzz laughed.

'Why the hell would a scientist get involved with UFOs?'

'Beats me. I'm surprised the Cradle lot would want anything to do with him. He must be bloody good at whatever he does for them.'

Edward nodded but he wondered what the connection could be. This was getting weirder with each search. He said, 'See what Kip thinks of it. If he's poking around in that world get him to look at our professor.'

As he left Buzz, he remembered Judith's last words. He realised she hadn't been saying "muffin" at all but "MUFON". What the hell was going on? He tried to remember exactly what she'd tried to say; there had been something about Warminster...

Edward stuck his head back around the door. Buzz looked startled.

'Ask Kip to look at Warminster too, in connection with Stephens.'

'Warminster? That's famous UFO country. Don't you remember the stories?'

Edward shook his head. He'd never taken any interest in that mumbo jumbo until now and was seriously puzzled as to why Judith Mulholland would. It must be something to do with Stephens.

After dinner the four men relaxed in Marcus's living room. Although the weather was warming up at last, the house was cold, and he'd lit a log fire in the huge hearth. Buzz refused alcohol but the others drank wine from the cellar that Marcus had built up over the years. Gareth appeared to have found something else in common with the man he professed to dislike.

Edward nursed his drink and thought about what to do next. He felt like he was treading water and knew Abby felt the same. Her messages were sad and full of a longing for them to return to their life before all this. He sipped his wine and caught Buzz looking at him. The youngster had cleverly sidestepped any attempts to find out how he was getting on. His answers were truthful enough to satisfy the other two but for how long? As Edward was musing, he saw Buzz look at his phone, frowning.

'Everything okay? You look worried.'

Buzz said, 'I've had a weird message from Kip's sister. He's been taken ill and he's in hospital. Food poisoning or something...'

Gareth and Marcus stopped their conversation and turned around to listen. Edward put his drink down.

'Do you want to go back? How bad is he?'

'I dunno. I'm going to ring her. Excuse me, I'll let you know in a minute.'

He left the room with the phone to his ear and Edward heard the concern in his voice as he connected to Kip's sister. The other two shrugged their shoulders and carried on with their chat but Edward was less relaxed. Why would Kip have food poisoning? He was very particular about what he ate. He stood up, stretched and walked to the door.

'I'll just see if Buzz is okay.'

Marcus refilled Gareth's glass and emptied the rest of the bottle into his own.

'There's another bottle of this in the kitchen while you're on your feet.'

'Okay, no problem. I'll be back in a minute.'

Edward took the empty bottle and headed for the kitchen; he heard Buzz talking and found him standing by the back door, looking into the yard. He put his hand up in acknowledgement as Edward came into the room.

'... Okay, Sam. I'll be there, and don't worry. He's in good hands. I'll let you know which train I'm on and you can pick me up.' There was a pause while he listened to whatever she was saying, then he said, 'Yeah, sure. I'll be there, okay? Got to go. Don't worry. See you tomorrow. Bye, bye.'

Buzz put his phone away and sighed, running his hands through his thick mop of hair.

'How is he?' Edward asked.

'Shit, man. It sounds bad. They don't seem to know what's wrong with him. It's not like anything they've seen before, and the drugs aren't helping. He's in a bad way. They've put him in an induced coma...'

'Christ, Buzz! I'm so sorry.'

Buzz stared at Edward. His gaze was direct and unflinching. Edward knew what was coming.

'Do you think it's something he found? He's been poisoned by someone...'

'Buzz, we can't speculate *but* I want you to be very careful. Don't tell anyone your plans. Be careful what you eat and drink and don't carry anything incriminating on you.'

212

'For fuck's sake! This is too heavy, man...' Buzz raised his voice and Edward put his hands on his shoulders to calm him, 'Kip is in hospital and he could die because I didn't take better care of him.'

'He's not your responsibility. He's an adult and he was doing what he enjoyed but he may have poked his nose into the wrong area and got caught out. He didn't say anything to you that might help us?'

'Help us?'

'I mean something that might help us find who did this to him, assuming it is manmade and not a viral infection?'

Buzz sighed. He looked worn down.

'No, nothing. He'd been chasing UFOs and had been poking around in the MoD and Pentagon files, but Kip would have covered his tracks I'm sure. And that's not enough to get him killed. Surely they'd have banged on his door and arrested him?'

Edward agreed with Buzz. It didn't fit unless the Russians were involved, and why would they be? What the hell would attract their attention and why attack Kip? He picked up the bottle of wine for Marcus.

'I'll take you to the station tomorrow and I want you to keep in touch with me. Any sign of trouble and you're to get out of there, okay? Anything at all that doesn't fit or makes you uncomfortable and you contact me straight away.'

'Fuck's sake. Yeah, okay.'

Edward put his arm around Buzz and said, 'I'll sort this. And I'm really sorry about Kip, even if it turns out to be just an infection.'

He knew it wouldn't be and he also knew that Buzz knew that too. *He has a right to be angry*, he thought; *I've got them into this and now one of them might die because of it.*

Chapter 28

Buzz left early next morning. Edward took him to Bristol Parkway, dropping him at the entrance. He didn't care about being seen anymore. It was almost as if he relished the chance of a fight whilst knowing there wouldn't be one; they would come after him quietly, stealthily.

Back at the house he messaged Abby, partly to see how she was and partly to make sure she was safe. Both women were fine and enjoying coastal walks, although he knew she missed him badly. He didn't tell her about Kip.

Gareth found him in the orchard, smoking yet another cigarette. He asked if he could join him.

'It's bad news about that lad. What do you think?'

Edward was surprised that Gareth was concerned and asking for his opinion. He inhaled deeply, which made his chest ache a little.

'To be honest, Gareth...' he paused to watch the reaction, 'I think it's been hand delivered and probably Russian. I just don't know why.'

Gareth stared at him, then glanced back at the house. 'That's the real question, isn't it? Why would those fuckers go after a single hacker? What did you ask him to look for, Edward?'

'Well, that's the thing, Gareth. I didn't. He was doing his own searching. According to Buzz he'd got obsessed with aliens and UFOs, got into government files chasing conspiracies.'

Gareth dropped the stub of his cigarette and cursed, sucking his finger. He pulled another one out of the packet and lit it straightaway.

'You're joking. Aliens?'

There it is again, thought Edward. His sixth sense was prickling. Gareth was rattled, although he hid it well. *What the fuck's going on?*

'I wish I was joking. Maybe he found something in one of those files…' He let the words hang in the air, but Gareth said nothing. He just stood there, looking at the view and pulling deeply on his cigarette. Edward decided to take the direct approach.

'Okay, Gareth. What do *you* think? Is there anything in Cradle that's connected to those files? Something that is so sensitive a man could die for it? We already have a list of dead men, after all.'

'How the fuck would I know?' Gareth shrugged his shoulders and looked Edward straight in the eye. *I'm flogging a dead horse*, he thought.

'I wonder what Sebastian knows,' Edward said, then added; 'Maybe I should contact him. We're getting nowhere and, you said yourself, he isn't the renegade type.'

'Are you mad? How do we know he won't turn up with a posse?'

It was Edward's turn to shrug. He finished his cigarette and turned to head back to the house. Gareth called him back.

'Look, I didn't meet that boy, but I feel for him and his family. No really, I do. But trusting Sebastian is a dangerous move. He was there too, you know, on the edge of Cradle.'

'So, what do we do? We can't sit here waiting for someone else to be picked off and not knowing why. You've got to trust me, Gareth, if we're going to beat them.'

'Without getting ourselves killed, you mean? I wasn't in the thick of it; I told you that—'

'But I'm more interested in what you *haven't* told me.'

Gareth stared at Edward, then he took a deep breath and seemed to shrink in the process. Edward waited while he stared at his feet as if deciding what to tell him.

'All I know is that there is a black project at the heart of Cradle with only a few people with the highest-level access codes allowed into it. One was Rayner and one was Professor Stephens. The others I didn't know. The rumour was that they had some extremely secret, high-tech equipment that was space age, I mean totally years ahead of the Russians, and it would give us such an edge for a generation or more. Maybe that's what Kip stumbled across.'

Edward watched Gareth's face as he spoke. This felt like the truth and it was seriously scary. If this was why Gareth had faked his death… Something occurred to him.

'You said a rumour was going around? The others that died, the ones on my list, were they in on the rumour?'

Gareth sighed and looked at Edward. He pulled out another cigarette then put it back again.

'Yes, they were all on the list. Do you get it now? We can't trust anyone. Not Marcus. Not Sebastian. Not even Buzz. We're on our own.'

Buzz messaged to say there was no change in Kip's condition. His sister, Sam, had visited him in the hospital, but Buzz had kept away as it was swarming with armed police. *There's deep shit going down here. The media are already talking about it being the same as Salisbury. Novichok. Kip of all people. Why him?*

Good question. See what you can find out but be careful. If it is a nerve agent, they might still be out there waiting.

Edward asked Marcus to put his TV on. He wanted to see the lunchtime news. If there were armed police at the hospital, it must be all over the media. MSN had been quiet on the subject, which seemed odd. The headline was a spat between the Prime Minister and several cabinet ministers, then a piece about the environment followed by some story about teenage gangs. Finally, an item labelled "News just in" saw a short report outside the hospital where the newsman said there had been reports of a man seriously ill suffering a possible poisoning. More to follow on this later as the police would not confirm whether a crime had been committed.

Marcus scowled at the screen. 'Fucking halfwits!' he bellowed at no one in particular. Gareth kept unusually silent but exchanged a look with Edward.

He said to Marcus, 'What do you reckon? Seems a bit dodgy to me.'

'Bloody Russians again, isn't it? Up to their old tricks.'

Edward kept his thoughts to himself but watched both men closely. Trust no one had become his mantra.

Marcus turned to face him. 'How's Buzz coping? What did Kip find that got him into this? Must be something big.'

'No idea. He went off on his own chasing after conspiracy theories. Even Buzz has no clue what he found. Do you think he's been poisoned, then?' Edward hoped that sounded suitably vague and not as if he was fishing.

'Fuck knows. It'll come out. The press is on the case. A few crumpled notes in the right hands works wonders.'

'You might be right. We'll just have to wait and hope the boy's okay.'

'Of course I'm right. The hacks will be feverishly working on it right now, scrambling to get the story first. I hope Buzz keeps out of it.'

Edward nodded. 'So do I.'

He pulled his phone out of his pocket. No new messages. He hoped Buzz was okay. He was one of the few people left that he trusted. He tapped out a brief message.

Keep away from the hospital. The news reporters are all over it like a rash. You can't afford to be connected to this. If you need any help message me.

Messages from Abby were coming in so fast he wondered how she could type so quickly. He was lying on his bed reading them by the light of the bedside lamp. It was past midnight and the house was quiet. The story had really broken out on the BBC evening news and almost instantly Abby had contacted him.

Where's Buzz now? Is he safe?

Yes he's fine. I told him to keep away. I've been trying to persuade him to come back but he wants to stay for the sister's sake.

I'm scared and so is Pat. Can't you come for a while? Please, I miss you.

219

Sweetheart, I can't leave the others and you're safer without me.

That's rubbish and you know it.

He sensed her anger and closing his eyes could see her glaring at him, her dark eyes radiating annoyance. Maybe she was right. Perhaps he should pay them a visit; distance between him and the others might help clear his head.

Let me think about it. There's a lot going on and I want to keep you out of it.

Isn't it a bit late for that? Have you heard anything from S?

No.

Good. I'm going to bed now. Please, please think about what I said. Love you xxxx

Love you too. Sleep tight xx

Edward sighed and put his phone on the bedside table. As he turned off the light he thought, *What the fuck do I do?* He felt very alone and no closer to solving the mystery.

Abby featured heavily in his troubled dreams: one moment taking charge and deciding what action they should take and the next as a frightened target for Russian spooks. He tossed and turned through several hours before waking fully at five thirty, hot and sweaty. Sleep would be impossible now he decided, so he got out of bed and threw on his sweat top and joggers. He hadn't run for several days and needed the exercise.

The house was still quiet; neither of the men were early risers. Both dogs wagged their tails at him as he entered the kitchen but stayed lazily on their beds. He patted their large black heads and opened the fridge. It wouldn't be light enough to see for another fifteen minutes so he had time for a drink.

The early morning air was cool and fresh when he left the house. A fine mist hung over the meadows and rolled down the lane in front of him as he jogged. He took the track that Marcus walked his dogs along, down towards the ridge that gave such beautiful views in daylight. Now he could only see enough to avoid tripping up. His breath enveloped him as he ran and he felt the tightness in his chest from smoking too much, a habit he must break when this was over.

As he climbed back up the slope he slowed. Plenty of time, he thought, so he came to a halt and turned to look across the fields to Marcus's land. He could see the buildings clearly. It was nearly full daylight now. A figure was moving about in the rear yard accompanied by two black dogs. Marcus must be up. He was waving his arm about and seemed to have his other hand to his ear, obviously on his mobile to someone. Who the hell would he be talking to at this time of the morning? Then he walked around the corner of the barn and was gone from sight. Edward jogged on up the lane, wondering who his friend had been in contact with.

There was the inviting smell of coffee wafting through the open door as Edward reached the house. Marcus was feeding the dogs and looked up as Edward came in.

'You're up early. Couldn't sleep, eh?'

'Morning. Yeah, I went for a run to try to clear the cobwebs. Any news?'

'Bit early yet. They're still repeating what they said last night. Anything from Buzz?'

'No, nothing. I'm going to have a shower then I'll be back for coffee.'

'Okay.'

Marcus turned back to his dogs and Edward headed for the shower room. Was he imagining it or did Marcus seem edgy? By the time he'd showered he convinced himself he'd imagined it; they were all strung out by the events in London.

When he came back down, Gareth was sitting at the kitchen table, looking tired and grumpy. He raised a hand in greeting but seemed absorbed in his coffee mug. Edward thought he'd been right to think this had affected them badly.

He poured himself a coffee and watched Marcus frying bacon. The dogs lay at his feet, brown eyes fixed on the frying pan.

'Did you guys sleep okay?'

Gareth looked up from his drink. 'No, not really. I couldn't switch off. I guess you couldn't either as you were up and out so early?'

'Yeah, I was wide awake at five thirty, so I went for a run. It didn't help. How about you, Marcus, did you sleep?'

'Like a baby; nothing keeps me awake.' Marcus piled the plates with food and carried two over to the table. *He certainly looks like a man without a care in the world*, Edward thought.

They ate their breakfast and sat chatting over coffee, then Marcus looked at his watch. He said, 'I'm going into town to get supplies in a while. Anything you guys want?'

Gareth shook his head and Edward said he couldn't think of anything. Then he said, 'Are you okay for money? Can I pay for the food?'

'I told you already, Edward, I'm fine, and you can pay me back sometime when all this is over.'

'I will,' said Edward. 'Can you get me some razors? I'm going to get rid of this.' He stroked his beard.

Gareth laughed. His beard was twice the length and breadth of Edward's.

'You won't catch me getting rid of mine. I'm too lazy to shave every day and it hides my ugly mug nicely.'

Marcus grunted but said nothing. He just winked at Edward as he grabbed his shopping bags from the cupboard.

As soon as he was gone Gareth stood up and turned to Edward. He jabbed his finger in the direction of the kitchen door.

'There's something going on with him. I'm not happy about being here, Edward. I can't explain why but it feels all wrong.'

There was a nervousness in his voice that Edward hadn't heard before, and he was being unusually polite. Should he tell him he'd seen Marcus on the phone at six thirty in the morning? He decided he had to trust him, at least for the time being.

'He was on his phone when I came back up the track. I could see him. Did he mention speaking to anyone?'

'Fuck! No, he didn't. Who would he be talking to so early?'

Edward felt the familiar prickle at the back of his neck. An idea occurred to him and he opened the food cupboards and then the fridge. There were plenty of provisions, even basics like bread and milk. Gareth watched him and they locked eyes.

'I think we'd better get out of here quick. There's something going down and Marcus doesn't want to be part of it.'

Gareth nodded and almost ran out of the room. When Edward returned with his bag hastily packed, he was waiting for him.

'What are we going to do for transport? Marcus has taken his car...'

'If I can find the keys, we'll take my mate's Land Rover. I left it here and it should be in the barn. Can you go and check while I hunt for the keys?'

Gareth flung himself out of the door and Edward started searching through drawers. The dogs stared at him with ears pricked, no doubt expecting to be taken out. He felt his pulse rising as he found nothing, then Gareth burst back in.

'I found them. He left them in the car, and it's got half a tank so let's Foxtrot Oscar!'

Edward grabbed his bag from the floor and slammed the door behind him. Gareth was already in the driver's seat with the engine running but Edward didn't protest. He just jumped in and said, 'Get us out of here.'

As they bounced up the track to the lane, he did a mental check of the contents of his holdall. He had his laptop and Buzz's memory stick, they were the two most important things; clothes didn't matter. The gun was in his jacket pocket and the rest of the stuff that Sebastian gave him was all in the bottom of his bag.

They reached the lane and Gareth turned right, away from the village. He put his foot down and raced through the lanes. There was nobody in sight and Edward relaxed a little.

'Where are we going? I'm heading towards the M5 at the moment.'

'We have two choices; we can either take this back to my mate's house and steal his other car or we can keep going and head south to join the girls. Either option is risky. What do you think?'

'I vote for heading south. Is there a map in this thing or can you plot a route on your phone? If we avoid the motorway as much as possible...' Gareth stopped at a junction and looked at Edward. 'Okay? Shall we go for it?'

Edward said, 'Yes, head for the M5 and we'll get off at Burnham-on-Sea and head south along the A38. We've just got to hope we can get onto the B roads before anyone spots us.'

'How long on the motorway?'

'About half an hour.'

Edward thought, *This is it. I've just got to trust Gareth now.* He was saddened by Marcus's actions and Gareth must have sensed it.

'Look, Edward, I know we haven't seen eye to eye but I'm sorry about Marcus. I really wanted to be wrong about him. He seemed such a decent bloke, but something was off. I kept ignoring it but...'

'Yeah, me too. Marcus and I go back a long way and I would have trusted him with my life. We can't both be wrong.'

They reached the motorway and Gareth drove pedal to the floor until they left it. Edward watched out for police or any vehicle that seemed to be shadowing them. It was only when they'd cleared Minehead and were crossing Exmoor that Edward felt safer.

He sent a message to Buzz saying they were on the move again and he'd be in touch later, and then one to Abby.

Looks like you've got your wish. G and I are on our way to join you both. Should be with you in about an hour and a half. I'll tell you everything when we get there.

Chapter 29

'How can you be so sure Marcus is working for the other side, whoever they are?' Abby was frowning again. Both Edward and Gareth had tried explaining but it sounded lame that their hunch that Marcus had gone rogue was based on slim evidence.

In exasperation Edward said, 'You just need to trust us, Abby. We can't tell you everything. It will put you in danger.'

Abby rolled her eyes and Edward was sure she actually growled. Pat stood quietly watching them argue.

'But Edward, just being with you puts us in danger. If it's that bad, we need to know! Perhaps we can help in some way—'

Gareth butted in, 'She's right, you know. We've done our best to protect them, but they need to know what's going on. Four heads are better than two; if we can't trust Pat and Abby who can we trust?'

'It's not a matter of trust. It's about survival.' Edward knew as soon as he'd said it that Abby would have an answer to that.

'Listen to yourself! Why did you come here, then? If survival is the prime consideration, then why bring the threat here?'

He was beaten and he knew it; he also had to admit he wanted Abby's sharp intellect to help them solve the mystery. But she didn't yet know about her husband's involvement and, if he was going to be completely truthful, he'd need to tell her.

'Gareth, can you give us some time alone? I'll bring Abby up to speed then we can all decide what to do next.' Edward hoped Gareth understood what he was saying, and he seemed to get the message.

'Yes, of course. I'll go for a walk with Pat and we'll see you here in half an hour or so.'

'Thanks.'

Pat smiled at Abby before they left the room, arm in arm. As soon as they'd gone, she rounded on Edward.

'What the hell's going on, Edward? What's happened to Kip, and is Buzz safe?'

He put his hands up and said he would tell her everything if she promised to listen. They could talk about it all afterwards. She nodded but still looked rebellious.

Edward carefully went through everything he and Buzz had discovered, skirting around Rob Rayner's involvement until he'd explained they thought there was a Russian connection.

Abby said quietly, 'What makes you think that? And there is something else you're holding back, I can tell, Edward.'

He sighed and said, 'Yes, I'm afraid there is. I have to ask you about Rob. What exactly did he do?'

She looked apprehensive. 'He was a project manager in defence procurement, worked on ships mainly. Why?'

'That's not entirely true, Abby. And what about his finances? Did you have a joint account, or did he have accounts of his own?'

She said quietly, 'Why are you asking me this, Edward? How was he involved? Don't sugar-coat it; I can tell you don't want me to know something…'

He took her hand and said, 'Yes, he was involved. How deeply we're not sure yet but he worked on some top-secret black projects with both American and British Intelligence. He also had a bank account he kept secret from you; one that handled large sums of money that ended up overseas. It's just possible he was taking bribes or being paid by foreign interests—'

'Such as the Russians? Are you trying to say Rob was a spy?'

'Not necessarily but it is a possibility. He may have just been laundering money, but selling secrets, unfortunately, seems the more likely scenario. I'm so sorry, Abby.'

Abby sat quietly, staring at her feet, then she sighed and stood up, taking Edward's hand. Her dark eyes were unusually bright, and he guessed she was on the brink of tears.

'Let's go for a walk to the beach. I need some fresh air.'

He said, 'Yes, okay.' He couldn't read her mind and knew he'd just have to wait for her to articulate her thoughts.

Their cottage was a short stroll to the small rocky cove. It was unspoiled and must be lovely in summer, Edward thought as they stood leaning against the wall watching the foam-covered waves roll in. Abby said very little and he thought it best to let her process what he'd told her.

The wind whipped her hair about her face and took her words away with the salty spray. He leaned closer to hear her.

'I knew something was wrong. I kidded myself afterwards that I hadn't; it made me feel less guilty...' she paused, 'less responsible. I knew and I couldn't stop him. I thought he was just depressed but now I can see it was more than that. I let him down, Edward.'

He put his arms around her and held her close to him. 'He let *you* down, Abby. He wasn't the man you thought he was.'

She lifted her face and looked him in the eye. Her words were soft, and he struggled to hear.

'Did he kill himself or was he murdered because he wouldn't play ball?'

Edward hesitated. It was a question he'd asked himself.

'To be honest, I really don't know. Why was he there? Did he meet someone, or did he intend to end it, or was it a genuine accident? I can't answer that but maybe we'll get to the truth.'

'When I first met you, I thought you seemed to know a lot about me, but I just assumed you'd heard the news just like everyone else, but I guess you knew more than I did.'

'No, not really. I took an interest in the case because I knew he'd been in the same line of business as me but that's all. I thought, like everyone else, that it was either an accident or suicide. I liked you and I felt sorry for you.'

'And now?'

'And now I love you and want to protect you. Abby, if I could turn the clock back, I'd tear up that bloody photo and ignore it all.'

'But we can't, Edward, and our only hope is to get to the bottom of it.'

'Let's go back and get out of this wind. I expect Gareth and Pat will want to know what we've talked about.'

'Gareth doesn't know all of this?' Abby looked surprised. 'What's been going on, Edward?'

'I didn't know who I could trust, so I kept most of what I've told you to myself...' he hesitated; 'I thought I couldn't trust Gareth. Someone was working against me and I thought it might be him. He seemed cagey about his connections but now I'm not so sure.'

Abby shook her head. They headed back along the path together, through the fields and past the local pub back into the village. She said nothing until they reached the cottage again, then she turned to Edward.

'Pat and I need to know everything now. Gareth was right, we must work together and trust each other. I don't see we have any choice. Let him see what Buzz found and what Kip has been up to. Perhaps...' she paused, chewing her lip, 'perhaps Sebastian wasn't compromised after all. Have you thought about that, Edward?'

Gareth leaned back in the chair and took in a deep breath. He said, 'I need a cigarette.'

Edward had let him read the files that Buzz had put on the memory stick and told him what Kip had been up to just before he was poisoned. He followed him out into the small garden, and they smoked together.

'I can see now why you've been so guarded. Fuck it, Edward! Russians and crazy scientists – it's like a bloody Bond movie.'

'I wish it was. Kip is still in a coma and I haven't heard from Buzz since we left Marcus's. What do you think of that? Did we overreact?'

'After what you just showed me? No, we didn't. Our instincts are good; we were trained to have good hunches. I'm just not sure how deep he's in or whether he's playing both sides, but either way we did the right thing. We've bought ourselves breathing space.'

'What do you make of this MUFON connection? Have you ever heard it mentioned before?'

'No, I haven't,' he ground the smoking stub into the grass, 'but I do remember people talking about space age technology. Nothing more than that; nobody seemed to know.'

'Abby questioned whether I was right about Sebastian. What's your take on it?'

'Sebastian? He always struck me as being slightly stuffy, a straight as a die kind of chap. Not somebody who would be turned, if you want my opinion. Marcus, however, rang bells for me as soon as I met him. I couldn't put my finger on it, but he seemed too helpful, too unquestioning. I'm sorry, I know you guys had history.'

'Yeah, we have, but after Sebastian I felt I was getting paranoid. I'm beginning to think I got it wrong.'

Gareth grunted. 'Whatever we do next had better be well planned and well executed. I don't know about you but I'm sick of running and hiding.'

Pat shook her head as they talked through what they'd found so far. Edward felt sorry for her; he knew she must be feeling completely out of her depth. Abby, by contrast, was listening closely and asking direct questions. He'd been right about her sharp mind.

'So, you're absolutely sure Sebastian is a threat? Based on what evidence, Edward?'

Edward thought carefully before he answered her. It was difficult to explain the intricacies of the intelligence world where hunches could save your life or someone else's.

'There were the secret phone calls at the Dartmoor cottage, the references to him as "the actor"—'

Abby butted in, 'And very little else except your hunch. What if you're wrong? He helped find me, removed the tracker that would have located us, watched your back…'

'Abby, we can't afford to take risks. Even if Sebastian isn't working for someone else, he could still have been compromised. The fewer people know where we are the better.'

'Okay, what about Marcus, then? He knows what car you're driving and that you're in the West Country. Let's assume Sebastian and Marcus are working together, pooling intelligence. What do they know?'

'Very little. I kept Sebastian out of it and by the time we reached Marcus I'd become, as Gareth put it, bloody paranoid.'

Gareth laughed and said, 'Very true, he kept us all in the dark. The key to this is Buzz. Seriously, we need to get that kid back with us for our safety and his own…' he added, 'if they haven't got to him already. Have you heard anything, Edward?'

'No, and it's bothering me.' Edward got his phone and checked for messages. There was nothing new. 'Give me a minute.' He tapped out a message.

Contact me urgently. We're worried about you.

Abby was talking again. Edward half listened with an eye on his phone waiting for the screen to light up.

'So, basically, we don't know whether Sebastian is "compromised", to quote Edward. We don't know for sure who Marcus is working with. It looks like my husband was selling secrets, and Judith... Where does she fit in? Oh, and Kip has been poisoned with a nerve agent, probably Russian!'

Gareth said, 'Yeah, it sounds fucking bad, doesn't it?'

'I think that's putting it mildly. So, what do we do next? We can't hide here forever.'

B, are you ok?

'Does your cousin have anywhere else, even if we pay for it? Somewhere a bit more remote, maybe?'

Edward thought, *That might be a good idea but it's not our first priority.* Pat remained silent, and he was concerned about her. Gareth didn't seem to have noticed her lack of involvement.

'Pat, what do you think? Are you okay?'

She looked across the room at him; he could see an alarmed look in her eyes he'd seen before in people unaccustomed to risk. Gareth turned to her and put a hand on her arm.

'All this is...' she searched for the right words, 'overwhelming and scary. I knew Gareth was involved in things I'd rather not know about, but I had no idea... I'm not sure I should be here, Gareth. I can't add anything or help you all.'

She took Gareth's hand and squeezed it. He leaned over and kissed her on the head. Edward felt sympathy for both of them and was glad Abby was more resilient.

'Pat, would you feel safer at home on your own or with us, that's the question. If you'd rather not be involved, we can keep the rest between ourselves,' Abby spoke up.

Gareth said, 'I understand, love, but I'd be worried to death at the thought of you being alone. Yes, they might discount you but then they might not.'

Edward had lost track of the conversation. Messages had appeared on his phone screen.

Kip is still in coma. His sister with him. I kept away. She was given his possessions and I've got his jacket.

Where are you?

I'm safe. Staying with a friend but need to get out soonest. Can I come to you?

Yes, and as quick as you can. They will be looking. How will you do it?

Can't travel by train or coach now. Can get a lift somewhere west if you could collect me?

How far west?

Mate with van doing deliveries so service stations good. Devon or Cornwall.

Okay. Give me five.

'Guys, Buzz is making a move. He can get west with a lift. Where can we meet him? Suggestions?'

Abby said, 'Thank God he's okay.'

Gareth muttered, 'Whatever you think. Pat and I need some time to talk things through so don't involve me.'

'You can use my car, Edward,' Pat said quietly.

'Thank you, Pat. That's very kind. I've an idea where we can collect him.'

When are you travelling?

Tomorrow early.

Ok, tell your mate to drop you at Hog & Hedge. If he comes west he'll know it.

Ok, I'll be in touch

'Abby, do you want to come with me? Another pair of eyes?'

'You try stopping me.'

Chapter 30

According to the satnav it takes one hour twenty-five to reach Whiddon Down from the north Devon coast, but leaving at six in the morning Edward got Pat's Honda there in one hour ten. Abby looked a little pale as they pulled into the near empty car park. Edward grinned at her as he parked under the trees at the far end.

'Sorry, did I scare you?'

'I didn't know this thing could go that fast.'

'Especially with an old git driving?'

'Don't start that again.' She laughed, digging him in the ribs.

'That's better, I haven't heard you laugh for a long time.' He leaned over and kissed her.

'That beard has to go.' She rubbed her face.

'Funnily enough, I was about to shave it off when we did our runner. Have you got a razor I could use?'

'I'm sure we can find one. I hope Pat stays with us,' she said, changing the subject; 'I'd be worried about her on her own.'

'Me too, and I'm sure Gareth will persuade her to stay. What about you? Are you okay?'

'I've got to the point where nothing can hurt. No, that's not actually true, but I'm not scared for myself.'

Edward looked at her. She was smiling at him, but he noticed the dark shadows under her eyes. He felt the all too familiar wave of self-loathing for getting her into this but pushed it back; negative thinking would get him nowhere.

The weather had changed again, a fine drizzle was coating the windscreen and the air was cool. They sat in silence watching the entrance of the car park, waiting for a white van to appear. Edward checked his phone again. He tapped out a message.

We're here.

The reply came back quickly. *See you in five.*

'He's nearly here. Are you ready?'

'Yes. Just don't drive so fast.'

'Depends on whether he's got a tail or not.'

Abby grimaced but didn't comment. The rain had set in now and Edward turned on the engine, wiping the screen to have a better view. He checked his watch.

'I'm moving up the car park so we're ready to go.'

'Okay.'

He sensed the tension in the car increase as he edged it towards the main building. Abby clicked her seat belt in and leaned forward watching for the van.

Then it appeared, driving slowly around the corner to pull up in front of the entrance. They both watched Buzz jump out, reach in for his bag and wave goodbye. Edward saw another car pull in a few hundred feet behind them. As the van pulled away the car moved forward. Edward put his foot down and pulled up in front of Buzz, who looked startled. He reached behind him and flung open the rear door.

'Quick, jump in!'

Without waiting for Buzz to fully close the door Edward raced away. Abby looked behind at the other car as he sped towards the exit. Buzz threw his bag on the seat beside him and struggled to do up the seat belt buckle as the car lurched forward.

The black car was following. Edward could see it in the rear-view mirror. He'd anticipated this.

'Hold on, guys. I've got to lose them.'

With Abby clinging to the seat beside him he put his foot to the floor and shot out of the service area, turning left onto the A road and then left again, just missing an oncoming car. He glanced in the mirror. Their tail had lost momentum, having had to brake to avoid the other vehicle. Edward knew every metre mattered if he was going to lose them.

The traffic was still light, and he crossed the motorway bridge at eighty. There was a turnoff into local lanes coming up and he prayed there was nothing to slow him down. The only other vehicle had already passed the junction when he slew the car across the carriageway and shot down the lane.

They were still behind but had lost more distance. Edward had scoured the online map the night before and fixed the terrain in his mind. He knew where he was heading but needed something to distract his tail. There was no traffic at all on this lane and visibility was good enough for them to be seen for several hundred metres. He'd only get one chance.

Another junction loomed and Edward took it, sliding the car almost off the road. He swore as he corrected it and drove on, hoping they hadn't gained on him. There were two sharp bends coming up shaded by thick trees, farm buildings on the right and then a sequence of twists leading on to several crossroads.

'You okay, you two?'

'Yeah,' they said in unison as the car lurched around the first bend.

Edward pushed it around the second bend and saw the farm entrance a few feet on. He glanced in the mirror; there was no sign of the other car as he hauled the Honda sharply into the farmyard and spun behind the barn.

He heard Buzz say, 'Whoa!' from the back seat.

'Hold on, we're not out of the woods yet.'

Praying that their tail had carried on chasing down the lane, he pulled the car out of the yard and turned back the way they'd come. Now he needed to get some distance between them before they realised they'd lost him and turned back. He put his foot down and raced back to the main road.

'I'll keep watch,' Buzz said; 'you concentrate on the driving.'

Edward grinned and increased speed. He saw Abby's knuckles turning white as she clung to the seat. 'Sorry,' he whispered.

They reached the A road again and he turned right, driving as fast as he dared without attracting attention. There was no sign of the black car, but he knew that meant nothing. If they had enough resources, they might put up a helicopter or a drone. He hoped they didn't.

'Abby, can you look at the map and see if there's an alternative route back? We could do with tree cover if possible.'

Abby found a road map in the glovebox, but she said there wasn't enough detail. Edward decided to carry on as planned. In a few minutes they'd be in Winkleigh; he could change direction there if he needed to.

'Buzz, let me know if you see any drones or a helicopter. I don't think they've got access to that level of surveillance but better safe than sorry. And I'm not sure if they got close enough to see the car reg either.'

'I doubt it, the speed you took off at.'

'Yeah, I know. I've already had a telling off from Abby.'

'Edward, this time it was warranted and I'm glad you can drive like that.'

The rest of the journey proved uneventful but all three kept their eyes open for any suspicious air activity. Edward felt relief when they turned onto the lanes leading to the village. The rain was getting heavy now, running down the edges of the road and taking soil and stones with it. Between the tall hedges they were protected, but as they got closer to the village the landscape opened up and Edward could feel the wind buffeting the car. By the time he pulled up on the drive the rain was lashing down.

'Quick, get inside, you two. I'll lock the car.'

Abby and Buzz ran into the cottage and Edward followed, after checking the lane for cars even though he knew they hadn't been followed.

'You did what? Bloody hell, I wish I'd been there.' Gareth was laughing as Buzz told the story of what he called his Great Escape. Edward grinned. He had to admit to himself, he'd needed some action; all the hiding and waiting had driven him nearly mad with frustration.

'You would have done the same, I'm sure. We're going to have to be extra careful now though. They'll be bloody livid they lost us.'

Abby brought in a tray with mugs and a packet of biscuits. Pat followed her looking gloomy. Edward thought, *She's realised she can't go back now; she's stuck with us.*

Gareth stood up and offered her his chair, then sat on the arm next to her. Edward decided he must say something.

'Pat, I'm really sorry but I don't think you should leave us. They probably didn't get your car registration, but I can't be absolutely sure…'

'Edward, it's okay. I already agreed with Gareth that I would stay. I just had a bit of a wobble earlier. I can't leave him.'

Abby smiled at her. 'I'm glad you decided that. They couldn't manage without us.'

Edward thought it was a nice attempt to lift her spirits, but her face betrayed her real feelings and he worried for both of them. Buzz, as usual, was more interested in the biscuits.

'So, what next? We've rescued Buzz from the jaws of the beast, and we need a plan now. I can't sit waiting for the fuckers to come knocking. Any ideas?' Gareth took the biscuit packet before Buzz finished the lot.

'Let's hear what Buzz has to say. He's been closer to the action. How's Kip? Any signs of improvement?'

Buzz looked up, swallowed a mouthful of tea and said, 'No change. They've still got him sedated. Sam was told it may be some time before they can assess him. Luckily he was found quite quickly, so they started the treatment soon after.'

'Who found him?' Abby asked.

'Sam did. It was horrible. She went to his rooms to surprise him and there he was, flat on the floor staring at the ceiling. She thought he'd had a fit or something. He doesn't do drugs or booze, so she realised straightaway that he was ill. She called for an ambulance and they came within minutes. Then she called me. I knew he'd been got at when I saw the police at the hospital. And I knew that Kip kept his research close to him. He told me he had this old padded jacket with holes in the pockets. He kept his memory sticks in the lining, just in case. I always thought he was paranoid until now. Sam went back to his rooms to get some clothes for him and she said it looked like he'd been burgled, stuff all over the floor. Then the police closed it off, once they realised it was a nerve agent. Sam had to stay in hospital for two days while they checked her out. She managed to get the jacket to me before it all kicked off. I told her it was mine.'

'Christ, Buzz! You could have been poisoned too,' Gareth almost shouted at him.

'No, I wore gloves, which I threw away in a hospital bin. I chucked the coat too after I got these out.' He held up two memory sticks. 'I'm hoping what's on here might help us find the bastards.'

'Well done, Buzz. Bloody good work,' Edward said.

Abby stood up and gathered up the mugs. She said, 'I think lunch first then we can see what Kip has been looking at. No, Edward, we *all* get to see this. We're all in this together now, you can't pretend otherwise.'

Gareth said, 'I agree; one of us might spot something the others don't. I've been going solo for too long; I'm happy to be part of the team.'

Edward noticed Pat didn't seem as keen. He said, 'And what about you, Pat? How do you feel about all this?'

She looked surprised to be asked, and with a brief glance at Gareth she said, 'If you all don't mind, I'd rather just be in a support role, making drinks, doing the shopping; I feel out of my depth and I'd rather know as little as possible...'

Gareth turned to her and tried to persuade her to "be part of the team". Abby intervened.

'It's up to Pat, Gareth. This is a strange world we've been thrown into. You and Edward have had training and years of experience, but we haven't. As Pat once said, we're amateurs. She's here with you. Isn't that enough?'

Chapter 31

Abby had sheets of paper torn from her notebook all over the dining room table. The brainstorming session had raised more questions than answers. They had a list of facts and a list of assumptions and a sheet for each antagonist. Edward had noticed her hand shake slightly as she wrote Rob Rayner at the top of one sheet.

Gareth was frowning again. He picked up the paper with *Facts* at the top and read through Abby's points.

'So, we've agreed – 1. Rayner was taking money from persons unknown; 2. He was working with a nutty professor who believes in flying saucers… What? It's true!' He paused to allow the reaction to die down, '… 3. Abby was abducted by persons unknown who tried to find out more about what he'd been doing; 4. Judith Mulholland knew something if not all about what was going on; 5. Edward was dragged into it by Judith; 6. Someone tried to grab Buzz; 7. Edward was put under surveillance; 8. The woman at the care home was killed and Edward framed for her murder; 9. Kip was poisoned. And we should put another point on here – we're all on the run!'

He threw the paper on the table. Edward could see his frustration.

'You know as well as I do that facts are not always the whole truth. Let's look at the assumptions and see if we can discount any.' He picked up the sheet. It was covered in writing.

Sebastian – who's he working for??? Marcus – ditto. Rob – was he selling secrets? Where did the money come from? Judith's involvement? Russian involvement and did they poison Kip & why? What exactly is Cradle? Professor Stephens??

Abby was speaking. Edward looked up from the list.

'… So, we need to focus on one thing at a time or two people working on different threads? I think Kip should be the priority; he obviously found something that raised concern. That might be the key…'

Buzz nodded. He had Kip's memory sticks in his hand.

Edward asked, 'Have you looked at them yet, Buzz?'

'No, I was in too much of a hurry to get away. I wanted to be somewhere safe before I did, and with you guys.'

'Okay, let's take a look and see what's on there.'

Buzz went to get his laptop while Abby cleared the table. Edward noticed Pat had gone to the kitchen; *She really doesn't want to be part of this*, he thought.

The first flash drive Buzz loaded revealed lists of files all in date order, and he quickly decrypted a few to see what they were. Edward watched as he worked. After ten articles about UFOs and suspected alien landings, he was getting bored. Buzz opened yet another one.

'For fuck's sake, Kip! How much of this stuff have you saved?'

Abby leaned over his shoulder. She stopped him closing it.

'Hang on, Buzz. This one's about Warminster. Didn't you say that Judith was muttering something about Warminster, Edward?' Abby turned back to the screen and began reading from the report, 'On August 17th, 1965, a "detonation noise" rocked houses on the town's Boreham Field housing estate before a "monstrous orange flame was seen in the sky, crackling and hissing".

'The phenomena then became known as the "Warminster Thing" after scores of townspeople reported in late 1965 seeing an array of inexplicable sights in the sky, accompanied by noises and odd occurrences that led to a meeting being held in the town hall.

'It was hoped the meeting would lead to answers from authorities about what was happening in the local area, but no explanation was forthcoming, and the case remained unresolved even at a 50th anniversary conference last August.'

She laughed and read on. 'Listen to this bit... The report added that the reasons for the formation, movement, separation and general activity of buoyant charged masses was not completely understood, but an "increase in atmospheric dust and emissions can contribute to the formation of dusty plasmas and may have been responsible for an increase in sightings". So, the MoD was trying to cover it up. What do you make of that?'

Edward rubbed his chin. What the hell was that all about and why was Kip so obsessed with it?

Gareth grunted and said, 'It's all shit. I seem to remember some local bloke selling his story and a photo to the newspapers and it came out later he was in it for the money.'

Edward said quietly, 'If you want to hide some activity the best way to do it is in plain sight, encourage the conspiracy nuts to come out with their stories so that in the ensuing news frenzy the original event gets labelled as a fraud. One speculator doesn't necessarily mean it never happened.'

'Fuck's sake! You don't actually believe this stuff, do you? We've been visited by aliens and the authorities have covered it up?'

'A very wise man once said if you discount the possible then the impossible must be true, or words to that effect.'

'Bloody Sherlock Holmes!' Gareth burst out laughing but Edward noticed Buzz didn't find it so funny. He'd opened another file and was reading.

'The thing is, Gareth, the military has been in that area for years and you can't access any of the land north west of the town for miles. It would easy to hide something or test a new weapon. And there's something else you've forgotten – Kip was poisoned because of something he found, and it might be buried in these files.'

'Fair point, Buzz, but it does all seem a bit far-fetched...' Gareth paused, then added, 'but I have to admit, that's the best way to hide something – by discrediting the original report. Is there anything else about Warminster that might give us a clue?'

Edward watched the exchange between them and thought that Gareth seemed tense. He remembered an earlier conversation about rumours within the projects and wondered if this was one of them.

Buzz looked up from whatever he was reading and said, 'Warminster? No, not especially.' Then he closed the file and took out the flash drive. 'Let's try this one and see what's on it.' He dropped the drive and Edward saw his hand tremble as he picked it up. Something was wrong and Buzz didn't want Gareth to know.

Abby had seen it too; Edward saw her face as she moved to stand next to Buzz. Edward wondered what had upset him.

'Shall we have a break? Abby, can you ask Pat to put the kettle on? Fancy a smoke break, Gareth?'

'Good idea. I could do with some unfresh air,' he joked and reached into his jacket pocket. 'It's a filthy habit and I must give it up before it kills me.' He was laughing, and Edward thought, *He's trying too hard.*

'Just pray it's the cigarettes that kill you and not the Russians.'

'Ha ha, very funny.' But he'd stopped laughing.

Edward followed Gareth outside and they stood in the shelter of the walkway that ran behind the building. The rain had eased a little but drops of water dripped through the polycarbonate roof and splashed onto their heads.

'What do you make of all that fucking nonsense, then?'

'Kip gets weird ideas and sometimes goes off down rabbit holes. Hopefully there'll be something more useful on the other drive.' Edward drew hard on his cigarette and watched Gareth do the same.

'We're not any closer to saving our skins though, are we? I think we should get Buzz to look into Judith's background. See what that throws up.'

Gareth reached into his packet and pulled out another cigarette, lighting it between his cupped hands. Edward stubbed his out and said he was going back inside.

'Okay, see you in a minute.'

Abby was in the dining room with Buzz and they both looked up as he came in; he didn't waste any time.

'Right, Buzz, I think you found something on that stick, and you don't want Gareth involved. We don't have much time; he'll be back in a sec so keep it close and you can tell me later, okay?'

Buzz nodded and slipped the drive into the pocket of his sweat top. Abby smiled, and he was sure she'd spotted it too.

'Perhaps Gareth and Pat could go shopping? They're the least recognisable of us and we need some food supplies now there's five of us here.' Abby stood up and gave Buzz a pat on his arm before disappearing into the kitchen. Edward heard her clear voice asking Pat if they had enough food to last them for a few days.

Gareth and Pat, after some discussion, agreed to go to the nearest supermarket some five miles away, although Pat insisted that Gareth stay with the car while she shopped. Gareth said if they found anything, he wanted to know about it.

'Don't worry, you will,' Edward said. 'But we're going to see what we can find on Judith and Marcus next. I think whatever Kip found is not here – all that little green men stuff…'

Gareth grimaced but held back on his view of Kip's obsession. He just said, 'Yeah, that lad had a bit of an obsession.'

As soon as Pat's car pulled off the drive Edward asked Buzz to tell him what he'd found.

'I saw your face when you opened that last file. What is it? What did Kip find?'

'I'll show you and you'll see why I didn't want him to see.' He put the stick back in the USB port and opened up the file list. 'Look at this. Judith said Warminster, didn't she? Warminster isn't just a place where things happened, it's a project.'

Edward leaned closer as Buzz opened the file. He read the title and then the list of project team players. Top of the list was G Maxwell, followed by R Rayner.

He said, 'Fuck.'

Abby, looking over his shoulder, said, 'Oh my God, Gareth and Rob. Shit, Edward, and we've brought him into this. Now what?'

'We tread very carefully. What exactly is this project?'

Buzz said, 'Have a read. It's umm… a bit scary…'

Edward read the text that Kip had extracted from a secret report.

Professor Stephens has completed his assessment and it is agreed a trial should take place as soon as possible. Gaia to be maintained and no contractors allowed on site during testing. Mr G Maxwell and Mr R Rayner to attend as representatives of Warminster ex-Cradle. Miss Mulholland to be briefed in person verbally after the event. No recording materials will be allowed on site. Mobile phones, cameras or any recording equipment will be held in secure premises. Individuals will be screened prior to admittance.

The material extracted from the crash site of 1964 has finally been replicated and has defied all expectations. It is impervious to any degradation and is resistant to change in temperatures up to and in excess of 2,000 degrees Celsius. It is therefore capable of surviving atomic reaction, volcanic activity or anything humans could submit it to. If produced in sufficient quantity, we will be able to create a military vehicle, land, air or sea, that will be able to withstand any assault in any form. Combined with the weaponry developed by the British project Cradle this will give USA and her allies a formidable advantage.

'Christ!' Edward was lost for words. Glancing at Abby he saw she had lost her colour and looked as if she wanted to be sick.

'I can't believe it, Edward. My husband was involved in something so…' She couldn't complete her sentence. He put his arm around her and murmured, 'Sorry,' into her hair.

'It's hardly your fault, but I can't believe I didn't know him at all, did I? He kept all this from me.'

'That's what we're trained to do, Abby. But it got to him in the end…'

'Or somebody did,' she said.

Buzz kept quiet and just stared at his screen. Then he said, 'Do you think that's what got Kit targeted?'

Edward frowned. The attack on Kit had all the hallmarks of the KGB or its successor the FSB. He thought, *Unless we've managed to produce something akin to Novichok and we're framing the Russians?*

'I suspect so, Buzz, but I'm not sure who is responsible yet. Kip definitely rattled somebody and it all smacks of Russian involvement but I'm keeping an open mind. Do me a favour and see what you can find on Marcus McKellen. What's he been doing for the last twenty years, and look at his finances too? That flash drive is dangerous, so I'll take care of it if you don't mind?'

'Jeez, it's all yours, man. Glad to hand it over. You'd better have the other one too.'

Edward felt an almost overwhelming responsibility for Abby and Buzz. He knew he had to keep focused and couldn't let his emotions get in the way. Professionalism and training would keep them safe, not sentimentality. But he couldn't help apologising.

'Don't be silly,' they said together, and Abby added, 'If you apologise one more time, I'll ring Sebastian myself.'

'That's a point, Buzz. Was there any reference to Sebastian in any of those files?'

'I haven't come across him; shall I look again?'

'Yes, please. Concentrate on Sebastian and Marcus and see if there's any cross reference between the two. This is going to be difficult with Gareth here, but we need to be seen to be working, so just avoid anything to do with Warminster whilst he's in the house.'

'Sure. I'll get started on it now.'

Chapter 32

Edward looked at his reflection in the mirror. A clean-shaven face stared back, but it looked older than the last time he'd seen it. The fake tan had faded, along with the temporary hair dye, so he was Edward again, but more careworn and definitely less happy. He sighed, dried his face on the towel and went back through to the bedroom.

Abby sat on the bed with a book propped on her knees. She looked up when he came in and said, 'That's better. I've got my Edward back.'

'Well, a slightly worn-out version of him. What are you reading?'

'What my mum would have called a pot-boiler, and to be honest it's rubbish, which is probably why it's been left here.'

Edward laughed. 'A pot-boiler? I've never heard of that before.'

'Oh, she was full of little sayings, my mum. My favourite is "empty vessels make the most noise", which I save for those with a limited intellect and a big mouth. And anywhere that sold booze, like a large pub or nightclub was a gin palace.'

'I like the sound of your mum.'

'Yeah, I didn't really appreciate her till it was too late.' She said it without emotion, and he knew better than to offer sympathy. Abby coped by shutting her grief away.

He changed the subject as he dropped on the bed beside her. 'I'm worried about Buzz. He's got a lot on his shoulders and with Gareth lurking…'

Abby swivelled her body to face him and said, 'I don't know what to make of that. Why did he tell you he hardly knew Rob? The fact that he faked his own death means he had something big to run away from.'

'It's like trying to finish a jigsaw and finding out there's a thousand pieces of sky to work with. Each time we learn something new I feel like I'm taking one step back. There's something about Gareth that doesn't fit…'

'I know what you mean. Pat is struggling with the whole thing. Since you guys turned up, she's been really quiet.'

'I noticed that.' Edward got off the bed and pulled on a clean sweat top. He ran his fingers through his damp hair and said, 'We'd better go back down for dinner, and catch the evening news.'

Downstairs, Gareth was lounging in an armchair with a large glass of what looked like whisky. Buzz was helping Pat in the kitchen, so Abby offered to clear the dining room table.

Edward turned on the TV just in time for the BBC news headlines. There was the usual political storm in a teacup, a piece about police cuts and then a reporter standing in front of the hospital where Kip was being treated. Edward turned the volume up enough to hear what she was saying. 'The victim has now been named as Kevin Peters, aged twenty-five from Ealing. It's not yet known how he came into contact with the suspected nerve agent and a hospital spokesperson refused earlier to offer any more details. Obviously, we will keep you informed as soon as there is any development on this worrying case. Questions are being asked about the safety of the public, but the police have not yet issued a statement other than to say there is no threat to the public at large. Over to you, John, back in the studio…'

Edward turned the volume down and turned to find Abby and Buzz in the doorway. He said, 'Did you hear that? He's still hanging on; no more news.'

Abby said, 'No news is good news, right?'

'I'll ring Sam later and see if they've told her anything.' Buzz turned to go but Gareth asked, 'Why's he called Kip?'

Buzz turned back and said, 'Kevin Ian Peters – Kip – and I got called Buzz because, apparently, I sound like a bee buzzing when I snore.' He gave a little laugh.

Edward smiled and said, 'Let us know what Sam says later. Remember the two Russians; they made a good recovery.'

Dinner was a quiet affair. Nobody seemed in the mood for making small talk, but the beef casserole was declared delicious and Gareth kept the red wine flowing although Abby and Buzz declined. As the women cleared the plates Gareth suggested he and Edward go for a smoke.

'I want to have a chat; something I need to run by you,' he said.

'Yeah, sure.'

He got unsteadily to his feet and Edward wondered just how much whisky he'd had before dinner. Gareth held his drink well, only the redness in his face gave him away; his eyes were as piercing as ever.

They stood in the small garden, outside of earshot from the house. Gareth drew in a lungful of smoke then proceeded to blow little white rings into the evening air. He coughed and leaned his back against the wall dividing the cottage grounds from next door.

'Edward, I know you reasonably well by now and I am aware that you've looked into my past. If you haven't already found my secret, I'm sure you will soon so I'm going to come clean. I can't do this anymore. It's destroying Pat and she deserves better.'

'What are you trying to say?

'Just fucking listen and I'll tell you.'

There it was, thought Edward, the old Maxwell anger. He waited in silence for Gareth to continue.

'That Warminster thing...' he paused to light another cigarette, 'that was the killer. I knew when Buzz mentioned it that Kip had found more than old UFO stories as I'm sure you've worked out. I wasn't entirely truthful with you before; maybe I was too ashamed of what I'd done to come clean one hundred per cent. Rob and I worked together on an extremely sensitive black project. Professor Stephens was the American technical expert who just happened to be a member of MUFON. The Americans had developed this spectacular material, not unlike carbon fibre to look at but a thousand times stronger, incredibly flexible and resistant to anything we could throw at it. They suggested we use it as armour, and because it's so light it can be fitted on any vehicle without compromising performance. Rob was initially the project leader but then, for some reason, they put me in charge. I never found out why, but a very short time after that he was found dead on that railway line. It scared the shit out of me, I can tell you.' He paused but Edward knew better than to interrupt and waited for him to continue.

'Anyway, they called the project Warminster, after the Warminster Thing. Stephens never admitted it, but the rumour was that the material wasn't manufactured by the Americans. It was *developed,* a subtle difference, from what we found on a crash site in December 1964...' he paused again, 'in Warminster – your neck of the woods, I believe?'

Edward nodded. His home was less than ten miles from the small market town.

'Anyway, at the time I refused to listen, and I think that's what saved my skin initially, but as people started to fall ill mysteriously or die, I got twitchy. That's when I hatched my escape plan. I was under a lot of pressure to deliver a vehicle for testing, complete with the new weaponry. It would have put us light years ahead of the Russians, and the complexity of the combined projects was horrendous. I do wonder if that's what killed Rob, the strain. I'm not sure he was on the take but who knows?'

'So, what exactly are you telling me? Do you believe we've had alien technology since 1964 and have been working on it all this time? Is that the big secret that might get us all killed?'

Gareth looked Edward directly in the eye and said, 'Quite possibly. If it's true and that got into the public domain, it would be catastrophic for government both sides of the pond. Who would trust them ever again? But think about it, Edward, what about the Russians? If they've heard the rumours and believe it...'

Edward felt a chill down his spine that had nothing to do with the cool air. He pulled a cigarette from the pack and lit it, drawing the smoke deep into his lungs. It was too incredible to be real, like being in some fantastic Hollywood film.

'Gareth, if this is true, the implications are huge. No weapon system is worth risking world peace for. The civil unrest... the international condemnation, it doesn't bear thinking about. Shit!'

'I think you get it now. I tried to keep it to myself because I reasoned nobody else need die. When you turned up, I thought I could deflect you. It was obvious you didn't know much, and I hoped you'd just flail about and lose heart, then I realised you had Rayner's widow in tow. For fuck's sake, Edward!'

'And how was I supposed to know when we met each other that this was going to happen? If you want to blame someone, blame Judith. She dragged me and Abby into this.'

'Well, that was why I got so angry. My plan to get Pat and me safely away from this clusterfuck was unravelling fast.'

'I'm sorry, Gareth, I had no idea what the old bitch had dropped me into.' At that moment in time any sympathy for Judith Mulholland evaporated. The seriousness of their situation seemed overwhelming. He swore again, banging the wall with the palm of his hand.

'I guess this means that Kip won't survive, whoever poisoned him.'

Gareth sighed and said, 'Yes, I suspect you're right.'

'Do you reckon it's the Russians or are they just scapegoats?'

'I really don't know...' He paused to light another cigarette. 'Sometimes I think it's just too convenient and then I'm not so sure...'

Edward resisted another cigarette and leaned his back against the wall looking up at the sky. The clouds were clearing to reveal tiny stars millions of light years away, yet they suddenly seemed far too close. All he could think was, *I'm living a nightmare.*

'So, what the hell do we do now?'

Gareth made a sound like a grunt or maybe a laugh? He threw the half-smoked cigarette down and stamped on it.

'Well, I'm going to go back to my Plan A of getting the fuck out of here, with Pat of course, and I'd advise you to do the same.'

Edward stared at the dying embers of the cigarette. He looked at Gareth and said, 'I can't. Someone has to stop this or expose it.'

'They'll kill you and Abby and Buzz.'

'Look, Gareth, you do what is best for you. I don't blame you, but I can't keep running. I've got to stand and fight.'

'You're fucking mad, do you know that?'

'Yeah, probably. Just one thing before we go in... Do you believe the Americans? Is it alien technology?'

Gareth grimaced, as if considering the question made him feel queasy. He stared at his feet and then Edward.

'For what it's worth I think it probably is. Why else would they go to so much trouble?'

'But how come we're still alive? Why haven't they thrown everything they have at us?'

'Two reasons, I reckon. One is, until Kip they didn't know what we'd found out, and secondly, daft as it sounds, austerity screwed them. They don't have the resources anymore and...' Gareth laughed, 'ironically they can't go to the Treasury for more funding because they'd have to admit why they needed it, and same goes for stateside too.'

'That's a real catch-22 situation, isn't it? Fucking hilarious.'

'Watch out, Edward, you're beginning to sound like me.'

Edward said, 'God help me. So, how does Marcus fit in to this? And Sebastian come to that?'

He shrugged. 'I have no fucking idea to be honest. When we ran for it, I thought he was working for the Russians, and as for Sebastian... I still can't square that one, but we're living in strange times.'

Edward nodded and stood up straight. He looked back towards the house.

'We'd better go back in. What are you going to tell Pat?'

'That we're both going to Spain. My contacts are ready to get us out. Are you sure you won't come with us?'

'No, not yet anyway.'

'You're bloody mad.'

'Yeah, probably.'

Chapter 33

Gareth had taken Pat to their room, no doubt to tell her his plan. Edward found Buzz and Abby watching some game show on the TV. He experienced a wave of anxiety; they both looked so young.

'Change of plan slightly. We're going to throw everything at Sebastian. I think he's the key. Forget Judith Mulholland; she's old news and we need to know what's happening now. And I've had a heart to heart with Gareth. He's leaving us and taking Pat with him, so it'll just be the three of us.'

Abby gave Edward one of her "what the fuck" looks but said nothing. Edward knew she'd grill him later.

Buzz nodded and said, 'Okay.'

'I'm going to finish that wine. Either of you want any?'

Abby said, 'No thanks,' and carried on staring at the screen. Then she looked up and asked, 'Do I need to find us another bolthole? Are we safe here?'

Edward said, 'I don't know but it might be wise if your cousin has anywhere else? He must be wondering what you're up to by now though. Buzz, wherever we go you'll need to come too. Things are heating up and you're not safe on your own anymore. They'll have made the connection between you and Kip.'

'Yeah, I know. He's not going to make it, is he? They can't allow him to recover.'

Abby looked shocked and put her arm around Buzz. She looked up at Edward for support, but he shook his head at her. Fleetingly he saw the look of horror in her eyes.

'Buzz, I owe you the truth and if you want honesty then I'm afraid I suspect you're right. He knows too much regardless of who poisoned him. I'm really sorry...'

Buzz said nothing and Abby hugged him, whispering in his hair. Edward didn't catch what she said but he felt the sympathy.

He decided he had to say more but wasn't sure how much to tell them. He sat in the armchair and pulled it closer to the sofa so he could look them both in the face.

'Gareth came clean with me out there. He admitted he did work closely with Rob for a while on a very sensitive project. I'm not going to give you the details... No, Abby, I still think the less you know the better, even now... but you both need to recognise we're in serious shit. Buzz, yes, you're right about Kip I'm afraid. We don't know yet who got to him, but they'll be looking for us. That's why Gareth is getting out of here and he asked me if I wanted to join him. Do either of you want to go?'

Abby exploded, 'Fuck, no! How could you ask?'

Buzz said quietly, 'No way, Edward. This is personal now. My best friend is lying in a hospital bed...' He couldn't finish his words.

Edward leaned closer. He felt anger on Buzz's behalf.

'We'll get the bastards. If I die trying, I'll nail them for what they've done.'

'And what exactly have they done? What are you holding back from us?' Abby had a hard look in her eyes that he knew spelt trouble. He opened his mouth to speak but Buzz got in first.

'What Edward's trying to hide from us is so obvious I'm surprised he's even trying.'

'What?'

'It's the Warminster project. While you were talking to Gareth earlier, before you took the flash drive, I copied a file and read it. Tell her, Edward. Tell her the truth.'

Edward knew from the look in her eyes that he had no choice. He should have realised; Buzz was always ahead of the game.

'Okay. It's just so fantastic I'm still not sure I believe it… but it seems the Warminster project was called that because of the Thing they found that day in December 1964. We handed it over to the Americans – I don't think we had much choice – and they've spent the last fifty-odd years working on it. Now they've got a terrible weapon and Gareth and I reckon the Russians have found out and are desperately trying to learn as much as they can about it. It all points to Rob having sold some secrets…'

Abby butted in, 'I don't believe he would!'

Edward continued, 'For what it's worth, Abby, I didn't think so either. Well, not for money. No, hang on! What I'm trying to say is that this goes beyond national boundaries and patriotism. Rob may have thought revealing it would actually stop any potential conflict. Not all spies are traitors.'

Abby shook her head as if she didn't want to listen. He tried to take her hand, but she pulled it away.

'Abby, listen to me please. Rob was in an impossible position. He was guarding possibly the biggest secret of all time and he could tell *no one*. Gareth was cracking up and planning his escape, not that Rob knew that but what could he do? If he continued the project, he may end up like some of the others. Did you know that eleven people who worked on that project died from cancer? I did some digging. What we found turned out to be the tip of the iceberg. He couldn't tell you, the one person he'd normally confide in. So, I think he took the option that seemed to him the only way out. He planned to sell the whole thing to the Russians to even up the playing field, but somebody found out and he was dealt with before it happened.'

Buzz spoke up before Abby could say a word. 'I'm sorry, Abby, but I agree with Edward. Your husband wouldn't have had any choice really. I'm sure he was honourable and a lovely man, but he was put in a spot that none of us should have to face. If I'd been in his shoes, I'd probably do that. Are you sure that he did try to sell secrets? Is there any chance it was just an accident?'

Edward watched Abby's face as he replied to Buzz, 'Nothing is set in concrete. So no, I can't be one hundred per cent sure but it's highly probable.'

Abby had tears in her eyes. She mumbled, 'Poor Rob.' Then she stood up and ran upstairs. Buzz put his head in his hands and groaned.

'Leave her for a few minutes, Edward. She's grieving again.'

Wise beyond your years, Edward thought as he watched Buzz struggle with the enormity of it all.

'It's not a game anymore. We started this, Kip and me, thinking it'd be fun to outsmart the spooks. I should have realised we might find something scary. I never trusted our governments, bunch of fucking idiots most of them, but this… this is beyond the pale.'

'Yeah, I agree. And I have to admit to you I haven't a clue what to do next, but we must stick together, Buzz, and I'll do my best to protect you both.'

'Sure you will, but…'

'I know.'

Abby lay on the bed curled up like a baby with her back to the room. He hesitated before closing the door behind him and stood for a moment not sure what to say or do. She turned over and looked at him; her face was stained with tears. His heart ached at the sight of those dark eyes staring back at him.

'Abby…'

'There's absolutely nothing you can say, Edward, that will take the pain away but…' she adjusted her position so that she was facing him, 'it's not your fault.' She said it slowly as if she wanted to emphasise how she felt. 'You couldn't possibly have known where this was leading us when you visited Judith. I encouraged you; it seemed like a game.'

There it was, the same words Buzz had used. He could kick himself; he should have known better. It was never a game.

'Abby, I should have stopped it when I could have. Now, I don't know what to do or who to trust.'

She climbed off the bed and wrapped her arms around him. He could smell the lavender in her hair as she mumbled into his chest, 'You can trust me.'

He squeezed her tight and said, 'I know.'

She wriggled loose and went into the bathroom. He heard water running and she came back with a damp face. He thought back to the first time they'd made love and was overwhelmed by a desire to protect her.

Abby gave him a small smile and said, 'Is Buzz okay? We need to make some plans; and no, I will not go with Gareth and Pat, before you ask again.'

'I wasn't going to but—'

'No buts! What Rob started, we're going to finish together.'

'I guess I have no choice.'

'No, you don't. Go and tell Buzz I'm okay and I'll be down in a minute.'

'Yes, ma'am.'

Downstairs, Gareth had reappeared and looked a little less frayed. He was talking to Buzz when Edward entered the room.

'Ah, I was just talking about you. How's Abby? I heard her... in the bedroom.' He was unusually careful about choosing his words. 'I'm guessing she knows the score?'

'Yeah, I had no alternative. Buzz was one step ahead and we couldn't keep Abby in the dark. She's refusing point blank to go with you and Pat.'

'Of course she is! You can be a plank sometimes, Covington. She's lost her husband, she's not going to risk losing you too.' He snorted as if he thought Edward was the densest person he'd met. Buzz smirked.

Edward put his hands up. 'Okay! But you'd have tried too. I'm sure you don't want Pat in danger.'

'Course I fucking don't. That's why I'm going. Well, and saving my own skin too.'

Edward thought it was all bravado. He knew Gareth better now and could see through the bluster. Gareth turned to Edward and pulled a piece of paper out of his pocket.

'If you change your mind, phone this number. Tell whoever answers you're a close friend of mine. I'll tell them it's possible you might be in touch. They will arrange everything and get you away. They'll contact me and I'll meet you. Tell them I'll pay. No, don't refuse… you may need it.'

He pushed the paper into Edward's hand. 'I don't need to say this is for your eyes only. Best if you memorise the number.'

Edward took it and put it in his pocket. He knew better than to reject Gareth's offer.

'Gareth, it's good of you. I am grateful but don't hold your breath.'

'Same old Edward!' Gareth chuckled. 'Well, you never know and the weather's better there.'

Abby came into the room and caught them together. She said, 'What are you three up to? You look shifty.'

'And you look beautiful…' Gareth bowed, and Edward realised he was still showing the effects of the large amount of booze he'd downed.

Buzz laughed and said, 'Gareth has been plotting his escape and I think I'll put the kettle on for some strong coffee.'

'Good idea,' Edward muttered.

Abby followed Buzz into the kitchen, leaving the two men alone together. Gareth plonked himself on the sofa. He put his hand in the air and said, 'I just remembered! I have something else for you…' and putting his hand in his pocket he pulled out a handgun and waved it at Edward.

'Fuck's sake, Gareth! I hope the safety's on?'

'Of course it is.' He was indignant. 'I thought you'd have more use of this than me now. It's a Glock G19, bloody good gun, not like the shit you used to use back in the day…'

Edward thought, *How do you know what I used to have*? But he put his hand out to take it from Gareth, reasoning it was safer in his hands.

'I've got three magazines for it too. If you get through that lot, you're in trouble.'

'I'm in trouble anyway, but thanks. Are you sure you want to give it up?'

'Where I'm going, I've got an arsenal. If they come after me, they'll get more than they bargained for.'

Edward wondered how true that was but didn't question it. *To be honest*, he thought, *I need the extra firepower*. He felt the gun's weight and remembered hearing how reliable these were and wondered how Gareth had come by it.

'Best slip it in your pocket before Abby comes back.' Gareth winked at him.

'I'll probably be teaching her how to use it soon.'

Gareth looked surprised. He said, 'Really?'

When Abby and Buzz came back with mugs of black coffee Gareth staggered to his feet saying he'd pop up and see how Pat was doing. Abby raised her eyebrow but kept her thoughts to herself.

Edward took his coffee and said, 'Thank you. We need to have some sort of plan. I think it's best we move on but I'm not sure how we do it. I'm thinking we should keep your cousin out of it, Abby. What do you think? We need somewhere remote but not too much so, and with a good view of the terrain so we can see anyone coming…'

'Oh my God! This is like some bloody film,' Abby said.

'Any ideas, then? No other relatives with empty houses anywhere?'

Abby smiled. She sipped her coffee then said, 'No, but I do have an idea. Steve's company covers the whole of the south west. He's always got places empty because they haven't been booked or they need work doing or are even up for sale. I just need to find one that I know won't be in use for a while.'

'Do you know of anywhere?'

'Not yet but I can find out.'

He didn't bother asking how. He'd learned to trust Abby's resourcefulness.

'Okay, but be discreet; and I hate to sound pushy, but we need to move as soon as possible.'

Abby rolled her eyes and tutted at him. He knew when to keep quiet and was just glad she'd regained her usual unshakeable manner. Seeing her tears had cut him to the core.

Pat put her bag on the back seat of the car and hugged Abby before getting into the driver's seat. Gareth was talking to Buzz, unusually quietly, as Edward came out of the house to say goodbye. They were driving to Falmouth and Gareth had opted to do the journey at night; he'd arranged to meet the boat that was taking them to Gibraltar at six am to avoid onlookers. From there it was a short sea hop to Estepona and a car inland.

He walked over to Edward and shook his hand.

'Well, this is it. Wish us luck. I'll message you when we leave Falmouth but that'll be it. I'm not risking any more communication. I'd rather stay dead.'

'Let's hope they still think that. Thanks for the gun.'

'You're welcome and I hope you don't need to use it.' He paused and shuffled before adding, 'I know you think I'm a gobby twat but that's okay, I can be sometimes, but… I do care and I really hope you all win through. Remember my offer if things get tough.'

Edward said, 'I really appreciate it and thank you. Take care of yourselves, and I hope we can meet up one day when all this is over.'

'Me too, and I'm sorry to take the car. I hope you'll be okay with that old thing,' he nodded in the direction of the Land Rover.

'Yeah, it'll be fine. I'm going to cover it in mud and only drive it in the dark so it's difficult to see the plates.'

Abby came over to give Gareth a hug. He looked pleased and embarrassed at the same time. Pat waved at them and started the engine as a signal to Gareth to get a move on. She was smiling, and Edward thought she looked happier than he'd seen her before.

As they disappeared into the darkness beyond the one solitary streetlamp, Edward felt a pang of anxiety. He was alone with two amateurs to look after. Then he reminded himself that they were both capable of great resourcefulness.

Chapter 34

Edward washed the breakfast plates while Buzz vacuumed. He could see Abby in the garden, talking on her phone to her cousin. She walked up and down, occasionally waving her free arm about. As he drained the soapy water, he hoped she'd got some useful information to enable them to move on. The longer they stayed in one place the more chance of something going wrong.

The vacuum had stopped, and a sixth sense told him to check on Buzz. He found him standing in the middle of the living room staring at the TV.

'What's wrong?'

The morning news was on and he saw the headline on the screen. He knew instantly it referred to Kip. Buzz was frozen. Edward read the words scrolling across the bottom of the screen.

The suspected Novichok victim identified yesterday as Mr Kevin Peters of Ealing has lost his fight for life. He died at two thirty this morning and a statement will be made shortly.

'Buzz, I'm so sorry.'

'I knew it was coming. It's just horrible to see his name on the screen like that. I must ring Sam…'

Edward took his arm and said as gently as possible, 'I don't think that's a good idea; they're bound to have her phone tapped and it wouldn't take them long to work out where you are.'

'Shit, you're right.'

'Just before we move on send her a message and let her know you won't be contacting her again for a while. She's probably suspicious of why he was targeted, if she's got half of Kip's brains.'

'Oh, she has; she's already been questioning me about it.'

'Good reason to keep her out of it, then.'

Abby came in with a smile on her face that froze as soon as she saw Buzz. She looked at the screen and gasped, 'Oh no!'

Edward left her to comfort Buzz and went to make him a cup of tea. He always defaulted to tea at moments like this.

Buzz remained remarkably calm. He said that he'd been expecting it after their conversation and the way to remember his friend was to complete what they'd started. They drank tea and Abby relayed her chat with her cousin.

'I told him I was moving on and thanked him for the use of the cottage. We talked about his business and I asked about what he was buying and selling, made it sound like I'd be interested in working for him in the future. Anyway, he told me about a place they want to buy on the moor near Manaton. The owner died and her heir lives in Canada and isn't sure whether he wants to sell or not. The place is standing empty meanwhile, and Steve was saying it's all taking far too long and could drag on for months. It's a bit remote and off the beaten track but with glorious views of the moors and Bowerman's Nose. I didn't show too much interest, told him I preferred Cornwall but…'

Edward said, 'It could be a good hideaway. We'd have to be careful not to be seen arriving or leaving.'

'Well, it's not on the market and not being maintained so there's no reason for anyone to visit. At the moment we don't have a better option, do we?'

Edward agreed but was concerned it may be a little too close to Ben's cottage in Lustleigh. They would have to be very careful.

Abby asked Buzz what he thought.

'Yeah, why not? We can't stay here. Pat's left us with enough food for a while, so we won't have to go shopping and mix with people. That cuts the risk down, doesn't it? Only thing I can think of is there probably won't be any Wi-Fi so it'll limit what I can do.'

Abby said, 'Shit, I hadn't thought of that.'

Edward said, 'We'll manage. We don't have a choice, and I suggest we pack up and be ready to leave as soon as it gets dusk. Gives us plenty of time to clean this place and for Buzz to do some research on Sebastian.'

Buzz put his mug down and said, 'I'll start straightaway. I need something to do.'

Edward wanted to say how sorry he was about Kip but left that to Abby. He couldn't carry on saying sorry and he had a hunch there might be more to say sorry for in the future.

Abby packed her few belongings into her bag and watched Edward shoving things into his. He'd hidden both guns in the bottom of his holdall. He didn't want her to know yet, figuring it would only scare her.

'Do you have a plan at all?' She fidgeted with the bedspread while he sat and pulled on his trainers. 'Any escape plan even, if things go badly wrong?'

Edward stopped packing and turned to look at her. He leaned in and kissed her before she had a chance to pull away. Since she'd learned about Rob, she'd been less affectionate, but he was willing to wait for her to recover.

'No I don't, and yes I do, to answer both questions. If it gets too scary, we'll bail out like Gareth did. I'm not going to risk getting you hurt. The thing is…' he reached out and tucked a stray strand of hair behind her ear, 'I wish this whole business was over and done with and we could just carry on as before, but it isn't, and we can't for a while.'

'If Judith Mulholland was still alive, I think I'd probably kill her myself.'

Edward was shocked. She said it as if she meant it.

'Abby! Really? You wouldn't hurt a fly…'

'You don't know me as well as you think if you believe that. Now, are you ready? Buzz will be wondering what we're doing.'

She jumped up and grabbed her bag, leaving Edward staring after her. She'd revealed a hard streak he hadn't seen before and desperately hoped was only temporary. He followed her down the stairs to find Buzz waiting in the living room.

'I've saved as much as I can find on Sebastian and Marcus too. I just looked for any references and saved it all. A lot of it will be worthless but you never know,' Buzz said.

'Okay, that's good. I'm hoping we can find something useful that will give me some inspiration. I'm getting like Gareth, sick of hiding.'

Abby gave him a look he couldn't interpret. Whether she was angry with him or disappointed, he couldn't be sure.

It was an easy drive cross country to Manaton, and when they got closer Abby directed Edward down the dark lanes towards the house. She peered at her phone screen to get her bearings.

'How do you know exactly where it is?' he asked as he drove carefully along the moorland road.

'Well, the way he described it we won't have any trouble identifying it, and I came here on holiday as a child, so I sort of remember.'

They'd reached the outskirts of the small village by now and Edward saw a signpost ahead.

'Which way now?'

'Take the right; might be signposted Hound Tor but if not don't worry. We carry on for about a mile then there's a track on our right.'

He followed her instructions and they left the few houses behind and crossed open ground. After just under a mile he spotted the track and pulled over to the side of the road.

'Do you think that's it?'

'It must be; there's nothing else for miles. He described it as a rough track, quite narrow, that climbs and twists over a low stone bridge then a final sharp climb to the house. He had concerns about big family cars making it up there because it's so narrow. It's called The View – very imaginative.'

Buzz said from the gloom of the back seat, 'Yeah, but I bet it's fantastic. Look at the stars!'

He was right. The sky had cleared, and the lack of light pollution offered a spectacular view of the night sky. Edward thought he hadn't seen anything like it for years.

Abby said, 'It's like the sky's closing in on us. I've never seen so many stars. It's beautiful.'

Edward clambered out of the car and stretched. The silence was complete, not a sound of anything. He leaned back into the car to speak to them.

'Okay, I'm going up on foot to suss it out. I don't want to drive this old thing off the road and get us stuck, and I want to see the place for myself first. Is that alright with you both?'

Buzz nodded and said that he was happy just to sit and look at the sky.

Abby said, 'Shall I come with you?'

'No, I'd rather you stay with the car. If anyone drives by, it will look better if there's two of you in it and you can drive off if needs be.'

He expected an argument, but she nodded and slid over into the driver's seat. He closed the door and started up the track.

It was pitch black here and the ground was uneven, so he was forced to use his phone torch to create a small pool of light in front of his feet. He understood why Abby's cousin had concerns; the track was indeed narrow, stony and suddenly twisted left then right. He came to the bridge which had very low stone walls, wide enough for an average car but it would be tight for anything bigger. He could hear the water splashing across the stones below. He guessed it must be a stream that fed into the Bovey, the river that ran close to Ben's place. Then he climbed up a steep incline to join a tarmacked driveway. He stopped to catch his breath and looked for the gateposts that would have the name carved into them.

He walked more easily now, and round the next bend he spotted the old stone posts. Drawing closer he shone his phone torch onto the stone and read "The View". This was definitely the right place, but he was surprised that the iron gates were wide open. He'd expected to find them closed and locked.

The house stood just out of view, so he stepped through the gates and followed the drive to the left and suddenly there it was. Edward stopped dead and switched off his torch. He saw a light coming from the house; someone was in residence; and at the same time he saw a small car parked in front of the dilapidated garage.

'Shit!'

He crouched down, even though he knew anyone inside wouldn't be able to see him in the darkness. The curtains were drawn and there was a light on upstairs too. Whoever was in there wasn't in a rush to leave.

Edward muttered profanities as he walked back down the track. He'd had his concerns but hadn't expected this. Crossing the bridge, he looked back. There was no sign of movement.

Abby jumped when he reached the car and pulled the door open. She slid back across the seat.

'What's up? You look annoyed.'

He took a deep breath and said, 'There's someone there; a car's parked outside and lights are on everywhere.'

'Oh no! Now what do we do?'

'We only have one option. Well, two, but I prefer the first.'

'Which is…?'

Buzz butted in, 'The cottage, your mate's place…'

'Yep. I think we have no choice.'

Edward waited for them to disagree, but both knew he was right. He started the engine and turned back towards Manaton.

Abby said, 'What was the other option, just as a matter of interest?'

'Ben's house, but that would have meant driving back into Wiltshire and too close to our homes for comfort.'

'Yeah, you're right. So, what's the risk now? Who knows about the cottage?'

'I'm hoping only Sebastian and possibly whoever he was talking to. I'll need to check for bugs before we go in just in case, but somehow I don't think I'll find anything. What do you reckon, Buzz? Would you expect us to go back?'

'No, but then I'm not a spook. Logically, we'd keep on the move. Why would we go back? There's nothing there for us. He'd need to know we'd run out of options. He might even think we've left the country like Gareth.'

'That's what I'm hoping. At least there's Wi-Fi there.' And in a strange way, he thought that it felt a bit like going home.

Chapter 35

E dward checked the cottage out while Abby and Buzz unloaded their bags and provisions from the car. He still had the key and wondered what Sebastian had done with the spare. It was cold and slightly smelly inside. The kitchen bin, Edward thought, as he systematically searched each room as quietly as he could. There was no sign of anything, so he called the other two in.

Abby said, 'Jeez, it stinks in here.' She walked through to the kitchen and shouted back, 'It's the bin and there's a carton of milk on the side. I'll get rid of it.'

Half an hour later they'd made themselves comfortable and Edward lit a fire to warm the old place up. The smell had gone, and Abby had emptied the fridge too. She came into the living room with three mugs of tea.

'I know this sounds weird, but it feels like home.'

'I thought the same. There's no point in trying to hide. If they come looking, they'd see the car anyway before we saw them, so we'll have to get on with it, Buzz, and work out what to do next.'

Buzz said, 'Yeah. Do you mind if I take the upstairs bedroom this time? Last time I was here...' he paused, 'I shared with Kip.'

Edward said, 'Yes, of course. I'm sorry it didn't occur to me. We'll just ignore that room.'

'Thanks. I'll take my bags up.'

Abby waited for Buzz to leave the room then said quietly, 'Poor boy, he's lost his best friend and he's probably scared to death.'

'What about you? How are you holding up?'

Edward avoided talking about Rob in front of Abby. He knew she was still raw, but she surprised him by wrapping her arms around his waist and saying, 'It's strange but I feel better being here. I don't know why, but it feels safe, as if the house is hugging us.'

He held her close and smiled. It seemed like that to him too.

Buzz came back into the room and caught them standing with their arms around each other. He grinned, and Edward let Abby go, feeling slightly embarrassed.

'Can't leave you two lovebirds alone for one minute,' Buzz joked.

Abby pulled a face at him and said, 'And you're the gooseberry. Is anyone else hungry? Is it too late to eat something, do you think?'

Edward checked his watch. It was ten fifteen. He thought, *Not too late for a snack*, and said he'd see what they'd got and went into the kitchen to unpack their food box.

He was surprised to find his post-its and scribblings still on the wall. Why he thought Sebastian would remove it he didn't know but he was glad it was still in place. He and Buzz could add to it. As he cut bread to make toast, his eye caught sight of a white note stuck in the middle of the board. His first thought was, *That's not my handwriting*, and his second was, *It's Sebastian's.*

Edward pulled down the note and read it.

Just in case you do come back here and I hope you do. You're a bloody idiot. What the fuck did you run for? I've tried messaging you but you obviously changed phones again. NOBODY knows about this place. NOBODY! I need you onside. I'm guessing if you read this you know what you're up against now. We must work together. There're very few people we can trust. For God's sake contact me and let me explain. S

'Shit.' Edward left the bread and carried the note into the living room. Buzz was setting up his laptop on the table in the corner and Abby sat curled up in front of the fire. She looked up when he came in.

'Read this.' He gave her the note and watched her face as she read. Buzz came over to see what it was.

Abby frowned and said, 'What do you make of it? He sounds genuine but annoyed.'

Buzz agreed but added, 'The thing is – and I've been thinking about it a lot – I haven't found anything to connect Sebastian with the project. He did help you rescue Abby too, so maybe he's one of the good guys?'

Edward ran his hands through his hair and groaned. Sebastian had been one of his closest allies in the service and now he didn't know what to think. The wrong call could get them killed, so the stakes were high.

'If we choose to believe him, then we have an ally and possibly a team, as don't forget Sebastian was in contact with someone and planning to move us somewhere...' Edward thought back to the conversation he'd overheard – "bring him in" were the words used – 'but I'm not quite convinced enough to make contact. Tomorrow we'll use that wall and brainstorm everything we know. Then we'll make a joint decision. Okay?'

Abby and Buzz both nodded.

Abby stirred slightly as Edward slipped out of bed. Dawn was breaking and he needed to get out and get some exercise. He left the cottage by the back door, passing the wall covered in notes without a glance. *That will come later*, he thought; *I just need some fresh air to clear my head*.

It had taken hours to get to sleep and it came with dreams so vivid he was glad to be awake. The air was clean here and loaded with the combined scents of woodland and riverbank. Edward jogged up the lane and into the woods, heading away from the river and up the slope towards Trendlebere Down. His breath came in bursts of misty vapour as he climbed. Even a few days of not running had affected his fitness. He gasped for breath when he reached the top and the path divided. He took the right and headed back down towards the river again, not wanting to be away too long. Smoking so much lately was doing him no good at all, he decided as he panted his way down the path, weaving through the trees.

When he got back to the house, it was still in silence, so he put the kettle on to make Abby a cup of tea. Ever since the day she'd been snatched from his home, he experienced a wave of anxiety if he left her alone. Before taking a shower, he checked on her – she was still sleeping. He could hear Buzz moving about in the other bedroom.

He was staring at the wall of notes when Buzz joined him in the kitchen, yawning and still in his fleecy onesie.

'Morning, Buzz. There's a mug of tea for you; I heard you moving about. How do you feel today?'

'Tired; didn't sleep well.'

'Me neither. Abby's still sleeping. I'll give her ten more minutes then I'll take her tea up. I was just looking at our notes and thinking not a lot has changed really.'

'Apart from the Warminster thing,' Buzz said, adding two spoons of sugar to his mug of tea. He saw Edward's face and said, 'I need the energy. Don't usually have sugar.'

Edward grinned. He said, 'I nearly did too. I've been staring at this thinking I'm missing something or someone.'

'I'm missing someone. I messaged Sam last night and told her I couldn't contact her again. She said it's awful there. They won't tell her anything, won't even confirm whether it was a nerve agent, but there are still police hanging around and nobody is allowed near his… body.'

'Poor girl.'

'Yeah, she's really upset, but she sussed I was in trouble and told me not to worry but just let her know I'm okay from time to time.'

'I'll do my best to get them one way or another.'

'And I'll help you. I'll have a shower then we can get started.'

'You'll have breakfast first; I can't have you keeling over.' Edward patted Buzz on the back and grabbed Abby's tea.

She stirred when he opened the bedroom door and gave him a sleepy smile. He pulled the curtains open a crack to let light in.

'Morning. Have you been out?' Her voice had the muted early morning tone he'd come to recognise. After a cup of tea, she'd be bright and alert.

'Yeah, I had a quick run before the walkers get up. You okay?'

'I'm fine. Is Buzz up?'

'In the shower. He's okay. I said we'd brainstorm after breakfast.'

'I can't believe I slept so well. Told you this felt like home.'

'Perhaps, when this is over, I can make Ben an offer on the place.' Edward smiled and thought, *I'm only half joking*, and Abby seemed to sense his mood.

'Wouldn't that be nice?'

'Abby, we have to believe there'll be a life after this.'

'Sure, but will it be the same? Do you reckon we can beat them, Edward?'

'I think we can, but not sure how quite yet.'

Breakfast was cleared away and the three of them sat around the kitchen table, paper everywhere. Buzz chewed his pen and Abby frowned at the scribbled notes in front of her. They had added a column to the sheet on the wall which read "motives" and Edward began sticking post-its under it.

'So, we agree that the undisputable facts are quite slim. We've made a lot of assumptions that may or may not become facts…'

Abby said, 'The biggest one for me is that Sebastian is not to be trusted. Our "evidence" is based on one or two phone calls…' she held up her fingers and ticked off her points: 'one – he made the calls to an unknown person or persons; therefore two, he's working against you; and three, we were in danger.'

'What about Marcus?' Buzz asked. 'You had a hunch but where's the evidence there?'

Edward was exasperated. *We're just going around in circles*, he thought. The only facts were that: the project was super sensitive; Rob and Gareth had both worked on it; Judith was managing it; several people had died in suspicious circumstances, including Rob; heads of government didn't know about it; and there was no reference to Sebastian being involved.

'Let's leave the facts alone and look at our assumptions. Abby is right to question them, and you too, Buzz. For me one of the big questions is – are the Russians involved and if so why? That leads us to whether they killed Kip and who was after you, Buzz.'

Abby leaned forward over the notes and said, 'Is it possible that Sebastian would work with them?'

'That's been playing on my mind. The Sebastian I knew would never work with them…'

Buzz stopped chewing his pen and said, 'How do we know the Russians are involved, apart from the supposed Novichok? And to be honest, we don't even know that it was a nerve agent for sure, do we?'

Edward frowned. 'No, we don't, although everything points to it. I still think we're missing something. Can you go through Kip's files again? Ignore the stuff about Warminster and focus on connections between people and any reference to Russian interference however ambiguous.'

'Yeah, sure.'

Edward stood up and paced the stone-flagged floor. Something was bothering him, but he didn't know what. He knew he was missing a connection somewhere and it frustrated him.

Abby cut into his thoughts, 'Tea anyone? It might help the brain cells.'

Edward stopped pacing. 'I'm sorry, I must be driving you mad. Don't get up, I'll put the kettle on.'

Buzz had opened his laptop and was searching under the mass of paper for the flash drives. Edward could see his home screen from where he was standing; it had the latest news on it. He moved closer to take a look at the headlines in case Kip was mentioned, but another story caught his eye.

'Buzz, hang on, don't load it yet. What's that story there?' he pointed at the item and Buzz clicked on it.

Body of woman washed up on Cornish beach early this morning.

A woman in her forties was pronounced dead after being found on Swanpool Beach near Falmouth by dog walkers this morning. Police are working to identify the body. No one has reported a missing person in the area. She was found fully clothed but without shoes, and the police are working on the theory that she may have fallen overboard from a vessel at sea. No cruise ships or ferries have reported a missing passenger. More on this story later.

There was silence for a moment as the three of them digested the report. Edward had a sinking feeling in the pit of his stomach and hoped he would be proved wrong. Abby obviously thought the same thing.

'It couldn't be Pat, could it? All they say is "a woman in her forties"; there must be other women… And she was found on a beach – couldn't she have died there? Overdose or something?'

Edward wanted to reassure her but hesitated enough for her to give him that direct stare he knew too well.

'We'll have to wait and see how the story develops. It's a bit of a leap to assume it's Pat.'

'But it could be, and if it is where's Gareth?'

Buzz continued working through the files and keeping a weather eye on the news, but by mid-afternoon there was nothing added to the original story and an online search found nothing either. Edward suggested they stop for a while and get some fresh air. The weather had improved, allowing the sun to break through the thin cloud cover.

'A walk by the river will blow the cobwebs away. Do you fancy it, you two?'

Abby said, 'Yes, I'd like that. I'll just pull on a sweat top and get my shoes.'

Buzz declined, saying, 'I'd rather carry on with this, if you don't mind?'

'Sure, no problem. See you later.'

They slipped out of the back door and followed the cobbled path to the gate in the wall behind the cottage. The sun had warmed the air and it felt like spring at last. Edward led Abby up the lane to a small stile by the side of the stream. They walked in silence for a while.

'So, Edward, do you think it's Pat they found?' Abby was slightly out of breath from the climb into the woods.

'I don't know. I really hope not, and I wonder whether we're becoming paranoid, thinking every death is linked to us in some way. Then I think it's an unusual death in a quiet place out of season and it made headline news so...'

He pointed her in the direction of the next stile, and they clambered into a meadow where the path dropped down to the riverbank. Abby stopped to catch her breath.

'I can't believe it, and I won't until it's confirmed. I'd hate to think it's Pat. I really like her.'

'Let's wait and see. This way...' He pointed right, and they walked along the riverbank for a while. 'I'm sure we'll know soon either way.'

He stopped to admire the view. Ben had chosen well, buying that cottage, he thought. He could almost imagine that he and Abby were on holiday, but then reality broke into his thoughts. What if it's Pat? Does that mean Gareth is dead too?

Abby said, 'It's beautiful here, isn't it? So peaceful.'

They stood still for a while looking down the valley, watching birds skim the river. He had no idea what they were; he'd never taken much notice of the surrounding wildlife before. Abby sighed and he guessed she was thinking of home again. He took her hand and pulled her in to lean against him.

'Let's do this every morning while we stay here,' he said. 'It'll be a bit like being home.'

'How did you know I was thinking of that? Spooky!'

Abby laughed and he joked back, 'Well, it would be, coming from me.'

'Let's go back to Buzz. I'll make us all some bacon sandwiches.'

Edward smiled and said, 'Sounds like a good plan.'

Buzz was still in front of his screen when they got back, and they had to persuade him to have a break. Edward wondered what rabbit hole he was chasing down to absorb him for so long. Abby made them both bacon sandwiches as she'd promised, and Edward watched Buzz give her sidelong glances. At first, he thought the old crush had resurfaced, then he realised it was more discomfort than attraction. *He's found something about Rob*, he thought.

'Anything new, Buzz? You were deep in cyberspace when we got back.' He hoped he'd made the question sound casual enough.

'Umm, yeah, might be…'

'It's fine to bounce your thoughts off us, if you're not sure what you've found.'

Abby said, 'Yeah, we might be able to help cast some light on it.'

'Well, I… umm…'

'Oh for goodness' sake! It's Rob, isn't it? It's fine, Buzz, really it is… whatever you've found…' Abby put her hand on his arm and smiled at him. Edward felt her kindness and loved her for it.

'Well, yes and no. I'm a bit puzzled.'

Edward said, 'Fire away. Let's hear it and we'll see what we make of it.'

Buzz said, 'I'll show you.'

He angled his laptop so they could both see it and, fingers flying over the keyboard, he brought up several pages. They looked like bank account details, rows of figures and brief descriptions.

'Okay, this spreadsheet on the left is the outgoings from the main Cradle project. You can see the payments to Rob? All straightforward and about what you'd expect to cover expenses, nothing out of the ordinary, right?' Then…' he opened another tab, 'there's this one, which is what Kip and I found, and this one shows a much larger sum – see here – and that's what we thought was the suspect money. It goes from here into Rob's account then out again the same day. Three hundred thousand…'

Abby gasped, 'How much? We never had that sort of money—'

'No, of course not, and…' he paused, 'I don't think Rob did either. I think it was a sham. Somehow, and I've got to admire the dude who did it, they diverted the money from the project into Rob's account and out again probably without him knowing. Then they covered their tracks and it was left looking as if Rob had mysteriously been the recipient of a large sum of money.'

Edward frowned and said, 'So, to anyone investigating it would look like Rob was taking a bribe? Shit, that's devious.'

'Yeah, isn't it just? And it could be what got him killed.'

'So, it's possible that Rob was completely innocent?' Abby asked.

'Quite possible.'

Edward stared at the figures. If Rayner had been framed, then who had the money gone to?

'Can you see where the money went? Is there a name against the payee?'

Buzz snorted as if Edward had asked him a really dumb question. He said, 'These guys are good, man. They've covered their tracks and only left what they want the world to see. The only thing I was able to detect is that there was a third party involved. The trail stops dead when it leaves Rob's account. They used him to launder the money. And like I said, he probably didn't even know.'

'But we can't prove that.' Abby spoke quietly. She looked disappointed, Edward thought.

'Okay, so what about Gareth? He was head of the project at this point. Could he have known?'

'There's no way of telling. I've found no memos, emails or anything between him and Rob.'

'Any more on Sebastian?'

'Very little. He has a really low profile in cyberspace. If anything, unusually low key, which means one of two things – he's either in an insignificant role *or* exactly the opposite and his online presence is managed. The only thing I'm fairly sure of is that he was never in the project.'

Edward leaned back in his chair and rubbed his chin. Could it be possible Rob had been used, and if so by whom? He knew he had a decision to make and that he'd been heading towards it for the past few days. Sebastian had to be contacted.

Chapter 36

That night, as they lay in bed, Edward told Abby he was going to contact Sebastian. He felt her shift her body to face him.

'Why? I thought you didn't trust him. What's changed? Have I missed something?'

'No, it's been playing on my mind. I made assumptions based on what I overheard that night, and today, when we were talking about questioning everything, I recalled exactly what I heard. Maybe I misinterpreted it. It might be Sebastian isn't the problem, but he may be able to help us find who is.'

'It's still a risk though, isn't it?'

'Everything is a risk, but I have to make judgements based on evidence and there is, as you quite rightly pointed out, very slim evidence that Sebastian is a threat. And then Buzz said that he thought he had a managed online presence and that made me think...'

'Well, what he actually said was that Sebastian might be in an insignificant role—,

'Yes, I know what he said.' Edward realised that sounded rude. 'Sorry, I didn't mean to snap, but yes, I heard Buzz, and I think, knowing Sebastian, that it's unlikely. Which means, if you remove that possibility, he's got some level of considerable power. And he did give me a bag of stuff that a civil servant wouldn't have access to…'

'What stuff?'

Edward was thinking hard. The gun and the camera were classic intelligence issue, not available to the role Sebastian had claimed he was in. He'd been an idiot not to realise that. Sebastian had talked about favours and he'd taken it at face value.

'Edward, what stuff?' Abby cut into his musings.

'Sorry, I was just thinking it through. A gun and some surveillance things.'

'A gun? You've got a gun?'

He was grinning and knew she couldn't see him. The shocked tone in her voice amused him.

'I've actually got two.'

'*Two?*'

Her voice went up a level and he smiled even more. He felt her fidgeting beside him. Then the light came on and he blinked against the brightness.

'When were you planning to tell me?'

'When I thought I might have to use them.' He said it calmly, but it did nothing to soothe Abby. Her eyes were sparkling dangerously.

'Edward Covington, you are the most exasperating man—'

He stopped her in mid flow by kissing her fully on the lips.

'I know,' he said.

They woke up late. A long discussion about Sebastian and the merits of firearms had eaten into their sleep time and now the sun was pouring through the gap in the curtains creating a warm stream of light across the bed. Edward had agreed to show Abby the guns and suggested she learn how to fire one 'just in case'. That had gone as well as expected but eventually she reluctantly agreed to have a go.

Buzz was already in the kitchen when they came downstairs and busy making tea and toast. He waved at them with a chunk of toast in his mouth and pointed at the teapot.

Edward poured two mugs full and gave one to Abby.

'You guys are late up this morning,' Buzz muttered through a mouthful of buttered toast.

'Yeah, we spent half the night arguing,' Abby said.

'Not really arguing, more a robust discussion.'

Buzz raised his eyebrow and kept quiet waiting for Abby to explain, which she obliged.

'Edward's got a gun – no, two guns actually – and he suggested I learn how to use one…'

'I think that's a good idea.'

Edward grinned and said, 'Thank you. Glad someone can see the sense.'

Abby dug him in the ribs, but he saw her lips curving upward. He knew she'd come around.

Buzz turned on his laptop and waited for it to load. Edward remembered the dead woman.

'Buzz, can you check the news? See if there's any more about that body on the beach?'

'Yeah, sure.'

He clicked on the BBC Spotlight web pages and scrolled down the page. There it was – the story had been updated.

The police now believe the woman found at Swanpool Beach on Tuesday may have been on board a private seagoing vessel. They have approached the Falmouth harbour master for a log of boats that left the Falmouth area recently and are waiting for dental records as they have been unable to identify the victim from personal effects. More to follow on this story.

'So, we're none the wiser. Keep an eye on it for me,' Edward said.

'It might be someone else,' Abby said but she didn't sound convinced. Then she told Buzz about Sebastian and how Edward wanted to contact him.

'Edward might be right. I can't find anything about him anywhere and his bank account was dead straight, no funny payments or receipts...' he paused and added, 'And for what it's worth, I like him.'

'I liked Marcus and Gareth but...'

Edward sat down next to Buzz and looked at their notes. He knew Abby was struggling, but he had experience and he knew sometimes you have to follow your gut and hope you've got it right. The heightened tension around Abby's abduction and rescue had clouded his judgement, and he thought now his actions may have been driven by emotion not reason; he hadn't followed his training.

'I'll set up a meeting with Sebastian, just me and him. Then if it goes wrong you can get away. I've still got that number Gareth gave me.'

'For God's sake, Edward! For the last time, I'm not leaving.'

'I'm not asking you to. It's an insurance policy, that's all.'

Abby was in the bath; Edward could hear her splashing about. He wandered into the kitchen and asked Buzz how it was going, any news? Buzz ummed and aahed, which meant there was something but he wasn't sure he was ready to share.

'Look, you've been beavering away, and I expect there's something you're not sure about, isn't there?

'Yes, maybe. There's no news on that body yet, by the way.'

'Okay and…?'

'What?'

Edward was getting exasperated. He said, 'Tell me what you've found today, and I'll decide whether it's important or not.'

'Oh, okay. Well, it's Marcus I've been looking at. I got a bit bored, so I decided to look into his finances – you know, just to see if there was a link. Anyway, I found a recent payment into his account, quite a big one, actually…'

'How recent?'

Buzz fidgeted and said, 'Two days ago.'

'And how big?' Edward was getting a sense of déjà vu.

'Well, err… it's two hundred thousand…'

'Did it leave the same day?'

'No, it's still there, or was yesterday. It's a bit odd, isn't it?'

Edward thought it was more than odd. First Rayner then Marcus – what was the link? Who was the link?

'Where did it come from? The project?'

'I'm finding it difficult to track back. Somebody doesn't want me to find out.'

Edward grimaced. This was becoming more of a clusterfuck, as Gareth would say. He said thanks to Buzz and asked him to keep digging. He needed to clear his head and decided he needed fresh air to do it. He always thought better when he exercised.

'When Abby comes down tell her I've gone for a jog and I won't be long.'

Buzz looked up from his laptop and grunted, 'Yeah, okay.'

Outside the air was decidedly fresher. A cold wind was blowing from the west and an earlier shower had dropped the temperature, but Edward didn't notice. He set off at a brisk pace following the path he'd taken with Abby yesterday. By the time he reached the place where the footpath divided at the top of the slope he was out of breath. He cursed his smoking habit and carried on, turning left this time to head towards Trendlebere Down. The wind was biting, and his cheeks were burning, so he turned back towards Lustleigh Cleave and started heading down again.

He was running along the edge of the woods now and sheltered from the wind, so he stopped and took his phone from his top pocket. Hesitating for a brief moment he checked the signal and sent a message to Sebastian.

I got your message. Over to you. E

He wondered how long it would be before he got a response. Walking now, he carried on towards the river, checking his signal strength as he went.

Good, I'm glad you're still in the game. We need to talk. Can we meet? S

Yes, I think that would be a good idea. I'm on the move so I'll pick a place and get back to you.

He didn't want Sebastian to know he was staying at the cottage yet. It was a pathetic attempt at subterfuge that wouldn't fool him; he knew that, but it made Edward feel better.

Make it sooner rather than later. Things are hotting up. You need to check the news.

I'll message later.

Edward put his phone away and broke into a jog. He was maybe ten to fifteen minutes away from the cottage. What news did Sebastian mean?

Edward burst through the kitchen door, making Buzz jump. He slammed the door behind him.

'I'm going to get a towel from the shower. Can you bring up the news on your laptop?'

Buzz said, 'Shit, man! You scared the life out of me! Yeah, will do. What am I looking for?'

'I don't know,' Edward said as he came through with a towel wrapped around his neck, 'but I think it'll be obvious.'

He brought up the front page and there it was. The story about Kip was now headline news. Police had confirmed his death was due to Novichok poisoning. It appeared they'd been forced to by the media who had somehow gotten hold of Kip's medical notes. It was becoming a major scandal, with the press looking for somebody to blame and whipping up hysteria about possible secondary cases, despite the PM and chief of police reassuring everyone that it was a one-off, localised incident and completely contained.

Buzz stared silently at his screen, and Edward noticed he looked very pale. He put a hand on his shoulder.

'Christ, I'm really sorry, Buzz. That's not what I was expecting. Somebody has leaked this to the press—'

'How did you know there would be a major story?'

'I've been in contact with Sebastian. He told me to check the news.'

Buzz shook his head. Whether it was because of Kip or his contact with Sebastian, Edward didn't know, and at that point Abby entered the kitchen and stopped in the doorway.

'What's wrong? What have I missed?'

Edward said, 'The police have confirmed Kip was poisoned with nerve agent. It's a major incident and everybody's flapping like mad.'

'Oh shit, sorry, Buzz.'

Buzz muttered, 'It's okay.'

'I thought maybe there was news on that poor woman when I saw your faces.'

For a second Edward thought, *Who's she talking about?*, then he remembered. There was nothing on the news page that he could see.

'No, doesn't look like it,' Edward said.

'You heading for the shower?' She pointed at the towel draped around his neck.

'Yes, I'm a bit sweaty. Just got back. I won't be long.'

As he left the room, he heard Buzz say to Abby, 'He contacted Sebastian.'

He stopped in the passageway to hear her response. She dropped her voice, but he heard, 'Yes, I know.'

After his shower Edward told them both he was going to message Sebastian again and arrange to meet. Buzz nodded and Abby shrugged her shoulders.

'To be honest, you'd just as well meet him here. I'm sure he knows where you are, doesn't he? What's the point in messing about?'

He thought, direct as ever and maybe she's right. All this running and hiding had only added to his paranoia and got in the way of analytical decision-making.

'If you two are okay with that? What if I'm wrong, if he's not on our side?'

Buzz said, 'We talked about it and we think you're right this time and the risk is greater *not* having Sebastian onside.'

Edward said, 'Okay.'

He noted the "this time" and felt guilty for his failing to be rational. He was on the edge of saying sorry again but pulled back. How many times must he apologise to make himself feel better about the situation?

Abby stood up, stretched and said, 'And before he comes, I want a practise with the gun. You never know…'

Edward looked at her face, trying to read her expression. Was she being serious? He wasn't sure until she grinned at him.

'God, you had me there for a second.'

'Oh, I wouldn't shoot Sebastian, but you never know who he might have in tow.'

'Now you're sounding like me. But okay yes, I did promise. We'll have to go up on the moor, away from people.'

Buzz said, 'Can I come too? I've never seen a gun in action.'

'I'm glad you've lived a sheltered life, and yes, why not? We'll all have a trip up onto the moor. How about later, just before dusk? Less risk of upsetting any locals or walkers.'

'Cool!' Buzz grinned at Edward.

We've all agreed we'd like you to come here to the cottage. E

   Good. When? S

When suits you? Are you coming alone?

Yes, I will be. I'm tied up today. Can make it tomorrow 1100?

   Okay. See you then.

   Okay.

Short and sweet, Edward thought as he put his phone back in his pocket. He told Abby and she chewed her lip.

'I hope we're doing the right thing.'

'I don't think we have a choice. Sebastian is right, things are hotting up. Now, let's give Buzz a shout and get up on the moor for your shooting lesson.'

He watched her eyes light up and wasn't sure whether he was amused or disturbed by her enthusiasm. She dashed off to tell Buzz and he got the guns out of his holdall along with a spare magazine. He didn't have ammunition to waste, so he'd have to be strict about how many times she actually fired it.

Edward put the gun in his inside pocket and the second in a small bag along with the magazine. He didn't know how to feel about this, thought he'd left the days of using a weapon behind him, and now he was about to teach Abby how to shoot. And potentially how to kill, he thought, and that really didn't sit well.

Downstairs they were both waiting for him. Both looked slightly wide-eyed, like kids about to go on a trip to the fairground. Abby was fidgeting – a sure sign she was nervous.

'You two ready? I've had a look at the map, and I think I've found somewhere that should be nice and quiet.'

Edward ushered them out of the front door and locked it behind them. They had an hour or so of daylight and it was drizzling, so he thought they shouldn't see anybody else up there.

'Where are we going?' Abby asked as they clambered into the Land Rover.

'Near that house we nearly broke into but the other side of Bowerman's Nose. It's very quiet up there, no pubs or anything nearby, and I'm hoping the walkers will have gone.'

Buzz said, 'Cool.'

Edward smiled. It reminded him of Kip. He carefully edged the car out of the narrow gateway and drove slowly up the lane. There was nothing on the roads, and it seemed his idea of leaving it till late afternoon was sound.

Fifteen minutes later he pulled the old car onto the verge of the road that passed under the tor. The rock stack stood on top of a hill and a well-worn track led up to it and beyond towards Manaton. It was a beautiful area, well loved by walkers, but Edward had guessed right and tonight it was deserted.

He climbed out of the driver's seat, grabbed his jacket and slammed the door shut. Abby had already jumped out and was admiring the view.

'It's lovely. I couldn't see it in the dark the other night but what a view that house must have.'

'We'll be able to see it from the top. Come on,' Edward said and started to stride up the slope. 'We'll be able to stand behind the stack and shelter from the drizzle. Plus, we can see anyone coming from quite a distance.'

They clambered up the path and across the scattered rocks to the stack of boulders known as Bowerman's

Nose. Abby stood looking across the moor while Edward pulled out the handgun and worked out where they would stand.

'Buzz, can you stay over there where's there's a good view back down the path? If we stand here, I can see in that direction.' Edward pointed back down to the road where they could just make out the house they'd nearly broken into. He looked at Abby. She was very quiet, he thought.

'Do you still want to do this? We can't stay long...'

'No, I'm fine. I mean yes, I still want to have a go. I need to know I can do it.'

'Okay. Come and stand next to me and watch what I do. Then I'll let you have a go.'

Edward pulled the Glock from his inside pocket and slotted the magazine into place. He looked for a target and chose a small rock balanced on a larger one about two hundred feet away. The gun felt so familiar in his grasp and yet so unsettling. He shook away the memories and raised his arm, gripped the gun with both hands and squeezed the trigger. There was a slight kickback, a small flash, and he glimpsed the cartridge fly to his left. *That felt good*, he thought, turning to look at Abby. She stood open-mouthed, staring at the rock.

'Wow! You made that look easy.'

'You have a go. Hold it first and feel it in your hand, weigh it and then hold it up but don't squeeze the trigger. Okay?'

Edward gave Abby the gun and she gingerly took it from him. He watched her face as she turned it over in her palm. He recognised that look of wonder; he'd seen it years ago in new recruits.

'It's not what I expected. I don't know why but I suppose I've watched too many old films. This is like... something made out of Meccano!'

Edward laughed. He'd never heard a handgun described like that before.

'I've heard it described as being like something Action Man might carry. Are you ready to try it?'

'I think so...' Abby lifted the gun and wrapped her right hand around the grip. Edward stood behind her and told her to use her left hand to steady her right.

'Your right hand does the work and your left hand acts as a brace, okay? Lift the gun, look down the barrel, bend your elbows slightly and squeeze the trigger just once...'

The Glock fired and Abby gave a little shriek. She didn't drop it or lower it, but just stood looking across at the rocks she'd aimed at.

'Oh my God! My heart's beating so fast. I don't know whether I'm scared or excited. That was weird.'

Edward asked her to lower the gun. He put his arm around her and took it from her grip just in case.

'What do you think?'

Abby turned to look at him and he noticed her cheeks had turned slightly pink. She looked like a little girl who'd just had her first rollercoaster ride.

'Bloody amazing but I'm not sure I could aim at someone. It's a bit different pointing it at a rock.'

'Yeah, it certainly is.' Edward called to Buzz, who was watching them from a distance, 'Are you okay up there? Any sign of anyone?'

Buzz called back, 'No, we're good.'

He let her have another go and watched her taking careful aim at the rock. *She's a natural*, he thought as she fired the gun; no panic, no wavering and a good aim. He let her fire several more times then said they'd better not push their luck. Buzz had sat down to watch and wasn't paying attention to the path, so Edward called it a day and they started back down the path to the car. Abby was excitedly chattering to Buzz as he walked behind them, having scooped up the spent cartridges.

'It was amazing, Buzz! You should have had a go.'

'No, it's okay, I'm fine. I've got you two to protect me,' Buzz laughed, and they carried on walking side by side.

The light was going fast and the rain was coming in, so it was good to get in the car. Edward started the engine and pulled back onto the road.

'Do you fancy a drink? Shall we risk a quick pint in the local pub? If they stare at us too much, we'll just leave.'

Abby said, 'There have been too many stories since us, I don't imagine we'd be recognised. I expect everyone's talking about...' she paused and looked at Buzz.

He said, 'About Kip? It's okay, Abby, I've got to get used to it. That's going to be a top story for a while yet.'

Edward looked in the rear-view mirror to see Buzz's face. He looked calm, resigned even.

'You okay with that, Buzz? We'll just stop for one and then go back to the cottage. Let's pretend we're holidaymakers just once.'

Chapter 37

I t was ten o'clock and Edward was on his third mug of
coffee. He felt slightly jittery and wasn't sure whether it
was the caffeine or the anticipation of Sebastian turning
up. He thought, *What if I've done the wrong thing and he
turns up mob-handed?* Abby had been quite sure they were
taking the right action when they discussed it last night.

Buzz was sat at his laptop as usual. Edward noticed he
seemed more relaxed when he worked, and hacking into
others' secret worlds was work for him.

'Any news about the body on the beach yet?'

Buzz said, 'Hang on a mo, let me just close the doors
behind me.' His fingers flew over the keyboard and screens
changed rapidly till he stopped and said, 'Right, let's have
a look.'

Edward walked up to the table and looked over Buzz's
shoulder. They both checked the local and national news
but there was no mention of the dead woman. He frowned;
how long did it take to identify a body? It would be helpful
to know, if only to rule Pat out.

Abby came in with a towel wrapped around her head
like a turban. She popped some bread in the toaster and put
the kettle back on.

'How's it going, boys?'

'Fine,' they said in unison.

Edward smiled at her. She seemed in good spirits, he thought, and looked better for it. He recalled last night's conversation. In the dark they'd talked about the past and the future, daring to even plan a little; it gave them both some comfort. He told her selected snippets of his past life: his younger years in service in the navy and how he'd been recruited into the Special Boat Service. That's where he'd met Marcus and saved his life. After that he'd been approached by British Intelligence and that had been his life for a number of years. There was a lot he didn't tell her, but it was a start. One day maybe he'd tell the rest of it but not now.

They heard Abby singing. Edward didn't recognise the song, but Buzz did and joined in. Then they danced around the kitchen giggling like children. Suddenly he felt old again, excluded from a culture he'd ignored. He shook it off and Abby caught his eye and danced over to him, wrapping her arms around him.

'Come on, grumpy, have a dance with me!'

'What's in that coffee?' he joked, lifting her off her feet and swinging her round.

'I feel good! Na na na na na, knew that I would now!' she sang in his ear.

'James Brown! I know that one.'

She laughed and carried on dancing, with Buzz humming along. 'Let's have some music, Buzz, while you work.'

Edward left them singing in the kitchen and went to get his phone, on charge in the bedroom. There was a single message from Sebastian to say he'd left and would be there on time. He looked at the holdall on the floor, hesitated and pulled out the Glock, balancing it in his palm before putting in on the bed. *Who knows?* he thought; *it doesn't hurt to be cautious.* He left the other one and a spare magazine in the bag as back-up, just in case.

Then he pulled on his sweat top which hung loosely enough to hide the gun's shape in his pocket and went back downstairs. Abby was still singing in the kitchen, so he slipped out into the garden for a smoke. Drawing the nicotine deep into his lungs soothed his jitters and calmed the adrenaline coursing through his body. He had to keep reminding himself that Sebastian was an old friend.

The black car edged carefully between the stone gateposts and turned in a circle before stopping in the middle of the grassy parking area. Edward watched from the window with one hand in his pocket, his fingers on the cool metal of the gun. It helped keep him calm. He couldn't understand why he was so edgy.

'Is he here?' Abby's voice at his side made him startle. 'I'm sorry, I didn't mean to creep up on you.'

'No, it's not you. I'm just a bit jumpy. Yes, it's Sebastian and he seems to be alone.'

'That's good,' she said and added, 'Let's go greet him.'

Before Edward could stop her, she was out the front door and striding down the path. He caught up with her as Sebastian got out of the car. He smiled and waved at them.

'Edward! Abby! Nice to see you both again.' His voice was friendly as he greeted them.

'Sebastian,' Edward nodded, and Abby just smiled back and said, 'Lovely to see you again, Sebastian.'

'Right, that's the awkward bit out of the way. I could do with a drink, Abby, if you don't mind? Edward and I have some catching up to do. Fancy a smoke with me, Edward?'

Abby said, 'Of course.' She went back into the house and left them alone.

Edward felt the slightest twinge of resentment at Sebastian's dismissal of Abby. He realised he'd come to look on her as a partner and had forgotten she was still a civilian.

'Sure, let's go and sit on the garden chairs; they should be dry.'

Sebastian nodded and pulled out his pack of cigarettes. Edward wondered if he was carrying a gun too.

'So, bring me up to speed. What's Buzz found?'

Edward countered with, 'Who killed Kip?'

Sebastian blew a cloud of pale smoke into the air and squinted at Edward through the haze.

'Okay, fair's fair. Let's agree to share information and trust each other. I know you have a problem—'

Edward cut in, 'Actually no, I don't. I reacted without stopping to think. I should have questioned you instead of running. It was... unprofessional. You're right and we do need to trust each other, so how about you go first and tell me what the fuck's going on? I know about Cradle and Professor Stephens, I know about Rayner and the money, so you tell me what you know.'

'I'm guessing you found out about Warminster, then?'

Edward nodded.

'Okay. Well, it's become apparent we have a mole in the project. I was tasked with finding and neutralising him. It looked as if Rayner was the man we were after. We found out about the money transfer far too late, in fact after he'd died...'

'So who killed him?'

'We don't know but suspect it was the Russians. They've been very active of late – I'm sure you've noticed – and it's all been authorised at the highest level. So, of course, the logical explanation was that they disposed of Rayner once he'd handed over what they wanted, but...' he paused to light another cigarette, 'the leaks continued after Rayner died and I expect you know there's been another money transfer recently? Yes, I thought you would. So, I suggest you and I go and pay Marcus a visit and find out what's going on.'

'Okay, so let me ask a few questions. Who had me under surveillance? Who kidnapped Abby and why, specifically, was Kip killed?'

Sebastian grinned. He said, 'I'm surprised you haven't worked that out yourself.'

'I've got some idea, but I want it confirmed.'

'Our intelligence had you watched because Judith contacted you. I was asked to keep an eye on you because we wanted to keep you out of it as you were now a civilian but that proved difficult. I did warn them—'

'But *you* gave me the list of names...'

'True,' Sebastian shrugged; 'that was before I knew the full extent of what was going on, and I wasn't put in the loop until after we'd met. Judith gave me the list a while back when she was still compos mentis. Then, of course, the shit hit the fan when intelligence realised you were making connections. I was asked to bring you back in so we could reinstate you and get you to work officially with us. Then you did your runner.'

Sebastian sounded amused and Edward thought back to what he'd overheard that evening. *I've been a fucking fool*, he thought. He ground his cigarette stub on the grass and asked Sebastian for another one.

'Well, that explains the poor quality of the tail. The lad didn't have a clue.'

'Budget cuts; new recruits are sent out before they're ready and half of them have no fucking experience of life.'

They laughed together, then Edward remembered his other questions. He said, 'What about Abby? Who took her?'

'Not one hundred per cent sure but we think it was something to do with the Russian connection. They wanted to know what Rayner had said, did she know what he knew. It looks like it was a semi-professional job, certainly not SVR but probably some Russian collusion. We're not sure who planned it, but it definitely wasn't us or the Americans.'

'So, it wasn't a direct result of my contact with Judith?'

'Probably not, though I'm sure whoever it was knew of your relationship.'

'And Kip?'

'Poor boy. He was too damn smart…' Sebastian paused. 'We think it was the Russians but something about it doesn't stack up. I take it you have his files? We searched his room and there was nothing. His sister had no idea and thinks it was a random attack; he was in the wrong place at the wrong time.'

Edward decided honesty was the best policy as Sebastian was clearly happy to share information. He saw Abby coming out of the cottage with two mugs.

'I'll tell you what we found but here's Abby with your tea.'

Sebastian turned and smiled at her. 'Ah, the lovely tea lady. Thank you, my dear. We'll come in when we've finished our smoke.'

Abby gave Edward one of her direct stares but didn't comment. He knew he'd be grilled later. She left them and went back inside.

'Okay. Kip had two flash drives which Buzz managed to retrieve. It was just loads of stuff about UFOs. It seems he became obsessed with conspiracy theories and that's how he stumbled across the Warminster thing. But surely they wouldn't have killed him for that? My thinking is that he made a connection we haven't found yet...' Edward stopped. A thought struck him – Kip had worked out who the mole was and somehow they found out.

Shit,' he said, 'I think Kip was killed because he worked out who was passing the secrets.'

'That makes sense, I guess.'

'So, who was tailing Buzz when I collected him?'

'That was American Intelligence. They've been proving difficult to control. I believe they paid Maxwell's girlfriend a visit too.'

'Yeah, I saw them. We were there checking on Maxwell.'

Sebastian looked surprised. 'Really? Nobody said anything...'

'I was observing from afar, let's say. They had no idea I was there.'

'So, what's your opinion of Maxwell? I'm assuming you found him?'

Something about Sebastian's tone made Edward cautious. He made an instant decision to keep to himself the extent of his dealings with Gareth. It was a loose end he hadn't resolved yet.

'I think the guy is damaged, a bit of a loose cannon. And before you ask, I've no idea where he is now.'

Sebastian looked at Edward, holding his gaze as if he wanted to drill into his mind. Then he said, 'Okay, let's go in and say hi to Buzz.'

Abby and Buzz were huddled together over his laptop when they walked into the cottage. Edward saw Abby move away quickly and Buzz change screens. He thought, *They're playing safe, not sure how much to trust Sebastian.*

'Oh hi, we're putting a playlist together to work by.' Abby lied so smoothly, Edward thought, as Sebastian said hello to Buzz and took a quick glance at the laptop screen which, conveniently, was on a music download site.

Abby winked at Edward behind Sebastian's back and he knew for sure they'd not been choosing music. He smiled back.

'I'd like to buy you guys lunch, to make up for your… difficulties over the last few weeks.'

Difficulties? Edward almost laughed at the choice of words but said, 'That would be nice. We can recommend the local pub; we were there last night, and the food looked good.'

Abby said, 'I'll go and change my top if we're going out for lunch.'

She disappeared upstairs, squeezing Edward's arm as she passed. He took that as a signal to follow her. He chatted to the other two then excused himself.

'I'll just pop up and see what she's doing. Probably putting a whole new face on.'

Sebastian laughed and said, 'Tell her the one she's wearing is just fine.'

Abby was waiting in the bedroom for him, and as soon as he appeared she closed the door and hissed, 'What does he know? I don't want to put my foot in it.'

'The only thing I haven't told him is that we spent some time with Gareth. So keep quiet about him and Pat. He knows I found him and that's about all. There's still something not quite right about all of this; and also, he wouldn't expect me to have included you as much as I have.'

'Okay, I'll be careful. What about Buzz, though?'

'Buzz has a built-in self-preservation chip. He wouldn't say anything.'

'Edward, you're carrying the gun, aren't you? Please be careful...' Abby looked him straight in the eye. 'I mean it. You still can't be a hundred per cent sure who's the enemy, can you?'

It was a question Edward had been asking himself. Since their conversation he suspected Sebastian of holding something back. He knew he had no choice but to trust him but there was definitely information being withheld.

'That reminds me, what were you and Buzz doing when we came back in?'

Abby said, 'Oh yes, I was going to tell you... that money, the two hundred thousand, moved from Marcus's account into the same Swiss account as before. So, either Marcus and Rob were both on the take or neither of them. They've been framed and it's being laundered at the same time.'

Edward frowned. Then he remembered something else.

'There was something Sebastian said about your kidnap. Did any of the men have Eastern European accents? Maybe Russian even?'

Abby stopped putting her make-up on and frowned at him. She hesitated then said, 'No, I don't think so, but maybe one... The one who did the questioning had a bit of an accent, but I can't say what it was. I was out of it most of the time...'

'I'm sorry I had to ask. Don't worry, it doesn't really make any difference.'

She went back to applying her mascara and gave the impression of not being bothered, but he knew better. He could read her now. Leaning over her shoulder, he turned her face and gave her a kiss.

'Don't give it another thought, promise? I'd better go back down. See you in a minute.'

Chapter 38

The heat from the log fire had a soporific affect. Edward could feel his face warming up as they sat and chatted at the pub table. Sebastian had gone over to the bar for another round of drinks and was talking to the barman.

'You'd think we were on holiday,' Abby whispered to the others.

'That's the impression he wants to create,' Edward said.

Sebastian came back with a tray of four drinks. He put it down and passed Abby her diet cola and the men their pints.

'Cheers!' He raised his glass and they nodded back. 'And here's to a successful future for all of us.'

Bit rich, Edward thought but said nothing. Abby kicked his leg under the table, and he knew she felt the same.

'So, you guys, what next?' Sebastian sipped his pint and looked directly at Edward.

'You want to pay a visit to Marcus, don't you?'

'Yes, if you don't mind. I thought we could do that tomorrow. Is it okay with you three if I stay the night?'

Abby said, 'We assumed you would be. You'll have to sleep in the downstairs room this time as Buzz is upstairs.'

'That's okay. I just need a bed to sleep in, doesn't matter where.'

Edward thought, *Let's cut to the chase*. All the small talk was driving him mad.

'There's something that occurred to me earlier and I forgot to ask... That woman from the care home...' he dropped his voice, '... you remember, the one I was supposed to have murdered? Who *was* responsible for that and why?'

Sebastian's manner changed abruptly. His face took on the stern no-nonsense look Edward recognised.

'That was most unfortunate.'

'A strange choice of words; Judith said exactly the same thing.'

'Did she now?' Sebastian raised his eyebrows and added, 'I thought she was out of it when you saw her?'

'Not completely; there was a spark of the old Judith. But to answer my question...'

'Ah yes, the poor woman. It was a classic case of sending the wrong person to call on her. They misunderstood their brief and went too far, I'm afraid. Very sad.'

Abby opened her mouth to say something, but Edward caught the look on her face and stepped in quickly.

'So, it was an accident? She wasn't supposed to die? But why was I framed for it, Sebastian? And then Abby got dragged into it as well.'

'It was decided you needed a reason to be put under pressure, pushed into being open to an offer of help... from me.'

'And you wonder why I became paranoid and ran.' It was a statement not a question. Edward knew how twisted intelligence logic could be but had never experienced it as a recipient. He felt irritated that he hadn't sussed what was going on.

Abby had gone a little pink in the face, which might pass for being too warm, but Edward knew her well enough to see she was angry. He put his hand on her knee and squeezed, willing her to keep her cool.

'It was kind of you to buy lunch. Shall we go back to the cottage now? We can plan tomorrow.'

Sebastian murmured something like 'my pleasure' and swigged the last third of his pint. Buzz had hardly touched his but said he was happy to leave. Edward knew he was annoyed too.

'What the hell was that all about?!' Edward almost shouted at Sebastian. They were in the garden, smoking; Abby and Buzz had gone for a walk together, which was unusual behaviour for them.

Sebastian blew smoke in the air and smirked. He said, 'I have no idea what you mean.'

'Don't be an arse. Why are you playing games? They've been through a lot of grief in the last few weeks, literally. Buzz lost his best friend, Abby has been told her dead husband was a traitor *and* she was abducted. You tell them a woman's death was "unfortunate"! For fuck's sake, Sebastian, they're not service personnel. They're civilians caught up in a weird scenario that's totally alien to them.'

'Good choice of words, Edward.'

'Don't take the piss. You'll push me too far one day.'

Sebastian carried on smoking and waited for Edward to run out of steam. Then he put his hand on his old colleague's arm and said, 'I'm glad you've still got that anger in you. I was beginning to wonder...'

'Is that what this is all about? You were testing me again? You're impossible and you're an idiot.'

'I need to know that you'll be right behind me, watching my back, and you need to know I'll do the same for you.'

Edward looked at Sebastian, who stared back unblinking. What does he think is going to happen next? he wondered. Have I missed something important?

'Have you told me everything? What are we getting into tomorrow?'

'As far as I know Marcus is sound. This money transfer is looking very dodgy, but we can't work out who's behind it. There's been some clever hacking going on, and the only first-class hacker I know is...'

Edward jumped in, 'No way; Buzz is dead straight, if that's where this is going.'

'Can you be absolutely sure?'

'As sure as I can be about anything. Buzz is a clever, maybe naïve, young man, but I trust him completely.'

'Good, that's what I wanted to hear. Can he trace the money, do you think?'

Edward considered his response carefully, still not sure about what to reveal. He merely said, 'He's already on it, says whoever is doing it is covering his tracks and it's proving almost impossible to see what's going on. All we know is the money ends up in a Swiss account but we've no idea of who's taken it.'

Sebastian frowned and said, 'We'll see how it goes with Marcus. I understand you left in a hurry with Gareth.'

'Why do you bother asking me when you already know the answer? And no, I still don't know where Gareth

is. We parted company. I felt I couldn't trust him totally.'
Edward wanted to draw Sebastian on Gareth, but he
wasn't playing.

'Wise move. The jury's out on Maxwell.'

Edward lay wide awake staring into the dark; here on the
moor, nights were as dark as he'd known anywhere, and
tonight he was glad. It allowed him to think more clearly
without the stimulus of light. Abby's breath rose and fell
softly, which he found comforting knowing she was safe by
his side. Sebastian had got under his skin today with his
casual talk of death and duplicity. He felt tainted by the lack
of compassion that drove the intelligence world. Everyone
is dispensable. Worse still, he'd been that man once and
thought he'd escaped it.

His challenge now was keeping Abby and Buzz safe and
stopping himself from getting killed. There was more going
on than he'd been told, and he had a deep uneasiness about
what he might be walking into. He felt as if he were a fish on
the end of a line being slowly hauled in. What he couldn't
understand was why they hadn't simply disposed of him?

Abby stirred and he instinctively turned on his side and
put his arm across her body. She was soft and warm under
his touch and he thought, *Whatever happens I must protect
her*. Not for the first time he wished he could turn the clock
back and throw that bloody photograph in the bin.

Finally, as the first birds began to sing, he fell asleep, to
dream of Judith again. This time she was dressed in black,
her pearls around her neck and a diamond ring sparkling on
her finger. There was a strange smell in the air, sickly and
sweet. They were both standing in a fine dining room, the

table dressed for dinner with silver candelabras and white china plates. She fussed over the decorations while someone walked in behind her and whispered in her ear.

'Edward,' she said, smiling at him with her crimson red lips parted to reveal yellowing teeth, 'you must meet my most trusted servant. He has something to show you.'

Edward turned to see who she meant, and the smell got stronger as the figure approached. His face was hidden under the dark cloak, but he thought he knew who it was. Judith began to laugh, a horrible wheezy cackle like a death rattle, as the figure parted the cloak to reveal a large gun which he pointed directly at Edward's chest. There was a flash and a sharp retort, and he felt himself falling backward...

'Edward! Wake up, it's only a dream...' Abby's voice broke into the nightmare and he felt her hand on his arm. He opened his eyes to see her face inches from his.

'Are you alright? You were thrashing about and groaning.'

He took a deep breath and felt his heart beating strongly in his chest. Her lovely face was creased with concern. Edward swallowed, his throat dry as sandpaper.

'I'm okay, it was just a bad dream. Bloody Judith again.'

'I swear that woman's haunting you. Are you sure you're alright? You look pale.'

'I'll be fine in a minute. God, I hate that woman.'

He took a deep breath and turned to face Abby. He wanted to hold her and tell her everything was fine, but he couldn't bring himself to say it, so he just held her close, breathing in her scent. In a few hours he'd be leaving her again and he hated the thought of it.

Sebastian was full of charm and good manners over breakfast. He apologised for his behaviour yesterday.

'I was out of order. I forgot who I was talking to. Please accept my apologies, both of you. I've been in this business too long.'

Abby and Buzz said not to worry about it, they were fine, and Edward wondered if Sebastian had realised how heartless he'd sounded or whether it was simply an act to keep him happy.

'See what you can find out about Maxwell's finances while we're gone, Buzz, that would be helpful. All his accounts were closed when he "died" but there must be money sitting somewhere that he's drawing from.'

Edward thought, *Pat is managing his money*, but wasn't going to share any more information with Sebastian till he convinced him they were on the same side. Buzz nodded and said yes but shot a look at Edward that told him he had concerns too.

'Abby and I are going for a walk over the moors while you're gone but I'll get on it later.'

She said, 'Yes, we are, as it's such a nice day.' Then she winked at Edward and he knew they were up to something. He was worried now about leaving them; two amateurs playing at spying scared him. Sebastian wouldn't be impressed.

'Well, guys, we'll get going soon but hopefully we won't be gone too long. Try to stay out of trouble while we're away.'

'Yes, Dad.' Abby laughed at him, and when he frowned, she added, 'Don't be stuffy, Edward, you know we won't be doing anything silly. You're the one who should be careful.'

He saw Sebastian raise his eyebrows, but he ignored him. *It's just banter*, he thought, *nothing else; get over it.*

'Are you going for a smoke before we leave? We ought to be making a move.'

'Yes I am. Are you joining me?'

Edward said, 'No, I'll give it a miss now, trying to cut back. I'll go get my jacket, say my goodbyes and see you at the car.'

As soon as Sebastian left the house, he turned to the other two and said, 'I was being serious, Abby. We still have to be cautious. Anything at all that bothers you, any unusual activity, let me know straightaway. Okay?'

She nodded and said, 'Of course. Sebastian winds me up. I'm not sure why but he is a bit pompous, isn't he?'

Edward could see why she thought that and nodded. 'He can be but that's just his way. But he's also very sharp so don't play games with him, Buzz. After today I'll know how much we can trust him. Any news on that woman who washed up yet? That's gone quiet, which makes me wonder what's going on.'

Buzz said, 'I haven't seen anything. I'll do a search and see if anyone's talking about it.'

'Okay, let me know if you find anything. Right, I'd best get going.'

Abby followed him to the door, and he hugged her before grabbing his jacket. She looked up at him, her face suddenly serious, and kissed his cheek.

'Stay safe and try not to use that gun.'

'What gun?' he said, grinning at her.

'The one in your pocket. I'm not stupid, duh.'

'No, I know, and I'll take care, don't worry,' and as he opened the door he added, 'I only shoot people who really annoy me.'

He closed the door and walked up the path, grinning. He imagined Abby behind the door, frustrated with him.

An hour and a half later Sebastian pulled his BMW onto the track leading to Marcus's house. Edward had expected more grilling from him as they drove, but he was surprisingly quiet. Not always a good sign, Edward thought. As they bounced down the track, he wondered if Marcus knew they were coming and what their reception would be. The last time he'd been here he'd left in a hurry, but then he'd done a lot of that in the last few weeks.

The dogs barked furiously as they reached the gate and Edward said he'd get out and open it. Sebastian nodded okay.

'Rather you than me.' He nodded towards the dogs, who looked particularly cross.

'They're all bark, those two. Daft as their owner.'

He climbed out and went to the gate, speaking to the dogs, who instantly started wagging their tails at him. 'Where's the boss then, boys?'

'Right here, you bastard!' Marcus limped around the side of the house and bellowed at Edward.

'Nice to see you again, Marcus.'

'Don't try to be all polite now. You legged it without a backward glance. I was glad you took that fucking waster Maxwell with you but... really, Edward. Is that how you treat old friends?'

He waved Sebastian through the gate and showed him where to park, all the while berating Edward, who put his arms in the air in submission. The dogs danced around them both in excitement before rushing to bark at Sebastian as he got out of the car.

'Come on in, then. Here, dogs! Winston, leave him alone!'

They followed Marcus into the farmhouse and the dogs calmed down and settled on their beds while their master made tea. Sebastian looked around him at the cosy kitchen.

'Nice place, Marcus. Very comfortable.'

'I like it.' Marcus plonked the mugs on the table and found some biscuits. He gave them both a direct look then said, 'Okay, let's cut to the chase. Why are you here? I'm guessing this isn't a social visit to admire my home.'

'That's what I like about you, Marcus, you don't piss about,' Sebastian said, reaching for his tea. 'We're here to talk about the money.'

Marcus frowned at them. He looked at Edward and back at Sebastian.

'What money? Have I missed something?'

Edward said, 'Marcus, have you checked your bank account lately?'

'Not for a few days, why? What's going on?'

'Get your laptop and take a look at your account.'

Marcus went to find his laptop and Edward glanced at Sebastian, who appeared completely unconcerned. He thought, *This man doesn't believe for one second that Marcus is on the take.*

He came back in and opened up the laptop. They waited for it to load and watched his face as he accessed his bank account.

'Fuck me! What the fuck's going on? So that's why you came – you think I'm on the take?'

Edward noticed this was directed at Sebastian, who just smiled.

'Not at all but someone is using your account to launder money. Who's had access to it other than you?'

'Nobody.'

'Okay, has anyone had access to your laptop or seen you go onto your account?'

Suddenly it all made sense to Edward. *That's why I'm here,* he thought. *He thinks it's either me or Gareth.* Marcus must have come to the same conclusion because he shot Edward a look before answering.

'I did leave my laptop lying around when Edward was here with that bastard Maxwell. And there's that young lad of yours, Edward...'

'No way, not Buzz. He's not interested in making money from illegal activity. He'd be a millionaire by now if he was.' It seemed like he was continually having to defend Buzz.

'More likely to be Maxwell. How else has he survived the last few years? He needs money from somewhere,' Sebastian said.

'So, where's this money come from and where's it going?' Marcus stared at his laptop, still frowning at the figures.

Sebastian leaned over the table and grabbed a biscuit before saying, 'We think it's a deal between Maxwell and the Russians. It's looking more likely now that he was the one who was on the take, not Rayner, but what's he selling them?'

Marcus said, 'He's been out of Warminster too long now to have anything worthwhile...' he paused, 'unless he took more with him when he "died". Any more news on that lad who was given the Novichok?'

'No. All we know is it's highly likely to have come from Russia. It has the right signature. Kip obviously found something out that was highly damaging to someone, more than you found on that flash drive, Edward. I suspect this is connected to Maxwell.'

Edward listened to the exchange between the two men and realised he'd been kept in the dark. Marcus was clearly not on the outside.

'How long have you been working for Sebastian, Marcus? Why did you guys keep me out of it for so long?'

Marcus looked at him and hesitated.

Sebastian said, 'I asked him not to tell you anything. I wanted to be sure you hadn't been compromised. Let's face it, Edward, secrets don't get much bigger than this. You know it would be a political and commercial disaster if the public found out what's been going on all these years. And somewhere out there is a rogue operative who's busy selling secrets, little snippets of information that could help our enemies blow everything apart. Marcus has been intelligence gathering for me and keeping an eye on things.'

'Fuck's sake! Was it you who bugged my cottage, Marcus?'

Marcus fidgeted in his chair and Edward knew he was right. This was the worst-case scenario; an old and trusted friend who hadn't trusted him. He looked Marcus in the eye and asked again.

'Yes, okay, it was me. I was asked to do it and I thought, rather me than some stranger, but if you want to know the truth, Edward, I hated it.' He glared at Sebastian. 'It was completely unnecessary; you should have been brought onside as soon as Judith contacted you.'

'That's not much consolation. You could have told me.'

Sebastian said, 'No, he couldn't, and don't get all shirty about it now. It is what it is, and we move on. You have to be honest, Edward, you haven't been completely upfront with me either. Where's Maxwell? He spent more time with you than you admitted, didn't he?'

Edward thought, *Shall I tell him, or shall I wait and see if they reveal more hidden gems?* Then his phone buzzed in his pocket. It was Abby messaging him.

'Excuse me a second.'

Buzz has just found out the woman on the beach is Pat! And she didn't die from drowning. Police have launched a murder enquiry. What the fuck is going on?

Shit, I'm sorry, I know you liked her. This doesn't look good. Keep me informed. All ok here x

He put his phone on the table and looked at the other two. Sebastian was waiting for him to say something.

'That was Abby. Did you know about the dead woman washed up on a Falmouth beach? Turns out it was Pat Manders, Gareth's girlfriend. She's been murdered, and my guess is he had something to do with it. All I know is he's heading for Spain; probably there by now.'

Sebastian sighed and said, 'Thank you for that, Edward. Why didn't you tell me before?'

'Because I didn't entirely trust you; can't think why.'

Marcus said, 'Okay, let's move on. This whole bloody business has turned into a right bugger's muddle. We've known each other a long time so let's stop pointing fingers and start working together. How the hell are we going to get him? Do you think he's really capable of killing his lady friend?'

'I don't know, but if he didn't then one of his unsavoury associates did and…' a thought occurred to Edward, 'maybe they killed him too? Either realised he'd got nothing else to trade or he was becoming too expensive?'

'Get Buzz on it,' Sebastian said tersely.

'I can ask him to look into it. If it was Maxwell moving that money around and trying to frame Marcus, that would explain why it's still sitting there.'

Chapter 39

I've checked everything, including police records, and no sign
of Gareth or any unidentified male bodies in UK or Europe.
Ok, if anything changes let me know.
Will do.

'Nothing coming up on Gareth.' Edward frowned at his
phone.

'I think we have to assume he's still alive and is implicated
in her death.' Sebastian got his phone out. 'I'll get Interpol on
the case.' He stood up and went outside, taking his cigarettes
with him.

Marcus waited for the door to close and turned to Edward.
He looked unhappy.

'Edward, I'm really sorry how this panned out. I tried
to persuade Sebastian to talk to you but for some reason he
wouldn't. You must have pissed him off.'

'Yeah, I did. I didn't follow his game plan. It's okay, we'll
survive. He knows he needs me and Buzz. I'm sorry about Pat
though, she didn't deserve that.'

'Do you think he did it... Maxwell?'

'Well, if he did, he's a class A bastard; she adored him.
She's been looking after him for years. If he's capable of that
he's capable of anything.'

Marcus stared into his mug, deep in thought. Then he said, 'If that had happened to Suse I'd kill the bastard.'

Edward's phone jumped in his pocket. He took it out and read the screen. It was Abby again.

Edward, he's here! Gareth is downstairs. I can hear him threatening Buzz. He wants to know where you are.

Edward's heart jumped in his chest. Something in his face must have alerted Marcus. He leaned forward and said, 'What is it?'

'It's Abby. Gareth is there threatening Buzz.'

He typed rapidly, *Where are you? Does he know you're there?*

No, I'm hiding in our bedroom.

Stay hidden. Don't come out.

He's hitting Buzz.

Shit, Abby, stay tight. Don't go down.

Buzz has told him where you are. He's coming up the stairs.

Edward leapt to his feet as if he could run there and save her. He stared at his phone, not daring to type in case she didn't have it set to silent mode. Marcus stood up too but didn't say a word, just waited. It felt like forever before Abby sent another message.

I'm in the wardrobe. I have the gun.

Shit, Abby! Edward thought, and realised his heart was still racing. He willed himself to breathe slowly as he waited for what seemed like an eternity.

He's gone. OMG that was awful. Just going down to Buzz. Are you ok?

Yeah, I'm ok but Buzz is in a bad way. He's breathing but badly knocked about.

Make sure Gareth has actually left.

Sebastian walked back in and Marcus told him what was happening as Edward waited for Abby to confirm Gareth had gone.

He's gone. I'm taking Buzz to hospital. He's come round just about. I think I can get him in the car.

Abby, take care and keep me in the loop.

Edward, he's coming to Marcus's.

Abby, there are three of us here and we're armed.

Please take care. He's vicious.

Tend to Buzz. I'll be in touch later.

Okay xx

'Shit! The bastard!' A wave of anger washed over Edward; he hadn't been this mad for a long time. He gave his phone to Sebastian to read.

He said, 'Good girl, she did it just right. So, he's coming our way. We'd better be ready for him.'

'I'll hang the bastard out to dry. Thank God Abby had the sense to hide.'

Edward nodded. 'She's a clever girl. Poor Buzz, he didn't deserve that.'

Sebastian said, 'I think we can safely assume he's killed Pat. I'm concerned about his associates and where they might be. If he comes after us mob-handed, we could be in trouble…'

'Can we get help?'

'I'd rather keep this as tight as possible. We can't involve the police; they're as leaky as a sieve. The press would be all over it within hours.'

'Then it's down to us,' Marcus said.

'Indeed,' Sebastian said. He looked at his watch and patted his chest pocket, almost absentmindedly; then he caught himself and put his hand into his pocket as if searching for something. Edward thought, *He's carrying a gun too and he doesn't want me to know.* Had Marcus spotted that? he wondered.

Marcus turned to Edward. 'What do you think we can expect from him? Is he likely to be armed, do you think? Or is it just bully boy tactics against unarmed kids?'

Edward thought, *You spotted that too, then.* He said, 'Not sure. I've never seen him use a gun but who knows? I guess we'd better be safe than sorry. Have you got anything here, Marcus? A shotgun, maybe?'

Marcus grinned, followed by a guffaw. He said, 'Does a bear shit in the woods? Course I have; for shooting vermin, you understand.' Then he winked.

Sebastian seemed less impressed. He frowned at them and said, 'No guns. I want him alive and kicking. How long have we got before he gets here?'

Edward thought, *Why no guns?*, but just said, 'About an hour I reckon.'

'Okay, let's keep it cool and friendly if possible.'

Marcus gave Edward a look that said you're kidding me but neither argued with him.

'Plenty of time for a smoke. Are you joining me, Edward?'

'No, I'll pass, thanks. I'm trying to give up. I'll make another drink if that's okay with you, Marcus?' He hoped he sounded casual because he felt anything but.

'Please yourself but good luck with that.'

Sebastian stepped outside into the garden and they watched him walk down the path and round the side of the barn. Marcus frowned as he filled the kettle at the sink.

'What the fuck's going on? He's armed, isn't he?'

'I thought you'd clocked it, too. I'm not sure but I've got my trusty Glock so whatever happens...'

'Dear God, I thought we'd left all that shit behind us.'

'Yeah, me too.'

How's Buzz? Getting worried as I haven't heard anything from you x

It was nearly an hour since Edward had received the last message from Abby. They must be at the hospital, he thought, but nevertheless he was worried. He wanted to know she was alright before Gareth turned up and they were otherwise engaged. Abby was the only person who made him worry; he was usually rational and cool-headed, but with her he found it difficult to be calm.

'Any sign of Maxwell?' Marcus came to stand beside him in the garden room. They had a good view of the track from here.

'No, not yet. Where's Sebastian?'

'Smoking again. He's either got a death wish or he's running his phone battery flat.'

You too, thought Edward. He was getting more and more jittery about this scenario. Too many things didn't stack up. Marcus obviously thought so too.

'Did you sort out your shotgun?'

'Bloody right I did. I've put it behind the door in the downstairs loo, so if I say I'm going for a pee you know what to expect.'

'Let's hope we don't need it. I'm guessing you haven't told Sebastian that?'

'Told me what?' Sebastian had entered the room so quietly behind them neither had heard him.

Edward lied smoothly, 'Marcus found his shotgun but he's out of ammo.'

'Good job. I told you, no firearms. I know what you're both like.'

Marcus grinned and Edward just shrugged, but when Sebastian turned his back he winked. Despite the bonhomie all he could think was, *What the fuck is going on here?*

Another fifteen minutes dragged by. Still no message from Abby and no sign of Gareth. Even Sebastian seemed jumpy now, pacing up and down the floor before stopping to check his watch. Marcus had found an old copy of a motor magazine and was flipping through it, but Edward saw his eyes following Sebastian as he walked back and forth.

'I think I will have a smoke. I'll be outside.'

Edward opened the garden room door and was off down the path before either of them could open their mouths. He half expected Sebastian to follow but he didn't. When he looked back, he saw him standing with his back to the garden apparently looking at his phone.

There was a cool breeze blowing again so Edward walked around the barn to find a sheltered spot. He lit his cigarette and drew the smoke in before blowing it out in trails that dissipated quickly in the wind. He tried Abby again but still no response and told himself there must be a ban on mobiles in the hospital or, knowing Abby, her battery was flat. That thought reassured him even if it might not be true.

There was no sound of a vehicle so he took his time, hoping the smoke would calm his nerves. He hated having no firm plan or knowing what to expect from this encounter. He thought Sebastian was holding something back but wasn't sure what it might be. As Gareth had once said, this was turning into a clusterfuck.

After five minutes or so Edward flicked the butt onto the gravel and strolled back around the barn to the garden. He was more relaxed now. As he walked down the path, he noticed both men had left the garden room, which seemed odd. His training kicked in and he moved slowly to the door, opened it and slipped into the room as quietly as possible, listening for voices. He stood still and listened; Sebastian's voice came from somewhere within the house, followed by another gruffer tone that he instantly recognised as Gareth. Somehow, he'd gained access without them knowing, Edward reckoned.

He put his gun into the pocket of his sweat top and moved silently down the passageway that led back into the house. The voices were getting closer; they must be in the living room at the front, next to the bedroom Gareth had slept in. The door was ajar, so it was easy to listen in.

'So, where the fuck is Edward? Buzz told me he'd be here with you.'

'Well, he isn't, is he, moron…?' Marcus was baiting him, and it sounded like he got a slap for his trouble.

'Okay, fuck it. Let's do this without him. Sebastian, I want my money.'

'I'm not stopping you getting any money, Maxwell. What happened to your lady friend? I saw the news…'

'Pat, her name was Pat. Well, to use your terminology, it was unfortunate. She overheard something that she wasn't supposed to hear. It altered her opinion of me somewhat, I'm afraid, and we had a row. She fell overboard and that was that.'

Edward heard Marcus say, 'Fucking bastard! That poor girl probably adored you and that's what she got for her trouble?'

'Yes, she was a diamond was Pat. Anyway, like I said, I want my money.'

'Where did it come from, that money sitting in my account?' Marcus said.

Edward couldn't hear the reply from Gareth, so he edged closer to the door. Sebastian was speaking.

'... What's the Russian involvement, Gareth? How much do they know?'

'Cut the crap, Sebastian. How much longer do you think you can keep this up? That boy found out about you and it won't take long before someone else does too—'

'Shut your mouth and just answer the question.'

'Why? So that nobody else needs to die? First that care home woman, then that hacker and what about Edward? How come he's still walking about? Where exactly is he, by the way?'

Edward heard Marcus say, 'Tell me about Sebastian, Maxwell, and perhaps—'

'What? You'll cut me some sort of deal? Let me go? I think not. If you want to know about *him*... ask him.'

'What have you done, Sebastian? Did you go over to the dark side with this fucker?'

There was the sound of somebody scrabbling about, and Edward guessed Marcus was being roughed up, followed by heavy breathing. Then Sebastian said, 'Find Edward; he's here somewhere.'

Edward took a deep breath and stepped into the room. Marcus was lying on the floor with his face bleeding.

Sebastian was standing by the window and Gareth had his back to him.

'I'm here, so there's no need to go searching for me.' He remained calm although his heart was beating fast. He kept one hand in his pocket, fingers clamped around the Glock.

Sebastian turned and almost smiled. He said, 'Ah, there you are. I thought you wouldn't be far away. I think we all need to keep calm and talk.'

Marcus wiped the blood from his mouth and said, 'Don't trust one word that comes out of that fucker's mouth.'

Gareth stood over him. 'Shut up, old man. You're nothing but a has-been.'

Edward said calmly, 'You're not fit to wipe his boots, so I suggest you keep it shut or I'll help you close it.' He took a step closer and Sebastian sighed.

Pulling a gun from his jacket he said, 'I've had enough of this. All of you just listen.'

Marcus shifted himself into a sitting position and leaned against the wall, not taking his eyes away from Sebastian. Gareth remained standing over him but angled himself so that he could see all three men, and Edward stayed just inside the doorway, ready to charge or flee. His muscles felt tight as if he were about to run. *Fight or flight*, he thought.

Sebastian pulled a chair forward and sat down, crossing his long legs and resting the gun on his knee pointing at Edward. He smirked at him.

'You should have maintained your distrust of me. I can't believe how easy it was to persuade you we were on the same side. For a while I thought you'd save me the bother of dealing with Maxwell but that didn't pan out.

I even gave you the gun to do it. You were almost there; you suspected he was working for the wrong team, but you weren't sure, were you? Then that Kip had to get involved. God, I underestimated him—'

'It was you? But what about the Novichok?'

'Nice touch that, I thought. You suspected a Russian connection and there is, but not the state, just criminals out to make a quick buck. You'd be surprised how easy it is to buy that stuff; all it takes is money. That's all it takes to do anything these days. Want a government to pass the legislation you want, throw them a donation; want some cutting-edge weaponry, just pay enough to make someone a very wealthy man. The world revolves on money.'

Edward felt sick. This was far worse than he'd imagined.

'But why involve me at all? Why send me that list?'

'Simple – I needed to find Maxwell and I knew you were persistent at tracking down "the truth", and all I had to do was suggest that finding him was our top priority. Remember that conversation, Edward? The one you eavesdropped on? Did you really think I didn't know you were there?'

Edward was ready to make his move on Sebastian but saw Gareth out of the corner of his eye edging forward. *He's going to try to take Sebastian down*, he thought. Marcus must have thought so too because he moved back against the wall and wiped the blood from his eye.

Sebastian saw the movement and raised the gun. Several things happened at once. Gareth lunged forward, Marcus rolled onto his side to try to get to his feet and Edward pulled his gun out of his pocket. There was a sharp crack and Gareth went down; Sebastian fired a second shot and turned to Marcus, who had staggered to his feet. He put the gun against his temple and, without turning to look at Edward, said, 'One false step and your friend is dead. Throw your gun down.'

Marcus looked at Edward and gave a tiny shake of his head. Edward cursed out loud and inwardly too – how could he let his friend die? But if he gave up his gun, they might both die.

'I know what you're thinking. If I give him my gun, he'll kill us both. It was Maxwell I wanted, and you helped me get him. That's another two hundred k I can keep for myself – a nice little extra bonus and a treacherous bastard out of the way. I don't need to kill you, Edward. I'm out of here today and I'm not coming back. I just need you two incapacitated so you can't follow me. I'd rather not shoot you, you've both been so helpful. Drop the gun, Edward, or I *will* shoot Marcus.'

'For fuck's sake, why should I trust you now? You've lied like a cheap watch.'

Sebastian sighed. Edward saw him adjusting his grip on the pistol. *Shit*, he thought, then Sebastian raised his hand and hit Marcus hard on the side of his head with the gun. Marcus went down and stayed down. His gun was now trained on Edward. He stared at him with no flicker of emotion.

'Put the gun down or I will be obliged to shoot you.'

'I think we have a Mexican standoff; I could say the same to you.'

'Indeed, you could, but there's a difference between us, old friend. You won't kill me, but I am more than capable of killing you.'

In that moment Edward knew he had a choice to make. Sebastian was clearly a liar, a traitor and a murderer. He had to save himself and Marcus. He firmed his grip on the trigger; there was a loud bang and he felt a sharp pain in his chest. As he went down his last thought was, *The bastard's shot me*, then he thought he heard Abby's voice shouting his name, then more shots. Then blackness.

Chapter 40

He could hear voices; somebody was moving him. *I can't be dead then*, he thought, and tried to open his eyes, but somehow he couldn't. The pain in his chest was overwhelming and he heard a groan from somewhere. There was a mask on his face and a male voice telling him, 'Keep still; everything is going to be alright.' A sharp stabbing feeling in his arm was followed by the sensation of floating in a warm sea. He felt great; perhaps he was dead, and this was Heaven?

But somewhere Abby was talking; she sounded panicky. She wasn't dead too, was she? He heard her voice in the distance.

'Will he be okay? He's lost so much blood...'

Another voice, soothing but too quiet to hear, was talking to her. Edward tried to listen, but he was floating away in his warm sea. There were other sounds in the distance too – they sounded like sirens – then he was bobbing along, warm and comfortable under the bright sun. Shame he couldn't breathe, he thought, as he slipped away.

He came to again and found the pain rolling over him in waves, which confused him. *How can I feel pain if I'm dead*? he thought. And the noise too, all that shouting and beeping – then there was a bright light; his eyes hurt. He realised his chest hurt and he gasped for breath. A female voice told him to keep still, he was in hospital.

'Can you hear me, Edward? I'm just giving you some more pain relief then we'll sort you out.'

What the fuck? he thought, *I'm not dead*, and then he remembered, *I've been shot*. His eyes wouldn't open properly, his eyelids were so heavy. He felt his body being lifted and moved then all went dark again.

The next time he came around there was less noise, just a gentle beeping. Someone was there with him, he sensed it, but still struggled to open his eyes. He was aware of a mask on his face; he took in a tentative breath and the stabbing pain had gone, leaving just a dull persistent ache.

Edward opened his eyes and squinted against the light. His mouth was so dry, and his head felt as if he'd hit the whisky. He made a sound that alerted the person sitting by his bed. A familiar voice told him not to worry.

'I'm here, Edward. It was my turn to rescue you this time.' Abby leaned in close and whispered into his ear, 'You're safe. Sebastian is in a bed here somewhere too.'

He mumbled, 'Abby…'

'Shush, don't try to talk. You had a collapsed lung. You were very lucky. He shot you in the chest.'

'Marcus?'

Abby took his hand and said, 'Marcus is fine, a bit bruised and battered but fine. When you're a bit better, I'll tell you everything. Just rest now.'

It was two days since Sebastian had killed Gareth. Edward was able to sit up, propped on pillows. He felt like he'd been hit by a bus, but he'd survived. Abby had refused to tell him anything till she thought him well enough. Now he was waiting for her to come in. The one thing he'd learned was that he'd had a miraculous escape. Sebastian had shot him, but the bullet had ricocheted off one of his ribs and entered the lower part of his right lung, exiting through his back without serious damage to any major organs. The doctor told him it was a lucky escape; he must have moved just enough to avoid taking the bullet head on.

He sipped some water from a tube in a bottle that Abby had brought in for him. The ward they'd taken him to had only four beds and the others were empty; he guessed that wasn't a coincidence. He was sure there was a security presence outside the door. The doctors were refusing entry to anyone but Abby, who'd blagged her way in by saying she was his fiancée.

Abby came in and closed the door behind her. She was carrying a bag of fruit, he could see grapes, and his eyebrows raised. *Really, Abby, grapes?* he thought, as she bounced up to his bed looking as gorgeous as ever.

'Edward, you look so much better!' She kissed him before dragging up a chair and sitting next to him. 'I brought you some fruit,' she said.

'So I see. Grapes as well…'

She laughed and put the bag on the bedside table. He waited.

She said, 'You want to know what happened.' It was a statement not a question.

'Yes please.'

'Okay. I'll start with what happened after you left the cottage. We went for our walk and not long after we got back Gareth turned up, which surprised me. I couldn't work out how he found us. Anyway, I was upstairs getting changed – we got soaked in the rain – and Buzz let him in. I think he sussed really quickly there was something very wrong because I heard him tell Gareth that you and I were both out. I thought, that's odd, so I kept quiet and listened. It wasn't difficult. Gareth was shouting and threatening Buzz.

'The gist of it seemed to be about something Kip had found out, and did you know and where were you. He seemed to be angry with Sebastian too. Then he started getting violent. It was horrible to hear...' Abby paused, and Edward took her hand and squeezed it.

She continued, 'Then I heard him starting up the stairs, so I took the gun out of the holdall and hid in the wardrobe. He was bumbling about in the bedroom. I think he may have checked the bag, then he left.'

Edward said, 'Looking for the gun, I expect. He knew I had two.'

'Probably, that would make sense. He didn't have a gun on him when they took him away. He's dead, by the way. Anyway, I went down to Buzz and found him on the living room floor, blood everywhere. His face was a mess, so I took him to Newton Abbot hospital in the Land Rover. They wanted to keep him in for tests, so I left him there and came after you.'

Edward stared at her in disbelief. He said, 'You did what? So that was your voice I heard after he shot me?'

'I'm so sorry, Edward, I didn't act quick enough. He'd fired before I could—'

'The second shot! It was you? You shot Sebastian?'

'He was going to kill you. He was walking towards you to shoot again and I stepped in and fired. To be honest, I thought you were dead, and I was just bloody angry.'

'Oh, Abby.' He didn't know what to say. He was speechless.

'I got to the house just as he shot Gareth. I heard the shot and realised you were in trouble, so I crept in and followed the sound of your voices, but I got there as he shot you. He didn't see me because he was concentrating on you. I shot him in the thigh, apparently. He went down screaming and dropped the gun and Marcus picked it up. You should have seen the look on his face, well, what you could see with all the blood. He's a bit of a mess too.'

Edward lay back on his pillows and looked at her as if he'd just met her for the first time. This beautiful girl, who was prepared to kill for him.

'Marcus will be along to see you soon. They want to debrief you, apparently.'

'And Buzz, how's he?'

'He's fine, just very bruised but no lasting damage.' She paused and he knew she was keeping something back.

'What is it, Abby?'

'I'm not sure what's going to happen to us, me and Buzz. We know things... we shouldn't know. There're a lot of men in black suits about. I was cautioned but Marcus stepped in and vouched for me. They took my passport.'

Edward frowned. He didn't know who was in charge now.

'Where am I? Which hospital is this?'

'Bristol; they took you to the nearest one.'

That was good news. He hadn't been moved to a secure unit. Hopefully Marcus would be able to cast light on the situation.

'Don't worry, Abby. You shot Sebastian in self-defence, and if they grill you about what you know just say as little as possible. Don't mention the project, and I'll speak to Marcus. I'm not sure yet what will happen with Buzz once they know what skills he has…'

Marcus squeezed himself into the small hospital chair and grinned at Edward. His face was a mass of purple bruises, but he seemed cheerful enough.

'We live to fight another day, eh, Edward? That young lady of yours is one cool character. If you'd seen her…'

Edward couldn't help smiling. Marcus exuded positivity.

'Yeah, she is. What's going to happen to them, Marcus? I'm very worried she might be seen as a threat.'

Marcus stopped smiling and leaned in towards Edward; his expression became serious. He said, 'Trust me, I'll sort it. There's so much you don't know. I'm not supposed to tell you because they'll debrief you properly, but I can tell you Sebastian was being watched and Gareth was selling secrets to the Russian mob for huge sums of money. It was him who framed Rayner and used his bank account to move money; when Rayner worked out what was going on, they killed him. Apparently Pat Manders was disposed of because she overheard him doing a deal with his Russian acquaintances. When Sebastian found out, he saw it as a way of making himself a nice pension pot and getting rid of Maxwell as well. I thought I was working for the good of the country; turned out I was helping a complete tool. The corruption that's been exposed is deep, my friend.'

Nothing about what Marcus said surprised Edward. He was just angry with himself for not working it out sooner. He wanted to go home. He'd had enough of the intrigues, but he knew this would just be the beginning. They wouldn't let him off the hook so easily. He knew too much and was being dragged back into the fold. He sensed Marcus knew it too. But there were so many questions he wanted answers to.

'Do you fancy a drink to toast our survival?'

'A drink, Marcus?'

Marcus grinned again. He waved a bag under Edward's nose with a flourish and pulled out two small glasses followed by a bottle of single malt.

'Just a drop of scotch, old boy. For old times' sake and maybe new times as well.'

He poured two tots and handed one to Edward. They raised their hands and clinked the glasses together before downing them in one gulp.

'So, what's next? Who's in charge now?'

Marcus smiled and said, 'Some chap we don't know, but apparently he's very fair. I'm not supposed to discuss it with you given how sensitive all this is, but I heard he's horrified by what's been going on and quite a few heads are going to roll.'

Edward smiled too. He was happy to hear that. A new man with no baggage was good news.

Six months later

T he sun beamed down on them. It was such a beautiful day. Abby lay on the grass watching house martins swooping in the blue sky above. She rolled onto her side and grinned at Edward, who was struggling to open the bottle of sparkling wine they'd brought with them.

'Do you want me to do it? I'm guessing you haven't had much practice with fizz; not your choice of plonk.'

Edward grinned. 'Don't be cheeky. Here we go!' There was a loud plop followed by cursing as the wine fobbed over the top of the bottle, splashing Edward's white linen shirt. He poured two glasses and gave one to Abby, who'd pulled herself up into a sitting position, legs crossed.

'Here's to our new home! Health, wealth and happiness, etc. etc....' Edward laughed, and they clinked their glasses together. He felt lightheaded in a way that had nothing to do with the wine. Abby smiled back at him.

'It's a pity Ben wouldn't part with the cottage, I love that place, but maybe it's for the best. Too much happened there.'

Edward said, 'Yes, and thanks to your cousin we've got a fantastic bargain, and they were right about the view.'

'We must change the name though. "The View" is a bit naff.'

'Indeed it is, although it's accurate. Any ideas?'

Abby crinkled her nose, deep in thought. He loved the way her face creased when she concentrated.

'Covington Cottage or The Retreat, maybe?'

'I quite like The Retreat. It will be our haven, after all.'

Abby sipped her drink and unpacked their picnic basket. They hadn't exchanged contracts yet so couldn't get access to the house but a picnic in the garden was perfect. From here they could see the tor and beyond, almost to Manaton.

'Edward, do you think we are safe now? I know they said—'

'I've been promised an amnesty, and now I'm back on board I'm not a risk to national security and neither are you.' Edward thought how well Abby had slotted in. He'd told them she had a sharp analytical mind and they'd grudgingly offered her a job which she'd proved to be brilliant in. Buzz had been taken into the fold too. It was a no-brainer after he'd uncovered such a huge web of corruption. Now he was a security advisor and in-house hacker.

'When we settle in, we must have Marcus come and stay, with the dogs, of course. He's got so much time on his hands, now he's properly retired.'

Edward smiled at Abby and nodded. He looked at the house with its weatherworn paintwork, and despite everything they would need to do he couldn't wait to move in and get started. It had been such a strange year but overall a good one. The dust had settled on the intrigues they'd uncovered, and the mantle of intelligence security had protected the state yet again. But the price he'd had to pay was going back into a world he'd wanted to leave behind him. He hoped it wouldn't be too high a price.

Acknowledgements

Thank you to the team at Matador for making my dreams flesh and to Derek Jones for the cover photograph. I would also like to thank the following for their early reading of my manuscript and their helpful critiques – Grant Morris, Kath Fry, Jo Frayling, Pat Barber, Harriet and Derek Jones. This novel was written at my home in Wiltshire but was influenced by various places I have visited and love.

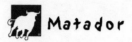